Discovery At Rosehill

Kathryn Brown

TO Margie
with love &
best wishes,
Kathryn x

Acknowledgements

My husband, James and my beautiful daughter, Amy, have embraced my enthusiasm and commitment to write this book. Their patience with me over the past few years has been amazing, both standing back to allow me the space to complete this life long ambition. I love them both more than life itself.

I have made so many good friends through my writing, one in particular. Lorraine Holloway-White is a gifted medium and has helped me to develop my knowledge of mediumship, learning about the wonderful world of spirit. I wish to thank her for helping me with research and giving me the opportunity to promote my work through various websites such as Authors On Show.

Nicole Scheller, author and editor, helped me to improve this book. Her suggestions and editing of my manuscript have made me realise that writing isn't just about having a good imagination. It's also about commitment, dedication and a good plot. My life has been made all the richer for having met her.

After four years of blogging, I have been fortunate enough to make some invaluable friendships with people all over the world. Their love and support has often been the encouragement I needed to get through the dark days of suffering with epilepsy. They have remained loyal and interested in my writing and I thank them all from the bottom of my heart.

And most of all, I thank our fascinating world of spirit; an existence that we all will one day experience as we begin to understand a life after death.

Dedication

This book is for you, Dad. You inspired me to write it, remained by my side as I wrote each word and developed each scene. I shall never say goodbye to you, for I know the day will come when you once more hold me in your strong arms, kiss my forehead then look into my eyes as you say, "mind how you go." In my heart and in my life, always.

Prelude

I hear someone walking up the stairs to my room. Footsteps urgently make their ascent to my first floor bedroom. I move to the door then stand in rigid poise. My eyes scan the stairs, the hall, eagerly searching for life amongst an empty space. There is no one there.

I smell freesias and perfume, a delicious aroma of cooking and the harsh scent of tobacco smoke. I hear my name being called, the cry of a child and a woman's soothing voice. I turn; my eyes see movement, flitting from one wall to another.

Chapter One

I fought back the tears as I turned the corner and saw the house standing proud on its hill, sheep grazing in the bottom fields. It was as though time stood still, nothing had changed. There was nowhere I wanted to be more. It drew me in by some kind of magnetic force, wrapping its soul around mine until I had no control.

I sat in my faithful old Land Rover for a while, as I watched the rabbits go about their business, totally oblivious to my presence. The wind rustling through the trees and the birds singing to one another was all I could hear as feelings of affection poured from my soul.

The farm house, a large stone building had an aura of warm colours around its walls. This was my dream come true. Relief and excitement besieged me as I realised that I had finally found the last piece of my jigsaw, the piece I had searched for all my life. I was complete. I was final. I was home.

"Your world you have to discover," my grandmother said. I looked at her sat beside me and saw tears in her eyes. When she visited I had to listen. I didn't always agree but she was wise, she spoke with sincerity. I didn't remember her passing. She often manifested before me, presenting as I would have recognised from her photograph which stood on the fireplace.

I looked longingly at the derelict building in dire need of love. It had a soul; a desire having lived on through hundreds of years. I knew it was where I needed to be. My life would unfold inside these walls as a future of certainty lay before me.

"It's beautiful," I said to the energy which occupied the passenger seat beside me. "But I don't understand why you've brought me here."

"You're ready to move on, Camilla. You're in your forties and you're lonely. I see it in your eyes every time I look at you." My grandmother knew so much.

"But look at it. It's derelict. I couldn't live here." We both stared at the cluster of buildings. "I was happy in Edinburgh. Why would I want to live so far away from civilisation?"

"You will find more civilisation in this house than you could ever wish to find anywhere else. Believe me, you're meant to live here. You have so much to learn about your life and it all starts here, at Rosehill."

I turned to face her as she too, turned to look at me. Her eyes were sparkling, her mouth curled up in a vibrant smile. I could sense the excitement within her heart as she impressed it upon my own.

"Go. Find yourself. Understand that what you have in your life is only a fraction of what is really there. I'll be by your side; I'll watch out for you." She began to fade. I reached out my hand towards where her spirit body had rested in the seat. But as the fabric touched my hands I realised I was once more alone, and a little frightened of the journey which clearly lay ahead.

***

It didn't take long for legalities to process, nor did it take long for my decisions to be made as to what I had planned for these ancient walls. My grandmother helped me to pack, all the while telling me about the home in which she lived with her beloved husband, my grandfather. It took longer than expected to fill the boxes which contained my life but I was grateful for her company. It was always such a pleasure to welcome her. She visited me often, usually at an appropriate time when advice was sought. I was never sad at not remembering her in our physical world. Her existence was much calmer, more sincere than ours. Her words were softly spoken, her smile forever worn. She never rushed, always stayed.

I moved with very little in terms of furniture and possessions, for the house already held such items; antiques from a forgotten age, ornaments belonging to the Ladies of the house. My heart raced as I passed the threshold, feet at a standstill to find my bearings. It was just as I'd imagined it as a dank and musty aroma reached my senses at an alarming rate.

Dust and crumbling plaster scattered about the floor, fallen from neglected walls, a dirt infested Aga stood against one wall; cupboard doors hung loosely; a drawer balanced precipitously, warning of danger looming with sudden movement.

Aged tiles clung in despair, no wallpaper adorned the walls. An abandoned room treated with dishonour, in need of heartfelt hands; now my room. No longer would it be abandoned. No longer would this room deteriorate into nothingness. It needed me. It needed my soul to revive its memories and bring it back to life.

As I made my way out of the once loved kitchen, I found myself in a long passage way. A dark, disconcerting space with several doors closed to hide remembrance within. I could smell tobacco smoke as it seemed to drift through the air, leading me to the bottom of a staircase. There was a white mist, wrapping itself around the handle of a closed door. Feeling coldness on my hands, my head began to pound, yet serenity filled my heart. I walked towards the door, curiosity beckoning me to turn the handle. My hand felt detached from my out-stretched arm as I watched my own fingers form their grip. The door opened slowly, its hinges old and piteous. It creaked, whined as it once more felt duty bound.

A large sash window was the first object my eyes caught in their frantic search, open shutters unable to withstand manoeuvre. No curtains hung, nor was there a carpet beneath my feet. A black and white wedding photograph sat upon an antique dressing table, its subjects unsmiling but proud. A few ornaments scattered about the mantel piece, a pathetic display of a no-doubt sparse life. Bed sheets were clumsily placed on a war-time bed, the mattress in desperate need of disposal. But apart from these few items, the room was empty. I could sense laughter at sunrise and pleasing dreams when the moon lit up the sky though I could feel no energy; no atmosphere prevailed. It smelt of a forgotten ashtray, of musty clothes and worn out leather; of a life from long ago that hung on for fear of being excluded. I caught myself in a worn out mirror which nestled on the dusty floor boards. Not a large item but big enough to reflect the middle aged woman I had become. I used to be slim and pretty, but the mirror portrayed me as frumpy, down-trodden and a little grey around the edges. It wasn't the image I wanted to see. The woollen cardigan I wore was perhaps hiding my curves but my pale face needed reviving, as if I'd only just awoken from the deepest sleep. I made a mental note to dig out my makeup bag and freshen up my complexion.

Gathering my thoughts I closed the door upon my exit, leaving the room once more in silent abandonment. The next space I was compelled to enter seemed hollow, an area once filled yet now containing empty shelves and a worn out fireplace. I was quite eager to inject some colour into the house and thought this would be the place to do it. I had never been artistic with a paint brush, but was determined to at least try to decorate a little by myself. This room had no life within its stone walls, it was quite eerie, even to me.

I was rewarded anticipating optimism as I removed ivory sheets from furniture in the guest wing. Dust particles took flight, settling gracefully upon wooden floorboards and a central rug. There was much work to do. Some parts of the house required major renovation whilst others would be satisfied with a lick of paint.

This was to be my home; my work; my life. I had to make plans. Bated breath and racing heart bestowed upon me as I thought about my grandparents and their wish for me to rededicate Rosehill.

As the weeks passed, the builders began their work and I looked on with bemused eyes. Wonder and intrigue filled my head as I touched walls and was graced with memories from a bygone age. I knew there would be tales to tell, mysteries to unfold, spirits to meet.

As units were stripped from their ancient bed, dust gathered and spiders retracted to safety. Three men removed four decades of memories to make way for new life. It was surreal to see a room almost bare, the decaying plaster and neglected walls, a record of family life beyond flesh and mortar. I could sense eyes in abundance, witnessing the demolition, heads shaking at the changes they would have preferred to avoid. Drilling and hammering, aggressive release continued throughout the day as a new room came alive, a room I had meticulously planned to alter, finally beginning to hold its head up high. No going back; it would only do to go forward, make progress, create something new and exciting, something I had thought about doing for so long.

Plaster was applied to walls. Old sockets were torn from their core; wires were fixed as modern clashed with old. Still so much to do yet confidence high, a nod of the head, no cursing or negative thought, just optimism ensued as workmen saw an end in sight. I sat at my laptop, trying in vain to concentrate on words which found it hard to reach the surface. Workmen up and down the stairs, in and out of the bathrooms, laying new wires, problem solving with little problem involved. I was impressed by their efficiency, their constant determination to complete the task in hand; they knew they could do it; I hoped they were right.

As the house lay silent once more, their vans departing in convoy, I stood and realised the fact that within days I would have that new kitchen I had so desired. My eyes continued to catch movement darting from one side of the room to the other, checking, approving, disagreeing. It was at that time that I heard the crying, a faint voice from the top of the stairs. The woman whom alerted my senses beckoned me as I continued to follow her voice; the stairs were empty, the landing mirror in a state of unclean. I ascended the first staircase where I stood in front of the looking glass, a grandfather clock to my left. I was disappointed.

Nearing the end of the week I could see a drastic change in the room with a view. It was remarkable; incredible; a wonderful feeling to finally be able to visualise this space worthy of time and effort. I wanted to paint the world a message, inviting them to see my new kitchen, informing them of a new birth in a country mansion. Perhaps that was why my calls were answered. Why, when I asked for my guests to knock, that they did, several times. I could not have been sure at that time exactly how many astrals were present but I imagined it was at least two, maybe three as footsteps became more distinct.

And when I stood at my new ceramic kitchen sink, looking at the distant orange glow of horizon lights, I was alerted once more to a soul with no face; the silence broken in the wake of a repetitive knocking on my new kitchen table. "Do you like it?" I asked after turning round to face the answer. The reply: two knocks, knuckle bound on ancient Pine.

***

I had finished familiarising myself with my new home, it was time to set up my reading room and begin my work. A small room downstairs sufficed, red velvet curtains already hung at large sash windows. The carpet would need replacing in time and perhaps the fireplace would need to be rediscovered but its atmosphere felt perfect for visiting spirits. I positioned a small solid oak table in the middle of the room.

Two chairs facing each other, currently unoccupied. A lace table cloth I draped in heavy splendour, of old fashioned appearance, found amongst a chest of antique fabrics. I placed my Crystal Ball upon pewter stand in the middle of the table. A large, silver candle holder with ivory candle adorning the mantle, alone and eager.

Perfect. All I needed now were people to grace me with their excited presence, looking forward to finding out which loved ones were able to bare their soul. I sat in that room for a while. Meditation came easy in such calm surroundings. Taken to a world of vivid imaginings, my mind's eye was able to distinguish between our earth plane and the plane in which our spirit friends had no choice but to reside. Lush green grass, morning dew still evident as sheep feasted upon blades and cud; a stream, gently flowing, carrying fallen sticks over rocks which had embedded over the years; blue skies; a yellow sun pointing her rays at poppies and wheat in the fields beyond.

I sat, flat-footed against the floor, my shoulders back and my hands resting on each lap. I couldn't hear the water in my imaginary stream, or the birds which chatted in their wake. I knew something wasn't right. Calm was upon me as a storm brewed in my head. I needed to come out of my meditative state, find reality once more, ask why I had been presented with this unwelcome feeling.

As I lifted my feet from the floor, moving my head to see the Crystal before me, the picture appeared, clear and instantly visible, my mind's eye drawing in to understand what was about to happen. A broken heart and tears. It was all too predictable; too corny. I had seen broken hearts before, many times. But there was no one else in the room. I could feel no spirits beside me, could find no explanation for a broken heart. I dismissed it. Put it down to the Crystal being in new surroundings; my own surroundings being new to myself.

As I opened the blue velvet cloth in which to securely return the Crystal, I wondered if my ears were deceiving me. I could hear the faint sound of a woman crying, so faint I could only just make it out. The woman sobbed as the sound became more distinct. Covering up the Crystal, the sound appeared much clearer; a haunting cry for help.

"Who are you?" My words prompted the sobbing to stop. "Spirit, come forward." I looked around the room, hoping a sign would appear of astral presence; anything; tapping, knocking, even poltergeist activity. I was eager to know whether my reading space had been appreciated by my spirit friends.

"Please give me a sign." I made some suggestions. "Perhaps knock on the table. Maybe you could push the candlestick from the mantle."

It was clear after fifteen minutes of patience that the crying woman either no longer felt comfortable in her communicative encounter or she simply didn't have enough energy to answer my calls. I hoped she would return, maybe she would realise she was able to draw from my energy and communicate with me in confidence.

That evening, the sun made her beautiful descent beyond the hills, lighting up the once blue sky with fire opals in abundance. I wondered how God could have created something so intense whilst allowing our neighbours to shed blood in battle. I wondered about God often. How some of us walked amongst the spirits, made friends with another dimension whilst others laughed, unable to understand their astral cousins. I thought about the world so breathtaking, abused by destructive hands, buildings of such captivating interest yet at the end of their existence as they lay destroyed by religious anger.

The television switched on by itself that night. It had often performed that highly amusing trick in my previous home but since I had moved here, it was my own hands that brought it to life. However, this time it had decided not to wait. Perhaps there was something worth watching, possibly a visiting soul thinking I might find its own favoured show of interest.

It switched onto a channel currently showing a film, a romance starring well known actors, one in which I would have chosen to avoid. I gave the film the benefit of the doubt and made myself comfortable. The remote control lay next to me, waiting with bated breath as I found it physically impossible to take it in my grasp. I didn't want to sit through this film. I wanted to watch a documentary which was due to be shown on the other side. I would find it more interesting, romantic films weren't my thing. The sound increased.

I found myself surrounded by voices, but not just the romantics who looked into each other's eyes on the magic screen. The walls around me had started to speak; women's voices, children laughing, men asking questions, a barking dog. The room had found life. Still unable to reach the remote control I had no choice. The picture on the television began to fade as new imagery presented itself to me, two new faces, radiant with bliss. But one of the faces was beginning to look familiar. The brown hair, hazel eyes, the long profile. It was me. I didn't recognise the other face; a woman's features, quite beautiful, elegant perhaps.

Spirit had appeared. An eager soul releasing energy insisted that I look into my own future. The voices and the dog's bark waned until I could hear nothing. No sound came from the box before me, there now remained just faces; mine and that belonging to a stranger. But who was she? Why was she appearing with me? I needed answers; I had questions which I suspected were not going to be answered during that visit.

"Who are you?" I asked. A faint knock came from the opposite corner of the room.

"Mum?" She didn't visit me often even though I knew she was able to. I hadn't mourned after her death. She had been deteriorating over many years after suffering an excruciating illness and we felt at the time that her passing had been a blessing. Still, after twenty years, I felt she had failed to forgive me for a lack of respect. We had so much catching up to do yet she made it hard for me when she refused to visit.

"Please give me a sign. Tap on the window. Is that you, mum?"

The faintest knock sounded once more. It was as though she was with me, yet she didn't know if she would be welcome or not. I wanted her to communicate, tell me about her journey from the earth plane.

"Knock louder, mum," I requested, becoming a little impatient with her modesty.

She did. It was a much more distinct knocking, hard against a table. My captor had released me from the chair and I was able to sit on the floor by the table in which I believed her to be near. I knelt on the floor, resting my palms on the table top. The woman's face on the television had become melancholy; my own face appeared to be fading. I felt cold. So cold. The heated radiators seemed to make no difference. Something touched my head. Unseen hands stroked the top of my head, running fingers carefully through my hair. Spirit was above me, guarding me from a future I had to unveil.

Chapter Two

I decided to get a dog. A local sheep farmer was selling border collie pups and my love of animals found me at his house, cooing over the litter of six. Unable to take just one I asked if I could have three, and as they hadn't been sold he agreed. It was two weeks later when he brought them to Rosehill, somewhat overwhelmed at their new surroundings but excited at the prospect of staying together.

When my client arrived on Wednesday night they showed me their true characters, high-pitched barking to protect me from the outside world. There were too many clouds in the night sky shading the moon and spoiling the atmosphere as Alice Baxter closed her car door. I welcomed her into my home. The heat from the Aga beckoned her to remove a quilted jacket from her back, as I reached for the kettle.

"It's nice to me you, Mrs Baxter. Can I offer you some tea?"

"Sounds lovely, dear," she replied. "But please, call me Alice."

I smiled. "Sugar?"

"No thanks, gave it up many years ago."

I could sense she was somewhat nervous as she watched tentatively while I filled the kettle. She was eager to get started. I needed to calm her, offer her a little psychological friendship. There was nothing worse than an over-enthusiastic client, forever expecting Spirit to appear.

"Let's sit down for a while," I suggested, placing two mugs of tea on the kitchen table. Alice's chair scraped across the tiled floor as she anxiously perched herself upon leather seat. Perhaps I should have offered her a brandy.

"Before we start the reading, I would ask you not to give me any names of family members, or indeed those departed. If we're fortunate enough to connect with spirit tonight, I'll give you confirmation by giving you information about them. But please don't be disappointed if no one comes through. It doesn't always happen. We can't order the spirits to connect, it is their wish only."

I think she understood. It was time we moved into the reading room, my peaceful space where I would welcome spirit into my home. This woman had come to me specifically to contact her husband, I knew this the moment we walked into that little room. He stood by the window, his hands stroking the velvet curtains in a bid for me to mention them. He only had eyes for his wife. I might not have been there but for my ability to communicate with him. I couldn't see his feet, his legs ended mid calf as he appeared to float several inches above the floor. A stocky man, tall and broad shouldered with grey hair, a few strands of which lapped over his head. His eyes seemed kind. He wore a black suit and tie, typical funeral attire.

"Sit down, Alice." I spoke softly.

"I'm a bit nervous." Her voice almost gave way to a fraudulent laugh.

"I want to ask you a few questions about your husband."

"Is he here?" Her sensational enthusiasm overwhelmed me as I tried hard to keep the connection. Trying to ignore her I continued.

"I feel you buried your husband in a velvet lined coffin."

"He's here isn't he? Please tell me he's here."

"Let me see if I can make a better connection," I requested.

William Baxter stepped forward, moving to stand beside his wife. He continued to stare at her then placed his hand on her shoulder making her shudder as if feeling a shiver in her bones.

"Your husband is at your side." I psychically encouraged her not to move. He was ready to communicate.

I looked up at him. So did she, her eyes scanning the corner of the room. She believed he was there, even though she couldn't see him. I knew I could communicate now that they were both ready.

His voice, strong and deep, emitted in my head. As his lips moved, the sound could only be heard by me, the sound of his breathing as he spoke. If he had not spoken I would have confirmed to his wife that he was happy and well. His eyes told me as much yet now I was hearing his words.

"Your husband wants you to know he's happy."

Alice began to cry. I should have known she would. It can be a very traumatic time to know a loved one is still around, even though they have left the physical world.

"Alice?" I asked, my hand resting on her arm. "Why did you put the clock in the hall?"

"He bought me that, just before he died. I wanted to look at it every day so I moved it near the front door."

"He wants you to replace it with a picture. He doesn't want you to be upset each time you use the front door."

She looked disappointed, perhaps annoyed. I begged this soul to relay more information. I needed something to make his wife smile again, something she could tell her children when they asked about her reading with the medium.

"Your husband is showing me your wedding photograph," I announced, relieved as her eyes began to sparkle. And then he showed me another photograph. "He now has a picture of a baby, a black and white photograph." But as I told her about the second picture her smile vanished. "It is your daughter, I believe."

I wondered why he was showing me this photograph and why Alice had suddenly become somewhat distressed. I didn't want her to tell me even though I knew there was something sinister in her husband's actions.

I glanced at my client, her face ashen as she looked at me. Her arms folded, legs crossed, William took a step backwards. He no longer wanted to comfort his wife. He no longer wanted her to feel his surrounding energy. His eyes had become harsh and the answer was staring me in the face. The manifested spirit began to fade but just as I decided to close the reading another energy entered our space. I was frustrated at being unable to work out whether it was a male or female spirit. The energy seemed to hover around Alice, seeming unsure whether to manifest or not. I sensed it was someone who hadn't come to terms with their passing, but I also sensed that the spirit was holding back from communication. I noticed Alice shivering as the room had got considerably colder. After being sure that the mysterious energy had left us alone, I once more decided to close the reading.

"I couldn't tell him." Alice sobbed as we made our way back to the kitchen. The reading had drained my energy, taken my soul and used it to punish this woman who wanted so much to make contact with her departed husband.

"Would you like some more tea?" I asked.

"No, I need to go home. How much do I owe you?"

"Alice, I don't want your money, it isn't the way I work." I had given her only half an hour of my time and she stood before me with an open purse. I refused her money. And she changed her mind about the tea.

"It can sometimes be a relief to talk to strangers about your inner most feelings. Your husband will visit again, I'm sure of it." More convinced than I was prepared to understand.

"The child isn't his," she began, trusting me to hear something she wished no one else to know.

It was no surprise. The look on spirit's face as he backed away from his grieving wife told me why he had come to see her. As he left, he impressed thoughts upon me. Thoughts I was certain would cause more pain for Alice Baxter after she had obviously been through so much already.

"My husband was away at sea," she continued. "His brother often visited me and we became close. I knew it was wrong but I was lonely. We had an affair and I had a daughter. William, my husband, believed she was his, I never told him the truth."

My vow never to judge remained and I sat down at the kitchen table that night until 1am, listening to my new friend reveal the truth about her life.

I knew other spirits may have come through but William stole centre stage. My head pounded. My muscles ached. Alice had come through my door eager and excited at the prospect of communicating with her late husband. She had left in tatters. Her heart broken once more. I doubted she would sleep that night and I felt she would be reluctant to seek solace in further mediumship. But I liked her. She knew she would never tell her husband about their child's paternity and having forgotten to ask, I wondered if she might have discussed it with the child herself.

A part of me wanted to see her again, to answer the questions I had little right to know. I even wanted to see William again. I decided, after I had slept, I would meditate and try to contact him.

Chapter Three

S piders and bats always had free reign as they roamed the attics of my house. Softly they moved, quietly making their hasty retreat for the tiny beam of light which gathered in the top eaves. I didn't use the attic space for fear of being eaten alive. Or perhaps my clumsy steps would falter as floorboards gave way beneath my feet. As I cleaned the bathroom with determined strength, my domesticity showing no bounds, I heard footsteps above me. It was the morning after Alice Baxter's anguished reading and I hadn't slept well having been awoken several times by tapping seeming to come from the window. I told myself it was the wind picking up beneath the crystals which hung innocently, a prism of light reflecting upon my walls.

But as my duties continued, as water washed away down a shiny silver plug hole, the creatures which lived in neglected space above my head became irritable, clamorous in their bid to escape. My longing to understand this unexplained movement left me anxious, yet a little excited at the thought of having discovered another visitor in my already affected residence.

Turning off the tap, I averted my eyes to the ceiling. Perhaps I expected it to disappear from my view, to reveal a party of ghosts walking about my attic space. I hoped it was not a spider of which I could not have contemplated moving.

But of course I was not so easily fooled, knowing the difference between earth and spiritual planes. I came to the conclusion that my attention had once again been required and I, being rather sensitive to such attentive gestures, had another reason to love my house.

There were cases of course when I had to smile, remembering I had my washing machine whirring its way around a full load. Air fresheners sometimes gave the game away too, their lavender aroma alerting my third eye to a paranormal being. But more times than not, the explanation always fell on my love of a spiritual realm, where my heart truly belonged. There were many more mediums and psychics far greater than I, with the ability to see far into the future, watch a person's life unfold before their eyes.

I continued to listen to the activity from my attic, knowing whoever was up there was demanding my attention. I had been found. My earlier inspection of the attic space had proved rather boring, just an empty area, ideal for putting those unwanted items which you didn't have the heart to throw away.

The bathroom sparkled. White aluminium bath, shiny taps. I didn't clean much, never saw a need. Living on my own had brought idleness to my already inactive bones. Yet it was becoming obvious to me now, spirit was eager to communicate so had impressed thoughts upon me to clean. Spirit worked in mysterious ways. I held a cloth in my hand, bleach in my other. Whoever needed my help also needed something clearing up. I thought hard. The soul who had previously sought my attention had made their way to the room in which I now stood. The cold water tap turned itself on as water began trickling down the ceramic sink.

"What is it?" I asked out loud. "Who are you?"

Not one to waste water, I turned off the tap. Shadows danced upon the opposite wall as the centre light flickered. The soul was restless. It was time I tuned in to its vibrations, discovered its reason for visiting me. I moved into the reading room where my meditating chair welcomed me. I sat down, my body feeling heavy, back beginning to ache. I blessed myself as I recited my words of protection, sat upright in the leather chair, my feet firmly on the ground, arms resting on the sides as my hands loosely fell, finger tips pointing to the floor.

"Protect me from darkness, show me the light." Within seconds the noises began, floorboards creaking to the rhythm of someone's footsteps.

"You have my attention. Are you William Baxter?" I asked.

My thoughts had already told me who this soul could be. I knew he would return, he had matters to discuss, business he needed to end. His wife had come to me for answers. She wondered if he would find out about her dishonesty once he had passed and now I had that confirmation. But another soul came through; a tall man. Handsome, sophisticated, features similar to those of William Baxter.

Yet this second soul had red pupils. An angry soul, determined and fired up. My heart missed a beat and I flinched. Two souls stood before me, Spirit men wanting my help. Having passed many years previously, the brothers had found each other and chosen me to help them continue their journey, an end to the torment of love and hate.

The names which came through were William and Harold. They had confused me. I wasn't sure if that was their intention but only one soul had come through the previous night. Alice had been quite sure that it must have been her husband and I now sat in meditative state looking at both men in spirit form, psychically asking questions. The second soul smiled, his eyes now piercing mine; I so wanted to keep the connection. But he began to fade. The manifestation which had appeared before me was leaving, to return I assumed, when Alice was present.

The first soul looked at me. His eyes were sad. The pain he had so obviously felt during his passing was being impressed upon me as the pain in my back was increasing. I can only describe it as being stabbed.

<hr />

I had been living more than forty years without knowing my real father. My mother had relationships, love affairs with men I would wish to be known as "dad" but nothing ever came of them. Since the twenty years in which she had begun her journey on the astral plane, I had wondered if my father would come forward, claim me as his own. I often made enquiries about his whereabouts and I had always given up. No one seemed to know him. My feelings remained that he perhaps lived in another country, didn't wish to know me, or was simply oblivious to the fact that he had a daughter who was now in her forties and lived alone. He could of course have been dead.

Some days I would sit silently and think about him. I would imagine a childhood with him around; taking me to the park on a summer's day or down to the rock pools, reading me bedtime stories while mum finished doing the dishes. I would imagine him giving me piggy back rides to school or taking me and my friends to a disco. Life with "dad" could have been wonderful, if only I had been given the chance to meet him.

My mother never talked about him. I sometimes wondered if she even knew who my father was. She was a wonderful parent doing everything she could to ensure I had a happy childhood. And I did. But there was always something missing, from her life, as well as mine.

I didn't feel sorry for her though. She had a man in her life for many years, Eric. I thought he was my dad for a long time while I was growing up. He used to play with me on the floor in the lounge. He often brought me presents, a new bike one Christmas, a beautiful doll another. We went on many holidays together. He loved to travel, introducing us to different parts of the country. But one day he travelled on his own and never returned.

Mum was devastated. I was twelve years old and took care of her for the weeks that followed his disappearance. When she announced to me that he was not my real father I began to hate him. My school work suffered for the next year and I remember mum sitting outside the Headmaster's office at least once a week. She blamed everything on Eric. And so did I. He had made mine and my mother's life a misery, yet had touched it with love at the same time.

I think mum used to write to his sister in the south. She thought he had gone to live down there but as time went by I had my suspicions that she was probably wrong. None of her letters were replied to and she didn't suggest going to look for him. Being a forceful and rather dynamic character, she preferred to see things through to the end. Eric must have really hurt her.

When I turned sixteen, I experienced my first spirit encounter, that of my grandmother. I had never known her yet there were many photographs of this beautiful woman positioned around our home. She had clearly been loved, having lived a wonderful life with my grandfather, another soul who had long since passed over. My mum often told me stories about them, about how proud they would have been of me. I always felt as though I had met them, knew them personally, even though their photographs were the only proof to me of their existence.

The only sound I could hear in my bedroom that night was of my fingers hitting the keyboard of my typewriter. It was an electronic machine, quite advanced with an eraser key. My mum had bought it as a birthday present. I hoped for a computer but in those days they were few and far between to the working classes. I bought my own paper with my pocket money.

For no reason, no logical explanation, the words of which I typed appeared differently on the paper. I didn't understand what was happening, cursing the typewriter for breaking down. I had no idea about electronic machines, my knowledge failing to stretch to such technology. As I looked upon the white A4 paper which rotated upwards as the keys were inflicted, I read the strangest sentence, one which didn't match the one I had intentionally typed;

"You have the gift," it said, bizarrely, causing my stomach to knot with excitement.

I was amazed. Each of the four words was perfectly legible. Had the typewriter broken down or my fingers hit the wrong keys, surely the words would form no sentence. But what did it mean? Was it referring to me? And if so, what gift was it talking about?

I removed the piece of paper from the machine then switched it off. I had almost finished my work and felt it was probably time to rest my mind. But my grandmother had other ideas. She stood before me, a full manifestation in my bedroom as I felt the hair on my arms stand on end and my heart begin to race. She wore a sleeveless navy-blue dress; a string of white pearls fell loosely around her neck. She had brown hair, short and wavy, like my own. She carried a white handbag, large handles held in her delicate hands. A smile lit up her face, kind eyes reaching into my soul. I couldn't help but smile back. I wasn't afraid but elated at her presence. She looked just like the photograph which sat proudly on our fireplace.

As her lips moved, no sound could be heard. It was like she mimed to me, expecting me to understand her every word. The silence in the room was deafening. I couldn't think about anything other than the words I felt she was speaking to me. Her voice was soft. Her accent seemed to be like my mother's yet with slight vibrations as she relayed the message of which she obviously intended me to hear.

"You have the gift," she said.

I looked at the piece of white paper. Amongst my words appeared those of legible statement. I was beginning to understand what the words meant having come across the paranormal before, once experimented with during my years at High School. Some of my friends had once partaken in Ouija Board. I didn't join in though, I thought it was childish at the time. Only two of the five girls arrived in school the following morning. The other three had been violently sick during the night and one had experienced a wine glass being thrown in her direction.

My grandmother continued to stand in elegance. Her smile comforted me and I knew she didn't mean harm. I even knew she was a ghost. My first ghost. The one I would never forget. That was to be the first of many times in which my grandmother would grace me with her presence. How grateful to her I was that night, for introducing me to the path of my life.

Chapter Four

*I*t rained. For once the forecast was accurate; a week of showers and heavy winds, a dreary week ahead. Having no motivation to venture out I decided to meditate. I was eager to contact my visitors from the other night, hoping they would give me more information about their purpose to manifest. Many souls who contacted me often did so to pass on messages to loved ones. They wanted their wives or husbands, sons and daughters to know that they still existed, albeit on an astral plane. I had the job of deciphering their message.

But this was different. I felt that the two spirits that had recently made themselves known to me had done so because the message was for me. Not for a loved one. Not even for Alice. I had spent most of the previous night lying awake thinking about my past, reminiscing about my childhood. As eventful as it had been, I could never have prepared myself for what lay ahead. The years passed by and my gift became more intense as I realised it had been given to me with no choice but to accept.

The house was quiet as I made my way upstairs. Part of me wondered whether I should have phoned Alice, explained to her that I would be trying to contact her husband and given her the option to sit with me. A séance might have been something she would fear but I could put her mind at rest, make her understand that, as a medium, I would never allow any harm to come to her. I went towards the phone which was on a table on the half-landing but when I reached it, I felt a significant blast of cold air rush past me. The communication with my spirit visitor had begun. I stood still, looking at the stair case, waiting for a soul to manifest.

A heavily scented perfume wafted around the landing, as a draught continued to blow on my face. She stood beside me, tall and elegant, beautiful in her feminine pose. Wavy brown hair fell against her blouse, a high neck with a dainty string of pearls on show. The name in my thoughts was Jane. Her face looked familiar, not of one I had seen before but of significant resemblance, perhaps to a family member.

As I continued to watch her, she began to glide across the landing, towards the top of the stairs. I moved to stand beside her but she seemed to be oblivious of my presence. Her eyes were sad and her expression confused. Emotion overwhelmed me as she started to run down the stairs, haste causing her to trip and fall. She tumbled, her body twisted as she lay at the bottom of the stairs, motionless. I could feel my emotions changing, the fear I had since felt subsided to allow thoughts of life's end to surface. Within seconds, her spirit vanished and she was gone. A breeze lifted the curtains at the hall window even though the window was shut. I wasn't sure what I had just witnessed but I went down stairs and stood in the space she had once lay. I wasn't sure whether another force had pushed her down the stairs, or whether she had simply tripped and fallen, to meet her demise unexpectedly. My tears ceased and calm once more resumed but I knew I had just uncovered a tragic event in days gone by. That night I knew I would have to conduct a séance.

Chapter Five

I decided to invite my friend Lucy to sit in on the séance. She had involved herself in spiritual exercises with me over the years and I knew this one would have interested her immensely.

She arrived at 9pm, a bottle of Chardonnay in her grasp. She wiped her blonde hair out of her face, beaming with pleasure at the prospect of a night in with the spirits. I welcomed her with open arms, our friendship had never faltered, even when she married. Lucy had two beautiful children, Jacob and Rebecca. I was Godmother to them both. Each having left home and living in halls of residence at Edinburgh University, she had more time to herself, more quality moments when she could allow herself those special treats that she had spent years going without. Her ex-husband had left long ago.

I had performed many séances previously, but this would be the first at Rosehill. I felt excited at the prospect of finding out who the mysterious beauty was and if any other previous occupants felt it necessary to make their presence known. I suspected I would hear from some but I was hoping that the Baxter brothers would appear again, bringing to light a little more information about their past.

The room was ready. Night had fallen and my candle stood, lit, upon the mantel. I arranged the letters, skirting around the outside, A to Z and the words, "yes", "no" and "goodbye" in between. Numbers 0 to 9 also lay in the circle but were rarely needed as I usually had a precise impression of dates, ages and numeric information. I placed a glass in the centre, blessing and encouraging it to be my guide to another plane. I was calm. I felt peaceful, if not a little hopeful. The candle indicated to me as it gently flickered insisting that I should take my seat and prepare for spirit communication. Lucy seemed nervous. I couldn't quite understand her mood as we sat perfectly still, our finger tips touching the other.

"Let the light shine within us, allow it to flow through our bodies, passing onto each other and let us imagine it now shining above us, banishing out the darkness that may wish to overwhelm our thoughts." Lucy was used to my opening calls which were essential to protect us from unwanted spirits, those of a more sinister disposition.

We both opened our eyes. The glass remained motionless. We waited. I was sure Lucy's anxieties were more pronounced as she released a tense sigh, prompting me to wonder why she was feeling so nervous. As the first spirit entered our space, I held my breath. Fear was telling me who the visitor was yet I preferred to ignore him, wishing him to leave us alone and allow those who needed to communicate to come forward. The room became cold. A sudden drop in temperature indicated spirit's presence.

"You know who's here, don't you?" My question to Lucy needed no answer. Her eyes glazed by tears, she tried hard to focus as the glass began to move slowly, spelling out a name, much to our regret.

P. A. U. L.

He committed suicide four years previously, unable to accept that his children had turned their backs on him. Leaving Lucy had been the biggest mistake of his life. He didn't need to use energy for his announcement. My psychic thought had already told me our first communicator could mean trouble. Yet I felt somewhat sympathetic towards him as it became obvious how much he wanted to speak to his ex-wife. I was his channel to help him do just that, and reluctantly, I gave in. I had never turned spirit away and I didn't intend to start there.

"Paul, how can I help you?" I was gentle in my manner.

The glass moved, first to L and then predictably to U. I too, became nervous. Paul was scaring my friend but I desperately wanted to continue. My legs were becoming numb, I was constantly aware of my aura as the draught became more intense. Over the years I had learnt to block out the coldness as spirit came forward but this was testing my mediumship. I wondered if Paul intended to weaken me, if he wanted to possess me so that he could speak directly to the woman he still loved.

"What do you think he wants?" Lucy asked, almost shaking in her seat.

"He just wants to communicate. He misses you," I replied, hoping Lucy would agree.

She shuffled in her chair, her discomfort now obvious to our visitor. He was reluctant to speak to me yet he continued to use the Ouija board, determined for Lucy to understand his reason for the visit.

I Love You. The glass moved around the table, spelling out its message as I put my hand over Lucy's, steadying her as she was in danger of breaking the communication. *Forgive me*, it continued, slowing down as it once more returned to the centre, waiting for a reaction.

Lucy looked at me, her eyes troubled. "If I forgive him will he leave me alone?"

"I don't know," I replied. "But you must only forgive him if that's what's in your heart."

I silently prayed for Paul to leave us, allowing Lucy peace after the pain he had put her through.

Within seconds of these thoughts another spirit entered the room. Another male soul reached out in our séance to attract my attention and allow me into his existence. His name was Arthur. He was 52 years old and had met his death in 1874. I felt he had once belonged to the house. Pains in my chest indicated that he had suffered a heart attack and I immediately felt that it had come about due to a sudden and tragic bereavement. I felt comfortable with him as I welcomed him to our séance. Something told me Arthur had come forward for no other reason than to introduce himself to me as a previous occupant.

"Has someone else come forward?" Lucy asked, her emotional state now almost back to normal.

"If there are any other spirits here with us, please come forward," I said.

My mind's eye could clearly see the attractive brunette whom I had since witnessed falling down the stairs, her brown eyes looked sternly in my direction. She presented about forty. Her clothes were modern and I suspected she had passed quite recently.

My head had started to throb and I could feel a sharp pain over my left eye as was usually the case when I was running low on energy.

Séances were often easier when my grandmother attended, her guidance advising me of visiting souls. She helped me to decipher messages, making communication clearer to me on the occasions when a particularly difficult spirit would come through. Why my grandmother hadn't joined us on this rather strange night I had no idea.

Paul seemed to have left us, perhaps realising Lucy's discomfort at his presence and Arthur had definitely gone. I still felt that Jane was hovering nearby but my pulsating head led me to make the decision that our séance should come to an end. It hadn't been particularly successful but so was often the case when trying to summon eager communication whilst expecting too much.

I closed the séance with the Lord's Prayer. Both Lucy and I were relieved when we were able to relax a little, cross our legs and shuffle our chairs away from the table. I switched the light on above us and blew the candle out.

"So what did you think of that?" Lucy, still somewhat perturbed, was the first to speak.

"I really don't know," I replied. "I don't know who Jane is. Arthur was a nice man, I'm sure he'll be back, and as for Paul, who knows. He obviously wants to contact you."

"How dare he turn up like that."

"You make it sound as though he's still living." I chuckled, hoping to make a little light of the recent activity.

"The way he communicated tonight, you would think he was. Shall I open the wine?"

"I don't think I could manage any. I feel drained." I sat with my head in my hands. I had experienced huge numbers of visiting spirits in a night's work but just three during that séance had washed me out.

"Leave it for another night then. I'll get off home and let you go to bed." Always thoughtful, Lucy stood up and went towards the door. "What's wrong with the handle?" she asked as she tried in vain to turn it.

"Nothing, here, let me try." I joined her, perhaps it needed a little persuasion.

But for the love of God, I could not open that door. The handle would turn yet the door wouldn't budge. My hand wrenched as I tried in desperation to free us. I knew we had been locked in the room, our séance had brought energy into the room which had been preserved within the flesh of the building. My only fear was that I had no idea where the energy would lead, whose spirit might manifest as forgotten souls tried to escape. I did not appreciate being haunted in this way. Spirit communicators would still be aware of my ability for them to use me as their channel to the outside world and now they were causing unnecessary frustration. Lucy once more took over the handle as I stood back. There was a light in the corner of the room, growing in eagerness to manifest.

"Who are you?" I asked, a little angry, somewhat anxious.

In the corner of my eye I noticed the glass begin to move on the table. Initially in a slow circle then it quickened its pace, moving round and round faster than I could keep up. Lucy turned from the door to stand and watch the glass. Fixated on its movement, both of us wondering whether it would begin to spell out a name, it suddenly shot off the table with amazing speed, flew across the room and smashed within a few inches of where we stood, against the door.

"Shit!" screamed Lucy. "What the hell was that all about?"

"An angry spirit, I suspect." I was quite sure it wasn't Paul. His spirit had been so easy to identify and even though I was sure he would visit again, this was definitely not a spirit that wanted to be easily distinguished. I prayed that I had not stirred up negative energy within my home. But who would wish harm on me? Or Lucy?

Chapter Six

I awoke the following morning, a distant headache threatening to spoil my day, but the vibrant colours of a nearby robin made me smile and remember I had Christmas to look forward to. I always enjoyed celebrating the festive time of year, usually with friends who were willing to take pity on me as I pottered about the shops buying last minute presents and a suitable tree. This year I had planned a little soiree at Rosehill. I had invited four guests, Lucy being one of them. Lizzie and Hamish I had known for many years after being neighbours in Edinburgh and then there was Richard, a friend from my University days. Having been married and divorced he lived alone, vowing never to fall in love again. I liked Richard, we had much in common and should he not have been engaged to Paula when I first met him, I might have been attracted to him myself. As it happened, our friendship became more important. We respected each other too much to have a frivolous fling only to become lifelong enemies.

My friends accepted me for what I did. They often questioned noises in my vicinity, asking if any of their long lost relatives had appeared or if I could sense activity in their homes. I had read for them individually on many occasions but I refused to do it if we were meeting for a social event. I will always remember one night in particular when Lizzie knocked on my door almost demanding that I go straight to her flat.

"There's someone in our bathroom," she announced, completely breathless and seemingly scared.

Traipsing across the landing in my pyjamas and slippers, I went into her bathroom to find an elderly gentleman sitting on the toilet. He looked up at me as though wondering why I had disturbed him.

"What do you want?" I asked.

"Can't a man have some privacy?" he answered.

"Who are you?" I suspected the man was a previous occupant of Lizzie's flat.

"Troy," was his abrupt reply.

"Why have you come here?"

"I live here!" I was grateful that Lizzie couldn't hear him. She could no longer see him either which was quite lucky as I didn't think she would take kindly to having an elderly man living in her flat, making himself at home.

"You have to move on," I told him, hoping Lizzie might leave me to discuss this in private. I turned to look at her and she raised her arms in defeat.

"Okay, okay, I'm going," she said.

Once she was out of earshot I began reciting the prayer of which my grandmother taught me, requesting spirit to leave our space and continue on his journey.

"Your life has ended. We thank you for your presence here but you need to leave us now, leave this life to us. Go now, go with our love." I shook. Not so long ago I had been ready to go to bed yet now I was closing the gates on a spirit entity, refusing to let him reside on a plane which no longer belonged to him.

The spirit left. Shadows danced around the room, my indication that Lizzie was no longer sharing her flat with an astral. I guess I came in handy that night. My purpose in life was always to help others, whether it was a friend in need or a spirit needing guidance.

She was more relieved than grateful I think, which prompted me to sit with her for a while, help her to understand she had nothing to fear.

Everywhere was locked up and I felt secure as I climbed beneath the duvet. The hour was late. Rosehill was quiet, dark and atmospheric. I couldn't sleep so I lay awake instead, thinking about my mother's blue eyes and her tender smile. Something heavy sat down at the foot of my bed. A visitor had arrived. Turning over and repositioning myself for comfort I was still unable to rest and seek peaceful state of mind. It was cold in my room even though I was already clad in winter attire. I decided to give in to the demands of my guest and got out of bed, reaching for my dressing gown. After leaving the room I chose to follow the footsteps which I had since heard descending the stairs.

The lounge was piercing, forcing me to pull my gown tightly around me. I switched the television on, a little company to assist me as I tried hard to beckon sleep. But I couldn't settle. I felt uncomfortable whilst sitting rigid on the sofa. My body however, was aching from cold and my mind felt overwhelmed by thought. Yet I couldn't understand why I was beginning to feel so emotional. My heart raced, my palms perspired, I could feel tears stabbing the backs of my eyes then a drop escaped, leaving me bemused.

The lounge door closed. My head immediately turned as I had a sharp intake of breath, relief washing over me. I had been drawn towards a forceful energy creating a wealth of emotions as I once more reached out my hand, this time to the soul who stood before me, her blue eyes drowning me in their intensity. Her beautiful smile helped me to feel at ease. I warmed. The room no longer pierced my skin with its chill. A rush of heat burned through my chest, my eyes closed, and tears flowed in a bid to escape the highly charged sensation.

My cries turned into a heart broken sob. I couldn't seem to prevent this powerful emotion. The television continued in its quest to comfort; yet failed. Noises screamed from the pictures which moved about before my eyes. They didn't register with me. All I could hear was the soul who encouraged me to leave my bed; the soul whom cried with me as we remembered the promises we had once made to each other many years ago; our pledge of unconditional love as we sat on my bed when I was eighteen years old, after a difficult time which had finally come to an end. My mother held me in her arms back then, her cries emitting around the room, her tears falling upon my silken gown. She almost gave up what she had achieved throughout her life, just to keep me warm and loved. My mum proved once more that she lived on, through me and with me. My only wish was that she would visit me more often. Introduce me to her new life as she watched me live mine.

Always our favourite time of year I was touched by her visit at Christmas. We would spend the whole day on our own, no visitors or interruptions, just the two of us immersed in each other's company.

Since her passing, Christmas had been one of the rare times I had felt her near me. Not that she needed to remind me of how much we enjoyed that quality time together, but it was as though she wanted to. I wondered if she felt lonely in her new world, finding it difficult to reach out to our earth plane.

Chapter Seven

*P*erhaps there was a reason for my mother's visit that night as the next day I answered the door to the local vicar. He stood on my door step dressed in full cassock and clerical collar; a sophisticated man, bearing slightly greying hair at the sides of his otherwise full head of dark brown hair. Tall and a little intimidating, he smiled at me, holding out his hand. A little perturbed, I acknowledged him, finding myself embroiled in a rather firm handshake. I liked him immediately.

Of course I had heard people speak of him but had never found myself in his company. I didn't attend church; too many regular parishioners would have thought it inappropriate for me to kneel in worship. The village was still quite traditional and the majority of its inhabitants were definitely on the wrong side of sixty. I ushered my guest into the kitchen, not really sure whether a sherry would have been more suitable or just plain tea.

"I hope I'm not disturbing you. I'm Marcus Calloway." He spoke with elegance, his voice gentle.

"Camilla," I replied. "Camilla Armstrong. It's always a pleasure to welcome people to Rosehill." I hoped my chairs weren't dusty as he parked himself carefully at the table. "Would you like some tea?"

"Sounds like a good idea."

I could sense him watching me as I pottered about the kitchen, forgetting where I had put tea bags and cups and wondering why I was about to look in the oven for a spoon. I had never felt this way before, not about a vicar.

"I was hoping to see you at the Sunday service." Hiding his expression with his cup, he looked in my direction.

"I'm afraid I'm not a church goer. Never have been."

"May I ask why?"

"I guess my mother never took me." I turned to him, his eyes continuing to bore into mine. He replaced his cup and clasped his hands together, elbows resting on the table.

"Then I'm inviting you to our forthcoming event this Sunday. A carol service."

"I'm sorry, not my thing, Reverend."

He smiled. "You have no need to apologise. And please, call me Marcus, it's so much less formal."

"More tea?" I asked.

"Why don't we go for a walk?" he suggested. "Make the most of this beautiful day." I agreed, starting to feel claustrophobic as my cheeks were burning up.

But something worried me. I couldn't stop feeling slightly guilty as this gentle man opened the door for me. Some people in the village knew of my mediumship yet I was doubtful that he did. Would he have been so considerate should he have known of my communication with another dimension? The view of Christianity in such instances did not agree with my practices, my delivering of messages in the form of passed souls. They condemned spirit communication, scorned upon mediums, psychics, clairvoyants and all those capable of future prediction. I was confused.

I wanted to get to know this man but I feared that once he knew of my "gift" he would turn away, never to return to Rosehill.

There was hardly a breeze to speak of. Blue sky enveloped us as the sun reminded us of summer days. The grounds of Rosehill boasted many walks of delight, eerie silences surrounding the trees and fields, unseen eyes following our every move. It was obvious to me that Marcus had walked through my land before I became familiar with its beauty; he almost led me along the path which took us into open countryside.

"Where did you live before you moved here?" he asked.

"Edinburgh. I lived in a flat, virtually in the centre. How about you?

"I lived in London. I wanted to move up here for the tranquillity. I've met some wonderful people so far." He looked at me, a smile forming, his eyes kind yet seemingly troubled. "So what brought you to the Borders?"

The question I didn't know how to answer. Was I supposed to tell this man of the cloth, thinking of his God with rose tinted glasses, that my deceased grandmother had brought me to this beautiful place? That she spoke to me with sincerity in order to assist my communication with the world of spirit?

"I have always loved the Borders, I decided to bid for Rosehill when it came up for auction last year. I heard a developer was interested in demolishing the house and building a hotel." I had lied to him. Perhaps if I kept the bit about my grandmother actually introducing me to the house he would think nothing of it. My life would remain pure. I could continue with a murky conscience.

"It must have taken a lot of time and money to get it back to its former splendour?"

"Money, yes. It took less time than I expected but there is still lots to do. The land needs attention of course as do the outbuildings." I stopped and pointed in the direction of a cluster of run-down sheds, most of which needed destroying and rebuilding. "Joey Taylor suggested I rent most of the land out. I feels it's a good idea but I've been so busy recently, I haven't got round to doing anything about it." Another lie was imminent.

"Busy? What is it you do for a living, Camilla?"

I walked right into that one. Pure didn't cut the cloth anymore. Holes and digging however, did.

"I'm a ....." I could almost hear my brain working its way around the next answer. "I'm a lady of leisure. I don't have to work anymore, my mother made sure I was well catered for when she passed."

"Passed?" He seemed concerned.

"Yes, twenty years ago." I could feel my answers coming together. There seemed no need to tell Marcus of my mediumship now. I was aware of him discovering the truth through village gossip, but of course being a vicar, I assumed he would never listen to such tickle tackle.

I pointed to a newly planted oak tree. "It's in memory of my mother. Her favourite type of tree. She planted one in memory of her own mother which gave me the idea."

"Were you close to your mother?" A large hare bounded in front of us, desperate to disappear from human sight.

"Yes. We had a wonderful relationship. She gave me everything she could, including a lifetime of love."

"A lifetime? Do you mean with what you have achieved here?"

"Well it's through her generosity that I'm able to live here. She will always be with me." He lifted his head, a strangely patronising expression appearing on his otherwise prominent face.

"I always think it rather sad when people say that." He surprised me.

"In what way?" I asked, the words leaving my mouth before my brain had chance to engage.

"It seems an obsession these days that our loved ones should live on after they have been entrusted to the hands of our Lord."

Feeling myself clenching as I dug my nails into my flesh, I realised I couldn't have a debate about my religious beliefs with a vicar, particularly one I hardly knew. He was trying to make me see his point of view and he wanted to see me in church on Sunday. Perhaps I should have told him the truth behind Camilla Armstrong there and then.

"It's a comfort to know my mother is here with me. I didn't want her to leave this life and I'm sure she would rather have stayed. I think we all have our beliefs, whether they be religious or not."

"Aha! But you think your mother is watching you now? Do you think she joins us on this walk? My parishioners have a loyalty to their Christian beliefs, they find comfort in attending my services on Sundays and integrating with the villagers. Why don't you think about it?"

He was beginning to annoy me. I couldn't think about worshipping Jesus Christ, kneeling before a life size statue as it loured over me, reminding me that I had sinned and I must therefore beg for forgiveness. This man hardly knew me. He had shared tea and biscuits with me at my kitchen table and now he thought he had the right to dictate to me what I should do with my Sundays. I wanted to challenge him. I wanted to annoy him the way he was doing with me.

"Church just isn't my thing." I stopped. My eye had caught something flit between the hedge. I stood rigid, listening to the leaves rustle on my right hand side. I knew it was not an animal, but my mind's eye was telling me I needed to concentrate. Marcus stood still, turning round to see why I had stopped.

I couldn't tell him that I had seen a woman following us; that a spirit person watched our every move, listened to our conversation and looked at us disapprovingly. But I could sense that this woman had connections with Marcus. She held her hand upon her chest, telling me she loved him. She was beautiful. Long golden hair cascaded down her back, her eyes were blue and her skin soft. She had the sweetest smile I had ever seen upon the face of an astral being. Yet she continued to look at Marcus as though wishing he would notice her.

Of course he knew nothing of the mysterious woman whom had suddenly graced us with her presence. I couldn't reach a name. Nothing apart from a television screen appeared in my head as I watched the spirit woman. And then it suddenly came to me. The woman's face was the young beauty I had seen some nights previously as I sat watching television in my lounge. Her elegance once more overwhelmed me. She was indeed quite breathtaking.

"Is there something wrong?" Marcus asked, a little agitation showing in his voice. My train of thought could only persist in view of this spiritual encounter. I couldn't comprehend his words or his thoughts as I began to feel the hold over which this woman had on him. I could not have been sure at that time, but as the woman pointed to her wedding ring it became clearer.

Trying hard to concentrate on someone other than our spirit guest, I failed to understand her reason for appearing before me. Perhaps she was warning me off, maybe she was simply telling me he was hers. Marcus had the potential of being a friend. But I would not be warned off someone by spirit communication. That kind of contact always spurred me on, encouraged me to a challenge and to know more about why I should be deterred.

I had made a vow when my mediumship first became clear that I would never let spirit frighten me. It was of course inevitable that sometimes I would get spooked by poltergeist and it had happened occasionally, but I was strong, stronger after my mother had passed.

"..... dinner sometime?" Marcus's voice rang in my ear as the spirit vanished.

"Sorry?"

"Would you like to come over for dinner sometime?" A distant chuckle became mixed up with his offer as he repeated his words and I smiled, realising I was back with him.

"That would be lovely, thank you."

It would also be a good time to tell him who I really was. I didn't want gossip stealing my thunder.

"Have you always been a vicar?"

"No, I used to teach. When I left university my heart was in teaching."

"Religious Education, I suppose."

"Physical Education, actually. I was sporty once, loved to be doing anything concerning fitness. Then I realised ten years into my teaching career that my real vocation in life was to serve everyone, not just kids. I guess you could say I was 'called' to do a job that I knew very little about." That handsome smile once more brushed his face as our eyes met, and I again felt myself blush.

"How long have you been a vicar then?"

"Twenty three years. It seems like yesterday that my ordination took place. A church packed with people, all willing me on. It was one of the most amazing days of my life." He gazed at the field on our left, lost in that service of long ago.

I tried to work out how old he must be. Definitely older than me.

"I'm fifty-eight, if you were wondering." A little telepathy had passed between us, I was surprised at his sudden announcement.

I smiled. There was no denying that this man could indeed be my friend. I had seen passion in his eyes as I opened the back door to him earlier, a sense of companionship eased my heart, comforting me to the face of a stranger.

He was fourteen years older. Not that age bothered me. I had never been deterred by the age difference in a relationship. It was a minor problem if a problem at all.

"I take it you prefer the priesthood?"

His eyes lit. The sun seemed to answer my question as I noticed a distinct glow on his face. Marcus believed in what he did more than anything. I didn't need my psychic mind to tell me so. He had found salvation in a life with God; the dream for him had come true.

"I wonder if I could have done anything else. It's just a shame my mother was never around to see it. She died just two months before I was ordained. There was a time during those weeks that I decided I wouldn't go through with it. I had a good family to support me and they made me realise that my mother would have been the proudest member of my congregation should she have been there." He smiled at me. "I knew they were right of course. And when I knelt at the altar, receiving my Holy Orders, I could almost hear my mother's voice telling me she loved me."

"I can imagine you did." I wished I had been there. I'm sure I would have seen her watching in boastful admiration.

"I know I should never talk about such things, but I have seen her, in the church. I had to pray for forgiveness afterwards just in case I had been possessed by the devil!" It was a surprise announcement indeed.

"Christianity can do strange things to a person. Do you believe you were possessed?" Surely not, I thought. Yet this man had already shown me he had telepathic abilities.

"No, of course not. I believe I had just been having a difficult time and she was on my mind. It was inevitable that I should imagine something more than I was capable of doing. We mustn't speak of the dead as though they are here. Their souls live on through our Lord, not through us."

A surge of disappointment rushed through my veins. He had no intention of believing a word of what I was then becoming desperate to reveal. Yet I had to tell him. I had never lied to anyone in my life, I could not have contemplated keeping things of such importance from Marcus.

Our walk came to an end as we arrived back at the house. Red cheeked and ready for a hot drink I invited Marcus in but he declined. He was in a hurry to get back and begin writing his Sunday sermon. Based on what we had talked about no doubt.

"Dinner then?" He shouted from the car.

"Just say when, I should be available."

"Thursday night? 7.30?"

It was agreed. I was to go to the vicarage and instructed not to take anything. I wondered if he thought of it as a date, my first in six years. After a brief fling with a guy which ended when I realised he already had a girlfriend I decided that men would have to take a back seat for a while. It occurred to me after two years of being on my own that I didn't need a man in my life. I had too much going on, too many aspects which were open to disruption.

Chapter Eight

*A*s I prepared myself for meditation that night, thoughts of the beautiful spirit woman kept flickering in my mind's eye. I wondered if she was near, had planned to visit me again, formally introduce herself. Red leather calmed me as I sat in my chair, encouraging the light into my heart. Protection was always necessary, particularly when I was alone. Yet right from the start of my trance I realised I was certainly not alone. My grandmother was with me. Her soft tones massaged my soul as she spoke.

"Thank you for being here, grandma." My feelings of delight were disturbed when I detected discomfort in her thought. Something made her unhappy as she wouldn't look into my eyes.

"What is it?" I asked, slightly nervous at my grandmother's aura.

"He's not right for you." It was clearly heard as I sat tall, desperate to interpret each and every word as she would have me understand.

"Do you mean Marcus?"

"No."

"Then who?"

"The man you think you love," my grandmother answered, leaving my thoughts racing for someone. But I couldn't think who she meant.

I could feel my stomach in a state of flurry. Then another spirit came forward. I was astounded when I realised who the spirit person was. Her beauty presented to me in perfect form. The woman who shared our walk earlier in the day once more appeared before me. I couldn't see a full manifestation, just a vision as though her energy weakened. The name of Anne stayed loosely in my head. I knew no one by this name and tried hard to think. But thought was constantly interrupted by my persistent grandmother who now stood in the middle of the room, shaking her head and wagging her finger; she looked at me as though I was a child again and needed to be told right from wrong.

The connection slowly became clear; Anne; her appearance; the face on the television screen, and finally, the spirit that had come forward during my previous séance with Lucy. It was obviously the same person. She had close connections with Marcus but I couldn't see what they were.

My time was booked shortly after by a journalist whom I felt just wanted a reading in order to write about it in her weekly column. However, obligingly I accepted her plea and booked her in, hoping I would make contact with someone close to her, finding the proof that she so obviously needed. I never felt as though I had to prove anything to anyone. My gift was true and those who wished not to believe were free to do so.

When I had first started practicing I would be visited by many sceptics who often frustrated me, leaving me drained after an hour's reading. It was of course initially embarrassing if no spirits presented before me but after a while I realised that I had no need to feel that way. My spirit guide was always present and more than not, the sceptic returned some months later for another try. I think it always helped them to step into my life as I never took money, even though some of the believers insisted I did and give it to charity.

Julia Henderson, tall, elegant, dressed in smart black trouser suit with her brunette hair gently falling against her shoulders, stepped into the house. She held a file under her arm and I suspected a pen within easy reach in the handbag which cascaded over her right shoulder. It crossed my mind whether or not she may possess a dictaphone or even a tape recorder but she didn't show me either.

"Can I offer you a cup of tea or coffee?"

"I think we should just get on with it. You call yourself a medium? We'll see."

I stared at her, asking myself if I should suggest she left. Clearly she had no intention of being here for a reading; her journalistic talent began to show no bounds. My initial reaction was to ask her to leave but I had to give the reading a chance, at least to prove to her I was genuine.

"Please take a seat," I suggested. "I'll get my Crystal." Placing it once more on pewter stand I looked into it. The only thing I saw was a newspaper; it was so typical for there to be no spirit present at that time. I glanced up at Julia.

"Would you like me to give you a formal reading? Are you here to see if we can contact a loved one?" My question was genuine, finding it necessary to ask sceptical clients how they felt.

"You should know I will be doing a piece on you. It won't be pleasant reading because I don't believe a word of what you do." Her rudeness angered me, particularly having to bear it in my own home.

"Then perhaps we should draw a close to the reading now. I don't wish any confrontation in my home." I touched the Crystal and alarmingly my hands came alive with electricity, a shock I had felt only a few times before during a difficult reading.

A picture began to form in my mind's eye and I could see Julia standing over a pile of newspapers, sorrow in her eyes as a man stood nearby. Unfortunately, I couldn't make out the man's face, yet he looked familiar. He was tall with brown hair, distinguished grey temples. An uncomfortable feeling was rushing through my stomach as I prayed hard for spirit presence to join us and show her that I was indeed a medium. Not for a long time had I felt this way.

"Can you see anything then?" she asked with sarcasm in her voice.

"I can see you and a pile of newspapers." I knew I sounded predictable but I never lied about what I saw, unless it was death.

"Has anyone joined us? Can you hear any noises?" She looked around the room, her smugness beginning to irritate the atmosphere.

"Please relax, I feel you are tense. There's no need to be." I decided to turn the tables, determined not to let my discomfort become obvious as she continued to sit cross-legged in her chair, completely unaware of the spirit that had come forward.

"You really are a fake, aren't you? I've never known such nonsense in all my life." She snorted, adjusting her jacket and folding her arms. I found her increasingly difficult to tune into. Many clients came to see me feeling nervous and I usually had the ability, and the experience, to make them feel at ease within five minutes. Julia however, was a challenge.

"You should know there is a spirit in the room with us. I don't yet know who it is and I would ask you once again to relax and try to help me determine them."

"How am I supposed to do that?" Another snort.

"By keeping quiet, just for a few minutes so that I can adjust my mind into understanding what I'm dealing with." The spirit made it almost impossible for me to communicate. I asked silently for my grandmother to protect me as I feared the soul was not to be reckoned with.

The problem was, I hadn't sensed my grandmother at all during the short time Julia and I were in the reading room. She looked at me, her eyes cold and questioning.

"You're not wanted in this village," she began. "Your ways are offending the residents and people are talking about you. When I send this to print you will be forced to leave."

"No one will drive me away from my home," I smiled, trying hard to make her see I wasn't easily intimidated even though my guard had been rocked and I was unnerved at her sudden outburst.

Upon standing from her seat, picking up the file she carried, she turned towards the door. I wanted spirit to communicate so that I could show this despicable woman that she was wrong about me.

"I suggest you stay away from the Reverend too," she began. "He's not right for you and I can assure you he will not want to know you once he reads the paper." These words shocked me more than any other she had spoken in the fifteen minutes of being in her company.

But the murky waters were starting to clear as I began to wonder if Julia was in fact a friend or indeed Marcus's lover.

As she turned on her heels, it all happened so fast; one of the candles on the mantelpiece fell to the floor, the small flame setting light to my hearth rug. I jumped up from my chair, frantically stamping my foot on the small fire which threatened to cause damage to my sacred room. Spirit had clearly found anger within its soul, perhaps at Julia as she started to scream. Her disbelief in me was finally being questioned. The central light flickered even though neither of us stood near the switch, whilst two books fell from the shelf, landing faced down with their pages spread. Julia was visibly shaken at the flurry of activity and I had become worried for myself. I didn't welcome angry spirits into my home, making sure my protective light deterred them from getting through. But it was now clear that this spirit was stronger than my grandmother and had manifested in order to prove to Julia that there is indeed a life after death.

Chapter Nine

*I*t went without saying that I was somewhat nervous about meeting Marcus again. Having been warned off him by Anne and then again by Julia I was unsure as to whether dinner with him was indeed a good idea. But being the independent woman I was, I fought my inner reservations and decided on a rare outfit in which to wear. Perhaps with age, I had expanded over the past few years and was struggling to fit into any of my clothes. I'm not a vain person and detested shopping in the eyes of vanity. However, I took myself into town, determined to find something suitable to wear.

I never had much to do on Saturday nights, life at Rosehill was far different from the one I spent living in Edinburgh. In general it didn't bother me but Christmas was only a week away making me slightly apprehensive about spending the day with a house full of guests. Anxious about the newspaper report that I had been threatened would appear, left me unable to concentrate on recent admin tasks, stupidly forgetting to invoice my tenant farmers. Having scoured the local press and found nothing remotely resembling Julia's article I hoped Marcus had not been filled in on gossip from around the village or worse still, from Julia's own mouth. It was the only and most honest way to confront the situation. Maybe one day I would look back as a lesson not to become attracted to a man of the cloth.

I arrived at the vicarage at seven thirty, somewhat surprised to see him standing on his doorstep. A young woman walked past the drive gate and I wondered if he had been waving to her as I approached, a little disappointment clamouring to the back of my mind. He looked deliciously debonair with his smile once again melting my heart. I noticed a small amount of silver chest hair peeping over the top of his open neck shirt and I needed to compose myself, stop staring as if intrigued by his manly appearance. Because of his church connection and my view of the spirit world, I was aware of the difference in our views, but I had to get to know the man. He fascinated me.

"Am I early?" I asked.

"Gosh no, Verity was just leaving. She's new to the village and I invited her round. Unfortunately, she chose an hour ago to turn up. Anyway, come on in."

I knew I should have taken a bottle. I felt rather cheap as I entered the wide and rather imposing hallway, following him into a large kitchen.

"I hope you like lamb. I've cooked a casserole."

"You shouldn't have gone to any trouble, but it smells delicious." I looked around his particularly well stocked kitchen, the slate floor and a rug placed in one corner where a two-seater sofa nestled in comfort.

"No trouble. It's a pleasure to have you here." He turned to face me, his eyes seeming to glide around my outfit. "You look fabulous, by the way," he said.

So did he, wearing a beige shirt loosely tucked into a pair of jeans, perhaps not as dressed up as I was but still looking incredible. For a short moment I forgot he was a vicar. He made me feel at ease, his hand resting on the small of my back as he showed me a bottle of red wine he had carefully chosen from his extensive wine rack.

"I'm surprised you have such a large collection of wine. Are vicars allowed to drink?" My question made him laugh.

"I think in years gone by it was forbidden but now, no, I don't think the Lord would worry too much if he caught me having the odd drink. After all, he drank wine at the Last Supper, didn't he?" He opened a drawer and began fumbling about amongst its contents.

It was my turn to laugh as I noticed car magazines and a newspaper scattered on the work top. Finding a corkscrew, he offered me a glass.

"Of course he did," I answered. "I think they preferred it in those days, to water I mean." I took the wine from his hands, our fingers overlapping slightly.

"Dinner will be about ten minutes, shall we sit in the lounge?" Holding out his arm he led me out of the kitchen.

His house interested me; it was beautifully decorated, not at all as I had expected. The kitchen appeared new, contemporary units neatly fitted whilst the Aga seemed to be the focal point.

In the lounge, floor to ceiling bookcases littered with books dominated, whilst two sofas faced each other with a long antique coffee table positioned between them. A cosy fire crackled in an inglenook fireplace, logs scattered on either side. He had lovingly put up a Christmas tree, decorated with obvious family heirlooms. A desk stood in the corner, overwhelmed with papers and a huge Bible. Photographs hung on each wall amidst paintings, some of which I suspected were originals. It was a very impressive room, comfortable and friendly, yet rather grand at the same time.

"How long have you lived in the village?" I asked.

"Three years, it's a great place to be. The people made me very welcome when I moved into the vicarage. I was a little nervous with it being a small village."

"You seem to have settled well. I thought you'd been here for much longer." There was an aura within the room, energy almost eager to make contact which made me wonder if one of the previous occupants would visit us that night. "The house is lovely, full of atmosphere." I waited for a reaction, slightly disappointed when he failed to pick up on my inquisitive thoughts. Even though beliefs would have some members of clergy disagree with my gift, they would still find time during their next journey to communicate with those able to comply.

I made myself comfortable on one of the sofas covered with a large ivory throw. I found myself wondering about the mysteries that had once lived in the house. Everywhere felt warm as I struggled to concentrate on the man who now sat opposite me on the other sofa. He unexpectedly slouched, throwing his arm over the top as he held his wine in his other hand. I was growing fond of him and could sense a part of me wishing he had sat next to me. But I had to speak to him about other matters, ones which would fade a conversation of casserole and wine into a distant past.

My eyes kept being averted to the tree lights, an abundance of colour, twinkling as I tried hard to look away. I wished life could have been simpler. There had been times at the beginning of my realisation of having the gift that I wished I was not able to communicate with passed souls. I had looked around me often, wondering why I had been chosen, why not the lady who stood in front of me in a queue at the chemists or the man who sat with his wife in my frequent hovel. My grandmother was always there in those days to make me understand that I had to open myself up to this incredible power; I had been honoured with a wonderful life and a journey in which I must continue to take.

"Penny for them." Marcus had caught me day dreaming. He wasn't the first. When I was a child I was known for it.

"I was just admiring your tree. I adore Christmas trees, they remind me of my childhood."

"Me too. That's why I always have one this big." He lifted his hand with the glass of wine in it, gesturing towards the tree. "Christmas is such a wonderful time. What's your favourite time of the year?"

"I love all times of the year but Christmas is one of my favourites. I also love the summer time when I can eat alfresco." I smiled. "Although last year wasn't too great when the house was being renovated. I was up to my eyes in rubble and dust with three skips parked outside. There was so much to get rid of inside the house they were filled in no time."

"You seem to have a love for life, Camilla. I suppose not having to work for a living makes your life easier?" He sipped his wine, his face once more mysteriously obscured.

"I sometimes wander around the house, finding something to do. I haven't yet become accustomed to day time television." A laugh ensued; an icebreaker.

"Don't you mind living on your own in that big house?" His eyes transfixed on mine.

"I love living at Rosehill, I wouldn't live anywhere else now. And as for living on my own, it's what I've done for such a long time. I would be too stuck in my ways to live with anyone." I bit my lip, asking myself frustratingly why I had needed to say such a thing.

Without warning he stood up, startling me somewhat.

"I think dinner will be ready now. Shall we?" Allowing me to walk in front of him, he once more rested his hand on my back.

He had set two places at the table, yet I felt there were three of us in the room. Having finished my glass of wine I tried hard not to mistake my psychic intuition with the giddiness that my head seemed to experience. He brought a large ceramic pot from the oven, placing it in the centre of the table. As he lifted the lid it revealed an aromatic vision of delicious stew.

The meal was exquisite. His company even more so. I took care so as not to embarrass myself in mess. He had cooked enough for two helpings of which I perhaps could have passed on, but I didn't.

"A man who can cook, I'm impressed," I said, replacing my knife and fork and pushing the empty plate aside in order to make room for me to lean on the table. "Do you entertain often?"

"I don't get much time. The life of a vicar is a busy one. I enjoy eating alone, doing my own thing.

"Same here." I was relieved that we had something in common. "When I lived in Edinburgh I used to spend a lot of time with friends but since moving to Rosehill I seem to have adapted to a quieter way of life."

Marcus nodded and smiled. "When I lived in London I didn't think about these small country villages. The cities and towns over populated as they are and my church full to bursting every week. I tried hard to make it work but it wasn't meant to be. That's why I moved up here; an easier life, quieter, simpler. But it's still busy. Better in fact."

"I haven't really made many friends since moving here, though I've met one or two of the locals." I thought it best not to mention Julia Henderson, or Alice for that matter.

Marcus too, brushed his empty plate aside as he once more filled up his wine glass. "More wine," he asked, raising his eye brows.

"I'd better not," I declined, "I have to drive home." He didn't seem any different in his ways than when first he had opened the door to me earlier in the evening, obviously a vicar who drank plentiful.

"Shall I help you clear the dishes?" I asked.

"Of course not," he answered "We can have coffee in the lounge. Go and make yourself comfortable and I'll bring it through."

I was grateful for his suggestion for my stomach was full and I needed to move away from the table. He followed me into the lounge, this time sitting beside me on the sofa, leaving a respectable gap.

Again, I could feel a presence in the room but was unsure as to who it was. There could have been a number of spirits gathered in eagerness at witnessing their vicar entertaining a woman. It might have been mocked. I could even have been disapproved by those of hierarchy.

"The meal was divine. It was very good of you to cook," I said.

"I don't cook like that all the time, just on special occasions." He flattered me and I smiled and sipped my drink. I was afraid to spoil a tender moment but I needed to tell Marcus who I was. He had been kind enough to treat me with respect, forming a friendship with a woman he hardly knew. I, in return, had to respect him too. My mouth dry, my stomach in knots, I turned to him, noticing once again the striking smile and the gentle eyes.

"Marcus, there's something I think you should know." I tried to make it sound less important, hoping he would continue to smile.

As his eyes met mine, I think I sensed the danger looming, tearing through me in destructive manner. I knew, before I carried on, that he would not take it well. Yet I had to continue. I was being encouraged by the presence that had now engulfed my thoughts.

"I haven't been completely honest with you." I shifted in my seat, anxiety getting the better of me. "I have what is known as a gift. Since I was sixteen I have been able to communicate with passed souls." The time seemed appropriate. "I'm a medium."

He stared at me. The silence almost drowned out the ticking clock as I sat and waited for him to speak. He picked up his glass and took a large gulp of wine before sinking back against the sofa, smiling at me, in what I hoped I had mistaken for a patronising glare.

"I am sorry, Marcus. I should have told you sooner."

"Do you believe in ghosts?" His question astounded me. Raising my eyebrows and shifting in my seat again, I nodded my head.

"Of course I do. I see them, hear them, and feel them. In fact ....." Before I had chance to tell him about the presence that had been hanging around most of the evening he stood up rather sharpish, a smile having formed on his lips.

"I'm surprised to be honest." He looked away, his gaze resting on the bright lights of Christmas. "You're an intelligent woman yet you believe in this paranormal clap-trap." He shook his head, the smile remaining but an unusual coldness overwhelming his eyes. I was offended. My sixth sense had already told me that he would have difficulty accepting my announcement but he was insulting my beliefs.

"I think I should leave." The only words I could find came hurriedly to the surface as I rose from the sofa.

"There's no need for you to leave. Let's just pretend this never happened and carry on where we were. Now, what shall we talk about?"

"We both know it won't make any difference," I replied. No change in conversation would have made him concentrate on anything other than what I had just told him. He had shown ignorance and had completely patronised me. I had dealt with far worse of course, through people's comments and behaviour during my years of mediumship but usually from those who didn't know me. Marcus, however, was different. I liked him and he seemed to like me. Now I suddenly felt as though I was in the wrong. I had done something so ridiculous that the village Reverend mocked me, hanging me out to dry.

I had questions to answer, questions I wanted to ask him. But I also had a spirit presence to contend with, the fact that I didn't know who it was worried me. I couldn't tell him that a lost soul had graced us for the evening, that we had shared our dinner with an unseen guest.

"I'm sorry, Marcus. I should go, it's getting late." I glanced at the clock. It was 9.30.

"Okay, if you must. But won't you come to church for crib service? You might like it."

I ignored him, my ears having heard his every word yet my head willing me from his home.

"Thank you for dinner," I said, whilst making my way to the front door. "I shall see you soon no doubt." I turned round to face him.

"May I come to see you?" His eyes seemed to plead with me like a hopeful child wishing for a candy bar.

"Of course," I found myself saying, before getting into my car.

Even though I drank no more than a glass of wine, the five minute journey home was a blur. I vaguely remember opening my back door and getting into bed. What I did remember was the visitor who stood in my bedroom. My eyes struggled to close yet my body couldn't move. I knew I had been joined by an unseen entity, one which I immediately felt sympathetic towards. She was a woman, silk robes covering her frailty. The level in which she presented made me realise she was connected to the clergy, perhaps even the spirit woman who had accompanied Marcus and I during the evening. The name, Anne came to me as I scanned the darkness. My mind began to focus on her demise which she seemed pitiful and detached from. It was becoming obvious to me that her life on our earth plane had ended at someone's hands. Someone she had trusted, perhaps even loved.

Historical facts of my beautiful home told me how a barn had been burned to the ground in recent years. It was an old building, empty, derelict and ready to be rebuilt. Yet it had been scorched, an open verdict as to the cause of the fire. No mention of perishing souls had been reported.

My thoughts were flitting from the fire in the barn to the uncomfortable ending experienced at the vicarage. I hoped Marcus wasn't angry at me and I started to mellow as I recalled my sudden exit. I expected him to take my news badly but I was hoping it wouldn't have resulted in us being irritated by one another. My eyes began to close whilst my mind at last made its journey into another mode. I knew I needed to speak to Marcus, try to help him understand that our differences of opinion could be overcome and that a friendship could, perhaps, be formed.

Chapter Ten

S till confused at the vision of a burning barn, I got up before sunrise to visit the place I suspected was at the heart of a tragedy. The door to the barn, an ancient slab of wood fixed upon pitiful hinges, was almost collapsing from wear. It closed with unwieldy action, sound emitting throughout infested stone. The door led into a series of rooms, all damp and covered with rat droppings. Cobwebs attached themselves to my hair and clothes like crawling fingers. A rustic latch fixed with obsolete screws, desperate to hold onto another day, gave character to panelled oak, bellowing clumsy action in a bid to fasten against a metal hook.

The atmosphere changed as I entered each room, colder and darker. The rats, having first scattered upon hearing human footsteps, resumed their hunt for food while spiders spun bringing the walls alive. Memories flashed before my anxious eyes as I realised I had invaded someone's space. A simple chore became impossible to achieve as sound carried from every crumbling stone in every wall.

The barn seeped energy from a woman's build. Activity had taken place leaving two hundred and fifty years of ambience as forgotten entities visited, wishing to be remembered on much loved ground.

I felt sorrow, loss and heartache. The atmosphere around filled me with dread. Tears stung my eyes as I stood still and sensed many characters having walked through the dilapidation, part of which lay in debris and cinders. I decided to sit for a while, upon a dusty stone, probably left after tragedy.

My surroundings echoed, voices emitted all around me, confusing me. But the name kept on repeating itself in my head. She had something to tell me and she was not about to rest until she was sure I understood.

"Anne, I know you're here. Please come forward, I mean no harm." I called out to her, my pleas encouraging communication. A stone was hurled in my direction.

"I know you need to tell me something, Anne. I'm here to listen."

But as I spoke I began to feel a negativity that I had never experienced before. Another spirit joined us, a negative force that was unhappy about my presence. Anne stood in the background, her humble pleas fading from my mind. I felt her energy beside me. The temperature had dropped considerably and I was also shivering with cold. I knew I couldn't help Anne at this time. More stones were thrown towards me, a seemingly unhappy soul requesting that I leave. Communication with negative forces had never appealed to me and I often called upon my good friend to help me rid them of their unwelcome presence. This one however, I wished to deal with myself. My suspicions about Anne went deeper than a woman burned to death. Somehow, I felt Marcus around me, his aura connecting with mine.

"You need to come forward, Anne. Step away from the negative energy, come into my space." But Anne wasn't ready. She faded from sight leaving me trying to decipher her reason for being in the barn. I believed she still had a message for me.

The negative soul deserted me too as the building once more became a haven for hideaway creatures. I went back to the house, the sun beginning to make an appearance over distant hills. My failure in realising Anne's presence weighed heavily on my mind as I reached the house, the dogs greeting me with enthusiasm.

<hr/>

It was the following day when I went to visit Lucy. She answered the door in her dressing gown, her eyes streaming as though full of cold.

"Hey, what's wrong with you?" I asked, not sure I wanted to go in the house for fear of picking up the virus.

"Bloody cold," she replied. "I've had it for weeks. Some days I feel okay then another I'm full again." She was terribly weak.

"Have you eaten anything?"

"Just had some cuppa soup. I'll be okay. Come in, I'll make us a coffee." I followed her into the house, making our way to the kitchen which was littered with dirty pots.

"You go back to bed," I suggested. "I'll clean up in here and make us a drink." I shooed her upstairs.

Lucy was always tidy so I was surprised to see such a mess. She'd seemed fine the night of the séance and I hadn't suspected an illness at all. I washed the pots and wiped the worktops before making us some coffee. I found her in bed when I got upstairs. Her eyes were closed when I appeared at her doorway and having heard me, she sat up and managed a weak smile.

"You spoil me," she said.

"You should have phoned me. I could have come to help you out."

"Oh, I'm okay, Camilla, really. I'd rather be on my own when I'm ill."

I drank my coffee. "Do you want me to go and leave you to get some rest?"

"No, stay for a bit. Tell me what's been happening with you."

I thought for a moment. I wasn't sure I wanted to talk about Marcus just yet. So I mentioned Julia instead. "A woman from the village came to the house the other day, for a reading. She's a journalist, full of herself she was, total sceptic."

"Why did she come for a reading if she doesn't believe?"

"She wanted to write an article about me."

Lucy raised her eyebrows. "And did she?"

"I don't think so. I haven't seen it in the paper yet. But before she left something really weird happened. Just as she was about to leave the room, the candle fell onto the floor, it was as though someone had thrown it. The lights flickered and the whole atmosphere became really angry. It wasn't nice. Julia was really scared. I think it was an angry spirit, someone convincing her that they exist."

"Sounds terrible. Did it do any damage?"

"No, apart from a burn in the hearth rug from the candle. Oh, and a couple of books were taken out from the shelves, too. That was classic poltergeist and I think probably scared Julia more than the candle." I laughed at the thought of Julia being so rude to me then almost being punished by someone from the spirit world. Lucy managed to laugh too, before she started coughing.

"Sit up straight," I said. "Let me pat your back."

She was almost choking and I reached for the water which was beside her bed. I held the glass to her mouth, helping her drink as I put my other hand behind her head. "Better?" I asked, as she pulled away and sank back against the pillows.

"I hate feeling like this. I hope it's gone by Christmas day."

"I hope it has too. Take it easy and you'll be okay."

"I hate phoning in sick. I feel really embarrassed. But I can't be sneezing all over the guests." I smiled at her as she made a weak attempt to roll her eyes. Lucy was a hotel receptionist. She'd always enjoyed her job and had worked for the same hotel for ten years.

"Of course you can't. You need to rest up, get yourself right. They'll manage without you for a few days."

"That's just it though, I've been off a few days now and I really need to get back. There's loads to do before the Christmas guests arrive."

"It's not like you to be off work. Have you seen the doctor?"

"I'm not seeing a doctor for a bad cold. They can't do anything."

"It might be something else. You might need a prescription."

"You sound like my mother. I'll be fine. Probably feel better tomorrow." But I could sense that Lucy was worse than she was making out. I wasn't satisfied with her excuse of a cold. She was forty-seven, a few years older than me, and I'd never known her to stay in bed because of a cold.

"You get some rest. I'll go and do a bit of cleaning downstairs," I said. "The place could do with a once over." I stood up, taking my cup of coffee, before walking to the door. I turned round to look at her. She snuggled herself under the duvet, closing her eyes, a weak cough escaping.

When I got downstairs I looked through her phonebook which sat on the telephone table. Then I dialled the number. A single tone, having dialled America, told me that I might be lucky and Lucy's brother might just pick up the phone.

"Hello," said the voice on the other end.

"Ross? It's Camilla." I waited a few seconds.

"Camilla? Hey, this is nice surprise. How are you?"

"I'm fine. How about you?"

"Never been better. What's your weather like?"

"Ross," I said, remembering I was on Lucy's phone, "it's Lucy. I can't shout because she's upstairs and doesn't know I've called you."

"Sorry?"

"I can't shout, Ross. Can you hear me?"

"Yes, just about. What's the matter with Lucy?"

"I don't know," I answered truthfully. "But I'm a bit worried about her to be honest. When are you coming back here?"

"I haven't got any plans to come over for while. I might do next summer. Why?"

"I thought it might be good for her if you came over. I just feel she needs someone here." There was a pause and I wondered if Ross had heard me. "Ross? Are you there?"

"Yes, I'm here," he said. "Is she ill or something?"

"She says she has a cold but I think it's more than that."

"What about the kids?"

"I haven't told them. I thought I'd ring you first. You haven't seen her for a few years, thought it might be nice if you paid her a visit. It might help her get better."

"Well, okay then. I'll see if I can get a flight."

"I think it might be a good idea to come soon, Ross. Be here for Christmas then she's not on her own too much." Another pause. I began to wonder whether Ross was finding his sister too much trouble.

"Leave it with me, Cam. Shall I ring you when I've got a flight?"

"Yes, ring me at home. Have you got a pen handy?" I gave him my number. "You can get me there anytime. I'll meet you at the airport."

"So how's things with you?" he asked.

"They're fine," I replied. "I have to go, Ross. I'm on Lucy's phone, she's upstairs in bed."

"Okay, give her a hug from me and tell her I'll see her soon." He hung up. I went back upstairs to find Lucy fast asleep. I decided to wait until I heard from Ross again before telling her he was coming over.

Chapter Eleven

*H*e rang me that night, giving me his flight details, and I arranged to pick him up at the airport in two days time. He had lived in America for twenty years, a bachelor with little responsibility and just himself to think about. Lucy often told me how she envied his lifestyle, his ability to do nothing and feel no guilt. I reminded her of the wonderful life she had with her children, Jacob and Rebecca, having almost brought them up single handed. Ross was a beach life guard and though he loved his job, Lucy always stressed how much he missed home.

He had always been a womaniser. He found women interesting yet his respect always seemed to falter in their company. At forty-nine he still bore a physique any man would be proud of. He had visited Lucy several times over the years, staying with her at her cottage in Lower Riverton, a little village half an hour away from Rosehill. I'd never known him to stay for more than a couple of weeks but I was hoping he would stay for longer this time.

I got to the airport half an hour before the flight was due. I loved looking round the place, feeling the hustle and bustle of busy passengers, the surroundings I sometimes missed from living in Edinburgh. The plane was on time and I made my way to the arrivals area. It had been a while since I'd last seen him, but I doubted he would have changed much. He hadn't. As people started filtering through the doorway, pushing trolley's with huge suitcases, Ross walked casually behind, a hold-all slung over his shoulder. I recognised him immediately, still the handsome man I had once admired. He looked amongst the waiting people until he saw me, a smile lighting up his face. He walked towards me, ruffling his hair and causing it to stick up at the sides. Not a grey hair in sight, still so conscious of his appearance.

"Hi!" he said, as he kissed my cheek. "Hope you haven't been waiting long?"

"Not really. I came a bit early but the plane was on time. How was the flight?" I walked beside him as we made our way to the main entrance. "I'm parked just over here."

"Good flight." He laughed. "Quite a good looking stewardess, too. Think she took a shine to me."

"More like you took a shine to her," I smiled. "Come on, let's get to the car, I'm freezing."

He put his arm around me after I said that, as though wanting to warm me. We arrived at the car and loaded his bag into the boot. The usual traffic jam on the main road meant we waited for a while before starting our journey back to Lucy's.

"How is she?" Ross asked.

"I rang her last night and she seemed okay. She said she'd got up but hadn't bothered getting dressed."

"Why are you so worried about her?"

"Because I've never seen her this bad. She's usually fit and healthy. Plus, I've noticed that she's been looking tired lately. I just think we need to keep our eye on her." I managed to pull out onto the main road at last.

"What did she say when you told her I'm coming over?"

"I haven't told her. I think it'll be a nice surprise." Ross looked at me. "It's time you two had a catch up, anyway."

"We keep in touch by phone."

"It's not the same though is it? Lucy's on her own most of the time. The kids are busy at University and they have their own lives."

"They still go to see her," he said, turning away and looking through the window. "I have my life, too, you know."

"I wasn't meaning to be rude. But she really misses you, Ross."

"And I miss her. But we have our own lives. We have had for a long time now." He turned back to me. "Anyway, how about you, what's this new place like that you've bought?"

"Rosehill? It's beautiful. Well, most of it is, I've still got a few rooms to do but it's looking more like it should."

"In what way?"

"When I first bought it, it was derelict. Totally run-down. Got an architect in and fixed it up."

"Is it a big place?"

"Yes, it's huge." I thought about my home and how much I adored it. "It's an old hall. Would have been built for Gentry once. I haven't learnt about its history yet, but I intend to."

"And is it haunted?" I laughed at Ross's question.

"Every where's haunted, if you're a medium," I said. "Yes, Rosehill is very much haunted. It's a wonderful place."

"I'd like to see it."

"You will. I'm having some friends over on Christmas day, including Lucy. You're invited too, of course."

"And will we be able to make contact with any of the ghosts in the house?" he asked, twirling his fingers as he spoke.

"Definitely not. It's my day off." We both laughed.

I turned off the main road and into the lane which led to Riverton.

"I hope she's in," Ross said. "Do you have a key?"

"Yes, I've got one on my key ring with the car keys. Don't worry, I'm sure she'll be home."

She was. In fact, she was in bed again. The kitchen was still tidy, as though she had either managed to tidy up or hadn't eaten anything. But I noticed a glass on the side together with a used cup.

"You wait there," I said. "I'll go and make sure she's okay before she sees you."

Ross waited in the hall while I went upstairs to find her once more fast asleep. I looked at her peaceful expression, another used cup on her bedside table. As I turned to leave the room she started coughing again. I went back to her and sat down on the bed.

"Lucy, it's me. Are you okay?"

She briefly opened her eyes and managed the tiniest of smiles. "What are you doing here?" she asked.

"I've brought you a surprise," I said. She sat up a little, resting her hands on the bed to help her.

"What is it?" she asked.

"Hang on, I'll go and get it." I went into the hallway and lent over the banister. "You can come up," I called down.

Ross reached Lucy's bedroom and stood in the doorway. I think he seemed a little shocked at her appearance as he suddenly realised that the cold she claimed to have was obviously something more.

"Hey, sis," he said, walking towards the bed. "I hear you've not been well."

Lucy looked at him, her eyes lit up and a smile etched on her face. She held out her arms as he embraced her. I knew I'd done right thing in phoning him.

"What are you doing here?" she asked him. Then she looked at me. "Is this your doing?"

I smiled. "I'm afraid so. I thought Ross should be here, just to look after you for a while."

"I don't need looking after. What are you like?" Fortunately for me, Lucy wasn't angry, but I suspected she was too weak to feel angry anyway.

"I'll leave you two to it," I said, backing away towards the door.

"I could do with some caffeine," Ross said, turning to face me. "Why don't you stay and have one?"

"Have you only just got here?" Lucy asked.

"Yes, I went to pick him up from the airport, we've come straight here."

"I take it you're staying for a while," she said, her eyes seeming to plead with Ross.

"Yes, I will. Not sure how long, but I've taken unpaid leave."

"Unpaid?" Lucy managed a giggle. "That's not like you."

"The way Camilla was talking on the phone it was as though you were on your last legs, sis. I thought it was best to just ask for unpaid, rather than be pushed for time."

"I'll be fine. Look at me; it's just a bad cold, probably flu." Ross leant over and kissed Lucy on the forehead.

"I'll go and make us a drink," he said.

"I should get up and have a shower."

"You'll do no such thing," I insisted. "Stay where you are. Ross is here now, he's going to wait on you hand and foot. Aren't you, Ross?" He didn't really have an option but to nod as he went downstairs, probably wondering what all the fuss was about.

I joined him in the kitchen. He'd already put the kettle on and got the cups from the cupboard and was just about to spoon coffee into them.

"Tea for me," I said. "So how do you think she looks?"

"I think she's just run down. Probably been working too hard."

"Could be. But she's definitely had flu, I'd say. She won't go to the doctors."

"She's never liked doctors. Here." He passed me a cup of tea. "Are there any biscuits around, I'm starving."

"I'll make you something to eat if you like. You must be exhausted after the flight."

"I'm okay at the moment. Probably feel jet-lagged tomorrow." He opened the fridge. "She's obviously not been shopping for a while." The shelves were almost bare as I peered in.

"I'll go and get some things from the supermarket. She's not been well enough to leave the house."

"Looks like it'll be a takeaway tonight. Are you staying?"

"No, I'd better get back."

"You're looking really well, Cam." He looked me up and down.

"Thanks, you don't look so bad yourself." I smiled at him, thinking how he still had his charming ways. "At our age, we need to look after ourselves."

"Speak for yourself," he laughed. "You should see some of the women where I live. It's like a plastic surgery walk-in centre in some of the bars on the boulevard." It was my turn to laugh as I imagined him being in his element as he struggled to avert his eyes from one woman to another.

"I'll just take this drink up to Lucy," he said.

"If you want to make a list, I'll do some shopping in the morning and bring it over."

He started walking upstairs. "No, that's okay, I'll go myself. But thanks for offering."

I stood in the hallway, watching as he approached the top of the stairs. My heart was beating unusually fast. I looked at my watch and realised I needed to go.

"Ring me if you need me," I shouted.

"Hang on," he said, appearing at the top of the stairs empty handed. He made his way towards me. "Is there any chance I could come over to your place tomorrow. I'd love to have a guided tour."

"Why don't you see how Lucy is first?"

"Well, okay. If she's feeling alright, I'll pop over tomorrow afternoon." He looked at me, a thought seeming to reach the surface of his otherwise tired mind. "How about you do a reading for me?"

"Oh, I'm not sure, Ross."

"Go on, it's ages since I've seen you work."

"It's ages since we've seen each other. I might tell you something you don't want to hear."

"Then you'll just have to control yourself," he said with a grin, wiping his hand against my cheek.

"So long as you're not just coming to take the piss," I said. "It's serious stuff. The house is full of spirits, you know."

"I won't be scared, I promise."

"How can I refuse. Okay, come late afternoon. About four-ish."

"You're on, I'll see you then." I opened the front door. "And thanks again for picking me up from the airport. It was a good idea that I came over. Christmas is a time for family, isn't it?"

"Yes, it is." I turned to him. "I just wish Lucy had someone in her life."

Chapter Twelve

I rang Lucy the following day and much to my delight, she answered the phone. She wasn't as weak as she had sounded previously but I could tell she was still full of cold.

"How are you?" I asked.

"Much better. Ross coming over has given me the incentive to get myself motivated again. I've phoned work and told them I won't be back until after the New Year. Ross insisted on it."

"That's brilliant, Lucy. A couple of weeks rest will do you the world of good."

"I believe Ross is coming over later, for a reading."

"Yes, you don't mind do you? Are you coming too?"

"No, I'll stay here. I got up and showered this morning but I'll get myself back to bed after Ross has gone. Don't want to get up too soon."

"Very sensible. I've never known you to be this ill before."

"Well I'm glad I didn't see the doctor. He wouldn't have been able to do anything."

"Just take it easy. Has Ross been shopping for you?"

"Yes, he popped to the supermarket early. I thought he might have had jetlag but he seems okay. Don't let him stay at yours too late, we don't want him being ill, too." I laughed when she said this, always the caring side showing through.

Ross arrived at four o'clock in Lucy's car. He kissed me on my cheek and I noticed, as he walked through the door, the same scent he had worn since we'd been in our twenties. It was a woody aroma, masculine, causing me to swoon like I used to do back in the days when I knew him best. As he entered the kitchen I realised he hadn't arrived alone.

Behind him walked an elderly man, a spirit of whom he had no idea was there. I suspected he was Ross's grandfather. His eyes were sad and he seemed eager to pass on a message of which I knew instinctively was important. Unable to concentrate on pleasantries with Ross I immediately tuned into the entity which now stood in my kitchen, and received the message he felt obliged to convey.

Lucy is sick, was all I could interpret. The message was so scrambled that even I couldn't understand its full meaning.

I turned to Ross. "Is Lucy okay?" I asked, trying not to alarm him.

"Yes, she seems much better, why?" But something told me the message meant more than even the flu she thought she'd had. The atmosphere was heavy and the air, cold. This spirit was giving me a warning; perhaps one I was to pass onto Lucy.

"When you get back, I want you to check on her," I told him.

"Stop worrying, she's fine." He seemed to show little interest in his sister's well-being, his eyes averting to my drinks cabinet.

"Can I get you a drink? A Scotch perhaps?"

"Thanks, Scotch would be fine." I poured him a drink and we went into the reading room, socialising would have to wait. My grandmother stood in the corner, her head shaking at the man who was so eager to hear of his fortune. My problem was that I could see nothing for Ross, only pain, and my heart ached for him; the womanising, the disrespect. I almost pitied him.

Another message became clear as I looked into my Crystal. Things were beginning to make sense to me as I remembered the night a few months back when I first saw the signs of heartache, my thoughts of it being a secondary prediction. I had ignored it back then as there had been no spirit presence at the time, and I wondered about my new surroundings. Yet experience should have told me that the image I received was not to be pushed aside, that it was to be noted for future communication. I looked at Ross who sat opposite me, waiting with bated breath for his future to be told. I had never, in all my years of mediumship, predicted someone's future without knowing the facts.

My grandmother continued to stand in the corner, encouraging me not to lie. But I didn't like to convey messages of bereavement to my clients. Death being inevitable to all meant mourning would happen to everyone at some time in their lives.

I kept looking over at my grandmother, psychically encouraging her to give me information to pass onto Ross. As always, she began to impress thoughts upon me, a future of love and companionship. Something at least I could convey. He may not believe me but it was a future prediction that I was confident about relaying.

"I can see true love for you." I smiled at him, watching as his expression turned to a snigger.

"You have to be kidding. Not for me."

"Seriously, there is a young woman here. I can see the two of you getting married." Ross burst out laughing, and I almost laughed myself.

"You know me, Cam, not interested in settling down."

"I'm only telling you what I can see. You never know, it might happen one day." I shrugged, struggling to believe what I saw.

"I'm assuming it's someone you met in America."

"What tells you that?" he asked.

"You'll laugh if I tell you."

"You can't not tell me who I'm going to marry."

"It's Barbie. I can see a Barbie doll in the Crystal." He looked puzzled. "Do you know someone who's called Barbie, or perhaps looks like Barbie?"

At this point he laughed out so loud I thought I would lose the connection with the Crystal. "Most women I know look like Barbie. You'll have to be more specific than that."

"Perhaps I'm being told you'll marry someone you already know. Time will tell." A white mist began to appear in the Crystal as the Barbie doll disappeared. But what worried me was the vision I had next; it was a coffin. I looked up at Ross who was still smirking.

"What is it now?" he asked. "Have you seen Ken?"

I laughed, realising that I couldn't possibly tell him what I'd seen. Not really understanding it myself I decided to try again to encourage my grandmother to pass on information. But she had left. It was up to me to tune into Ross's energy and work out for myself what the future held for this man.

"You have pain in your shoulder," I said. I think you dislocated it at some point." Ross glared at me.

I continued. "Your grandfather's with us. He's happy that you're home and wants you to spend time with Lucy and the children." Without thinking I continued, "they're going to need you" The old man stopped me from going any further, his eyes filled with tears as he shook his head.

"What?" Ross was curious.

"Sorry, I meant to say they're glad you're here, they miss you." The old man continued to stand over him, grief in his expression.

"Who's the lucky lady that I'm supposed to be marrying then? Is she from over here?" I couldn't help but to smile.

"She's very attractive and you're going to be very much in love so don't knock it."

"She better had be attractive if she's to marry me." He smirked. The spirit man faded from sight as his energy weakened, telling me it was time to end the reading. I didn't want to guess who the person was that Ross would mourn. Perhaps I already knew and my mind had closed the door to that knowledge.

I stood up and switched on the light before moving to the candle to blow it out, causing a thin trail of waxed smoke around the room. Ross followed me into the kitchen where he once more admired the contents of my drinks cabinet.

"Help yourself," I told him. I could tell he was reluctant to leave. The reading had been particularly draining and as my mind had been overwhelmed by grief I decided that inviting him to stay a while couldn't hurt, glad of some light hearted banter.

"I'm planning to stay for a few months, you know." Ross poured himself another Scotch. I watched as he half filled a large glass, wondering how on earth he planned to drive back to Lucy's.

"Oh, that's good. I imagine Lucy's really pleased. Do you have any plans while you're here?"

"Oh, I don't know, maybe a few visits to Edinburgh, catch up with what's been happening in my absence. You look good, by the way. Country life seems to be agreeing with you."

I grinned as I assumed the Scotch was taking effect. "You've been away a long time, Ross, there'll be a lot of catching up to do." I laughed a little, suspecting he had intended to live a life of leisure whilst Lucy pampered to his every whim.

"I thought I might take you out to dinner?" I looked up in surprise, the rise in his voice at least indicated that it was a question.

It was a tempting offer and catching up would be fun. I laughed again, a childish giggle which brought a smile to his face.

"What? What are you thinking?" he asked.

"I hope you don't think I'm the lucky lady whom you will marry?"

"You?" He was genuinely surprised. "Have you had plastic surgery?"

"Don't be cheeky," I said, with a smile. "Do I look as though I need it?"

"Not at all. You're perfect, just the way you are." I looked into his eyes.

"Okay then, dinner it is," I agreed.

"I'd like to try the new Indian in town, Lucy told me you and her had been a few weeks ago."

"It's very good, I'll enjoy that."

"I know you'll find it hard to believe but I don't go out much in Santa Barbara, by the time I get home from work I just want to relax in front of the TV." I did find it hard to believe.

"Do you have a girlfriend?"

"I did, we split up a short while back. Long story." I decided not to question him further, it was obvious from the reluctance in his voice and the way he gulped the Scotch that he didn't want to talk about it.

I'd known him with kindness in his heart. I fell for him once, many years ago, when in my twenties. A time I had chosen to forget. He was my best friend's brother and I had known him most of my life but the way his eyes shone reminded me of that time long ago.

"So what about you, Camilla, are you still single after all this time?"

"Yes," I sighed, reaching for the bottle of Scotch. I didn't offer any to Ross but just poured some into my own glass.

"I always thought you'd get married. Have kids. Why didn't you?"

"Maybe because I never met the right man."

"It must be hard work running this place. How many acres do you have here?"

"About five thousand," I answered, "but I rent most of it out to local farmers."

"Guess that's how you make the place pay. It's brave of you to take it on. Not the kind of thing a woman on her own wants to do I shouldn't imagine."

"So long as I get the rent every month, the farm ticks along nicely. I love Rosehill, I'm only sorry I didn't find it sooner."

"Oh well," he began, as he put down his empty glass and stood up. "I'd better go before I turn into a pumpkin. I've enjoyed tonight, thanks for having me."

"I wish I could have given you more information with the reading but sometimes the future just needs finding out for itself." I stood up too, hiding a yawn behind my hand.

"I'll ring you about that dinner?"

"Sounds great. I'll see you on Christmas day I assume?"

"Yes. I'm look forward to it."

He left, leaving me standing in the kitchen pondering why my heart had started to beat faster.

Chapter Thirteen

Worrying about Lucy after receiving information the previous night I made the half hour car journey to see her, praying all the way there that she would be okay and my concerns were for nothing. I rang the door bell before Ross answered, bare foot and holding a bowl of cereal.

"Come through," he said, "I'm assuming it's Lucy you want to see?"

"Is she okay this morning?"

"Seems to be, I haven't been up long so haven't really had chance to talk to her." I smiled at him, trying hard to hide my concern.

She was in the dining room, wrapping Christmas presents. The table was strewn with colourful paper and gift tags, an organised list by her side. Her expression seemed joyous as she looked up to greet me.

"This is a nice surprise," she said, standing up to hug me. It had only been days since I last saw her but I sensed she had lost weight, her body seemed frail and even though I wanted to hold her tightly I felt I should release her for fear of snapping her bones.

"I was thinking about you. Did Ross tell you about the reading I gave him last night?"

"I haven't spoken to him much this morning. What time did he leave your place last night? I never heard him come in."

I thought for a moment. "It must have been around ten, he stayed for a catch up after the reading." I watched her walk towards the kitchen door, struggling as if her back was in pain. "Are you okay?"

"Bit of a chill, that's all," she said. "Shall I put the kettle on?" She reached for cups and then picked up the kettle. But I took it from her hands, unable to continue witnessing her frailty.

"Go and sit down, I'll do it. You should be in bed."

"I'm fine. These presents won't wrap themselves."

"Ask Ross to help you." I nodded towards the kitchen door. "He isn't doing anything, is he?"

She managed a slight chuckle. "All right, all right, but I'll make the tea!" I laughed, though words swilled round my head as I thought of the best way to encourage her to take care of herself. The message I had received wouldn't go away. I finished stirring our drinks then took them through to the dining room where Lucy had sat down and continued wrapping presents.

"Have you seen a doctor?" I asked. "I know you say you're fine but you look weak. Maybe you need antibiotics or something."

"I've got plenty remedies." She was looking down at the wrapping paper. "So, how did you and Ross get on last night? Anything interesting happen?"

"That's partly why I'm here. Your granddad came through, he was worried about you."

"Typical granddad, being melodramatic. He always was over the top when grandma had anything wrong with her." She touched my arm and looked at me, a feeble smile appearing. "Really, I'm fine."

Ross came in, carrying his empty dish. He brushed his free hand through his hair and pretended to peep at the presents still to wrap. "Anything for me?" he asked, grinning like an excited child.

"I've already wrapped yours," Lucy said, outstretching her arm in a playful manner to shoo him away.

"See, I told you, she's fine, aren't you, sis?" He continued towards the kitchen.

"Of course I am. I'll be as right as rain in a few days."

"I can't ignore a message from the spirits," I said, wondering if Lucy was hiding something. Her fingers fumbled about with the sellotape, struggling to tear a piece off. "Here, let me help," I suggested.

"Leave it, Camilla!" It was now obvious to me that she was far from okay as I drew my hand away, turning to look at Ross who stood by the kitchen door.

"I'm sorry, I didn't mean to annoy you." Upsetting Lucy was the last thing I wanted to do.

"Well you are annoying me. I want you to stop fussing over me. Once I've done this I'll go back to bed and hopefully sleep it off." Her voice mellowed a little. "I'm coming to your place for my Christmas dinner and I'm really looking forward to catching up with the others."

"If you're not well enough to come over I understand." Ross came into the room and stood beside Lucy.

"We can have dinner here if Lucy's not well," he said.

"Ross, we're going to Rosehill for Christmas day and that's arranged. Now go and get yourself showered, I need you to go to the shop for me." He glanced at me, shrugging.

"I was thinking about shopping next week, during the sales. If you're feeling better maybe you could come with me." A full day in the city, lunch in a fancy restaurant and a long girly chat were something we had looked forward to between Christmas and New Year for the past twenty years.

"Oh yes," Lucy replied. "We have to go shopping in the sales." I noticed her expression lighten as the smile on her face broadened. "Do you remember that year we both bought the same coat because it was half price?"

I laughed. "Of course I do, it was a lovely coat but why we did that I'll never know."

"We must have been about twenty five I think, seems like a long time ago doesn't it?"

It was nearly twenty years ago and even though not so much had happened to me in all that time, a lot had certainly happened to Lucy.

"Then the year we took Rebecca and Jacob with us because Paul decided he had to work. And we ended up eating at that burger bar and Jacob got ketchup all over your new skirt."

"I'll never forget that," she gasped. "Why did I take it out of the bag in the middle of the cafe?"

"We could go to Newcastle this year if you like. The kids won't be around will they?"

"That's a point," she said. I noticed she didn't seem so drained any more. "We could take the train."

"See how you are after Boxing Day and we'll sort something out. What will Ross do?"

"He'll be alright. I doubt he'll want to come with us." I was quite relieved about that, shopping with Lucy's brother in tow didn't seem quite so appealing. "He can have the house to himself for the day."

"Something to look forward to," I said, before standing up. "I'd better get back." Lucy followed me into the hall, hugging me again before opening the front door.

"Thanks for coming over. I do appreciate you caring but I'm sure granddad was over-reacting."

"Possibly," I said, trying not to doubt myself. "But take care anyway, give yourself some me-time, let Ross look after you for a few days."

"I will, I promise. See you on Christmas Day."

"Come whatever time you like," I shouted, as I got into my car. "I'll be the one stood in the kitchen with the apron on." She smiled, a little enthusiasm showing in her expression, before shutting the door behind me.

❦

Upon arriving home, still dissatisfied with Lucy's explanation, I made the decision that after lunch I would go to see Marcus, try to see if a friendship could at least be salvaged from our awkward dinner the other night. I wanted to ask him about Lucy, too, assuming his experience of being a vicar might help me persuade her to see a doctor. There had to be a right way to approach the subject without causing offence.

He was cleaning his car when I arrived, dressed casually in jeans and a woollen jumper. Putting down the sponge he greeted me as I walked into the drive.

"It's nice to see you," he said.

"I hope you don't mind me turning up unexpected?"

He smiled. "No, not at all. Fancy a coffee? I could do with a break." I nodded and followed him through the front door, a feeling of déjà vu as I walked into his kitchen.

"I need your advice about something," I said.

"You aren't going to reveal another secret are you?" He asked, a tiny smile forming.

"Well, sort of," I replied, "but I could really do with your help."

"I'm listening," he said, his smile disappearing.

"I gave a reading to my friend's brother yesterday and we were visited by his grandfather." Marcus nodded his head, questions obviously arising. "I don't expect you to agree, I just want you to listen, as a vicar. Don't say anything, just listen."

"Okay, I'm listening." He lifted his arms in defence.

I continued, "Ross is going to experience heartache. Someone close to him is going to pass over and I'm worried about who it is. And then I got a message from his granddad telling me Lucy is sick."

"What's the matter with her?" He tilted his head to one side.

"She says it's a cold, possibly had flu, but I'm not sure." I bit my bottom lip. "I went to see her again this morning and tried to talk her into getting help, but she refused."

"And you don't think it is a cold?" he asked, taking a sip of his drink.

"It was the tone in her granddad's voice. He was worried about her enough to encourage me to do something to help."

"Why don't you ring her tomorrow, let her see that you're still concerned, maybe offer to look after her while she's ill. Her brother, Ross did you say? Does he live nearby?"

"He lives in California but he's over here for a few months." I paused. "I picked him up from the airport the other day. He's staying with her but I don't think he believes there's anything wrong with her other than the cold she claims to have."

"Oh well, I suggest you leave him to look after her. Maybe she wants to be left alone."

I drank the rest of my coffee. Marcus didn't know Lucy, he didn't seem to understand my reasons for worrying. I had every intention of ringing her the next day, still thinking about the message received from her granddad I knew I couldn't just let it drop. However, I decided to listen to Marcus, reminding myself why I had visited him in the first place. Perhaps he had a point about Lucy wanting to be left alone.

"What are you doing for Christmas?" I purposely changed the subject.

"I'm spending it with family, but most of the time I'll be here. It's a busy time for the church and I have a lot of sermons to write. How about you? Are you going anywhere?"

I almost wondered if I should have invited him to join us at Rosehill on Christmas day, but I decided against it.

"I'm having some friends over for Christmas dinner, people I knew when I lived in Edinburgh. So long as she's well enough, Lucy will be coming too. We always spend Christmas day together. Something we've done since she got divorced. Ross will be coming, too."

"Sounds good. At least you won't be on your own." He smiled, his blue eyes shining.

"I'm never on my own," I said, before standing up and putting my empty cup in the sink. "I'd better get going and let you carry on with your jobs."

"I'm only cleaning the car, it can wait. I've been thinking about ringing you, hoping our little disagreement the other night hadn't upset you."

Managing a rather false smile I lifted my eyes to the ceiling. "I was a bit upset." I paused for a moment. "But it was a nice evening, despite our differences of opinion." He laughed, the ice at last starting to break between us.

"It was a nice evening yes, and we're all entitled to an opinion." I wondered if he thought his opinion was right and mine was wrong but I decided not to aggravate the calm surroundings.

"You'll be taking the midnight service on Christmas Eve?" I asked.

"Yes. Hopefully we'll get a sober congregation this year. Half the pews were filled with people who seemed to have fallen out of the pub last year. It was quite loud, especially when we sang the hymns." We both laughed as I pictured the small village church overwhelmed by party animals, most of whom had probably never even been to church.

I looked around the room, thoughts racing as an unexpected breeze brushed past my face. It was spontaneous of me but I couldn't stop myself asking. "If you'd like to come for supper on Christmas Eve before the service, you're very welcome."

Marcus looked at me, his laughter having ceased. "I'd love to," he replied, a smile forming on his lips.

Leaving under better circumstances than the last time, he walked me back to my car, closing the door as I got in. I wound the window down after starting the engine.

"See you tomorrow night, then," I said. He nodded and waved as I drove away.

Chapter Fourteen

I wanted to be organised when Marcus arrived for supper on Christmas Eve, choosing roast beef with Yorkshire pudding. I had never been a great one for cooking but occasionally I made an effort. My grandmother joined me, standing by the dresser, her expression looking somewhat confused. I couldn't understand what she was thinking but I sensed it had something to do with Marcus.

"What is it?" I asked, whilst wrapping the beef in foil. "I know you're here for a reason other than being sociable." I giggled, the art of appearing to talk to myself was one I had perfected over the years.

Going into the pantry I heard footsteps behind me, my grandmother had followed me. She watched as I reached for the flour, her aura appearing less colourful than it usually did. There was something wrong though she didn't seem eager to talk about it. Making my way back to the kitchen I realised she had left, perhaps not wanting to engage in spirit communication.

At seven o'clock Marcus arrived laden with a bottle of Beaujolais. The supper was ready and I ushered him into the house, taking his coat and scarf then hanging them up by the back door. He seemed in good spirits, happy to be at Rosehill as he gave me the wine.

"Don't pour me any," he laughed.

"I won't. But I can't drink all this on my own." I opened the drawer to get out the corkscrew.

"Drink it up tomorrow at your dinner party." I gave him the corkscrew and encouraged him to open the bottle, then reached for a wine glass. "I'll have water," he confirmed.

"Supper's ready now," I said as I took out the sliced beef from the Aga. "Go through to the dining room if you like, I'll bring the food in." It was all very simple but deliciously aromatic as I took through roast potatoes, Yorkshire pudding, carrots and broccoli in china bowls with the beef on a matching platter.

It didn't take long for us to empty our plates, a roast dinner always one of my favourites and I assumed was one of Marcus's, too. I was aware that we seemed to be forming a friendship. Marcus was enjoying himself, telling me about his life in London and the early days when he first became ordained. His life had been so much different back then.

"It must have been a shock when you transferred from a large congregation to such a small village church. I imagine the place only holds about fifty people."

"About that, yes. St. Stephens, where I used to work, was enormous. Some Sundays there must have been about four hundred people there, the roof was lifted with the sound of voices."

"Do you miss it?"

"Not one bit," he said with a hint of relief in his voice. "Moving up here was what I needed to do."

"I miss Edinburgh a little, the hustle and bustle, the shops, but I don't regret moving to Rosehill. I wouldn't want to be anywhere else now."

"I don't blame you. You were lucky to find this place when you did, I heard a developer had his eye on it." I had heard that too and wondered if it had perhaps been one of the reasons why my grandmother brought me to it.

"I haven't got to know many people yet, just Alice Baxter from the village, oh, and Julia Henderson who I believe lives near the pub." He lifted his eye brows at the mention of Julia's name.

"There's some good people living in the village, they're mainly elderly but there's a few families too. I'm not sure if they'll be a small shop opening up soon. Some new people moved into one of those newly refurbished cottages." His voice rose and I nodded, acknowledging that I knew where he meant. "Mr and Mrs Kelly, I think they're called, they have a young son."

"The village is expanding." I laughed, a little sarcasm reaching the surface. He smiled in agreement, before finishing his water. "I'll just take these plates into the kitchen then we can sit in the lounge for a bit, have some coffee." I stood up, reaching for his plate. "Unless you have to go?"

"I need to be at church by eleven, open up and put the heating on otherwise we won't be able to concentrate on anything other than the cold. But I must go home first and put on the robes."

"Oh, well you have plenty of time. Would you like coffee, or do you prefer another glass of water?"

"Coffee will be perfect, it'll keep me awake before the service." Again, we laughed, the atmosphere so much lighter than during our previous evening together.

I left the plates on the worktops before leading him into the lounge with another glass of wine in my hand. I had already put the lamps on before he arrived, just in case he was able to stay after supper. It warmed the atmosphere of the room, just the dim light from three table lamps seemed to change the ambience to a gentle and relaxing pace, smothered in the soft ticking of the fireplace clock.

"I should have asked, how's your friend?" He put his coffee down on the table. "Lucy, isn't it?"

"I spoke to her this morning. She sounded cheerful enough. I think Ross is looking after her. I'm hoping it won't be the other way round."

"How old is he?"

"Forty-nine," I answered. "He lives on his own in California. He's had a string of girlfriends but never seems to settle down. Lucy just laughs at him now. He's a few years older than her."

"Sounds like he has the ultimate bachelor's life." I sensed a little envy in Marcus's voice, though I brushed it aside.

"I'm not sure. He's nice enough. I've been friends with Lucy most of my life so I've kind of grown up with him. I used to have a thing for him once!"

"Oh?" he said, "and?"

"And nothing," I smiled, a little embarrassed at divulging information about my long ago relationship with Ross. "It passed, we both moved on."

"Are they coming tomorrow?"

"I hope so, Lucy seemed to think she would be okay and I know she's excited about seeing the others again." I poured myself another glass of wine, realising there was probably only enough left for one more glass. I was tipsy and starting to get emotional as I thought about Lucy.

"Tell me about your friends, are they the ones you knew from Edinburgh?"

"Yes. Lizzie was my neighbour, her flat was opposite mine and we shared many a night with a glass in our hands, putting the world to rights. She's married to Hamish now but they don't have any children. Richard I've known since college. He's divorced and lives on his own on the outskirts of the city. His ex got remarried and moved down south. We don't see much of each other anymore but occasionally I catch up with them if I'm in Edinburgh. They've never been here though." Tears had welled up in my eyes and I wiped them away before they had chance to roll down my cheeks.

"Hey, what is it?" Marcus asked.

"Oh, I'm sorry. I was just thinking about Lucy. I'm worried about her."

"I can see that. You two are obviously close."

"We were childhood friends. I know her like I know myself and I've never seen her like this before. It was as though she was keeping something from me." I turned round and grabbed a tissue from the box on the sideboard. "Ignore me, it's probably the wine!"

"I'm sure she'll be better by tomorrow. If she's still coming then you'll have a great day. I never get chance to catch up with old friends these days. My sister's coming in the morning and staying overnight." He reached for his cup, finishing the last of his coffee. "Anyway, I'd better go, get myself ready for the service. Are you coming down later?"

"No, I'll clean up here then go to bed I think, big day tomorrow."

"Of course." He didn't question me further which I was grateful for. We hadn't talked about our differences of opinion all night and I hoped to end our time together on a good note this time.

I took his coat and scarf from the hook, passing them to him whist he stood in the kitchen.

"Thank you for a lovely evening, I've really enjoyed myself." He started to put on his coat, hesitantly fastening buttons. "I hope we can do this again sometime?"

"That would be nice," I replied. He threw his scarf over his shoulder then took his keys out of his coat pocket. His next move surprised me somewhat as he leant towards me, softly brushing my cheek with his own.

"Soon." He moved to the back door reaching for the handle. "Thanks again."

"See you soon," I said, as I closed the door behind him.

***

Satisfied that the kitchen was clean and tidied, I went to bed, my eyes tired and thoughts of my evening with Marcus still in my head. I found it difficult to get to sleep though, and at midnight switched my lamp on to read for a while. I was light headed from the wine and knew I was in danger of feeling the worse for wear in the morning. I can't have been reading for long before I heard the dogs barking downstairs, something they only did when someone arrived at the house. At half past midnight I was a little concerned as to who could be wandering about outside my house at that time. Knowing the dogs would protect me I got out of bed and put my dressing gown on, pulling it tight around me. I hadn't seen the lights outside, nor had I heard the car in the driveway but I knew someone was there, my dogs never made such a commotion for no reason.

Going to the back door I hushed the dogs and looked out of the window to see the figure of a man striding towards the house. My heart started to race and I became nervous, unsure as to whether I ought to phone the police and let them deal with my mystery guest. But when he tapped on the door, sending the dogs into a barking frenzy once more, I stood still, desperate to know who it was yet worried it was a stranger.

"Who is it?" I asked.

"It's me," he answered. "I hope you don't mind me calling back." It was Marcus.

I relaxed, unbolting the door before opening it. "What are you doing? It's gone midnight."

"I'm sorry, I just wanted to make sure you were okay. You were rather upset earlier and I felt as if I'd left a bit abruptly."

"Not at all," I answered. "You could have phoned me tomorrow. You must be tired." I moved aside, letting him walk past me into the kitchen. The dogs had calmed down, content that they had done their job of guarding me.

"I don't feel tired right now, I think the buzz of the Christmas service always gets to me. The church was half full but fortunately with sober locals."

"I was just in bed when I heard the dogs barking." Conscious I was in night clothes I once more tightened my dressing gown. But my heart was racing. A part of me was glad he had come back.

He moved to stand in front of me, reaching out his arms to touch mine. I felt a little uneasy as we stood together, neither of us knowing of our next move.

"I could have phoned you, I know. But you've been on my mind since I left. I was struggling to concentrate on the service at one point." He smiled as he ran his arms up and down mine.

"I think I drank too much wine. I don't normally drink so much in one night. I finished the bottle after you'd gone." I turned to walk further into the kitchen.

"I should have brought another bottle," he laughed.

"Gosh no, I'll never be able to cook dinner tomorrow."

Once more standing in front of me, he suddenly lent in, our lips just centimetres apart. I couldn't resist the temptation of drawing him closer and as his lips touched mine, my whole body shook. I became overwhelmed with passion as he continued to kiss me, gripping me lustfully. He moved his lips from mine, caressing my neck with his mouth, his hands now moving gently up and down my back, around my shoulders then settling in their grip around me. He eventually withdrew before taking hold of my hand. I was unsure, I couldn't see past the feelings of forbidden love, feelings I was trying so desperately to ignore. But I allowed him to take me into his arms once more. His touch was incredible as he kissed me again, sending shivers up and down my spine.

Before I knew what was happening I found myself leading him out of the kitchen and into the hallway, towards the stairs which would take us to my bedroom. He followed, obligingly. The quilt on my bed was pulled back and it seemed like an invitation to our lust. He took off his trousers, carefully removing the dog collar and his shirt.

He cupped my head in his hands, kissing me. "I want you, Camilla," he said, his tongue stroking my neck. Then he helped me to remove my pyjamas, forcing me gently onto the bed before lying on top of me.

It was pure lust; a feeling I had forgotten of how love making should be performed. I wanted him too, his voice in my ear, his touch against my aroused body. And I had him. Upon moans of pleasure and his satisfied claims, he lifted from me, settling by my side.

His head turned towards me and he smiled. "You were wonderful," he sighed, his eyes once more sparkling like blue diamonds. We got beneath the duvet, his arms wrapping themselves around me as he pulled me into him. I rested my head upon his chest, running my fingers through the silver hair which threatened to arouse me once more.

Marcus's heart was beating fast. I could feel the rhythm against my cheek. He stroked my face whilst I rested in his arms, wondering what I was doing with the village priest in my bed.

"Merry Christmas," he said softly, kissing my forehead. "I won't stay, I know you have a busy day tomorrow." But I didn't want him to move. I was so warm and having a man in my bed was something I hadn't had for a very long time.

I was tired as I glanced at the wall clock, noticing it was already one-thirty. Sitting up and moving away I gave him the opportunity to get up and leave. What had just happened was a passionate encounter I hadn't expected but I hoped would happen again.

Chapter Fifteen

On Christmas day, Lucy and Ross arrived first. She seemed a lot better though I still sensed she was tired. I knew she would be missing Jacob and Rebecca who had arranged to spend the holidays with their friends in Switzerland. Their love for her always shone through and even though Lucy would have preferred them to be around, she agreed that a skiing trip was something they couldn't turn down.

"You look nice, Cam," Ross said, handing me a bottle of Chardonnay and looking particularly handsome.

"Come on in," I suggested to them both. "Here, let me take your coats." I held out my hands in gesture and Lucy gave me the bag she carried which contained wrapped presents. "Put these under the tree, can you, there's something in there for everyone." I took the bag, putting an arm around her back to hug her.

"Yours are in the lounge. Shall we wait for the others?"

"We may as well," Ross replied.

I left him in charge of the drinks cabinet after he had shown so much interest in it on his previous visit and Lucy kindly assisted me with the lunch. Lizzie, Hamish and Richard arrived soon after, making themselves comfortable in the lounge. I left Ross to entertain them after having been assured by Lucy that her brother had always admired my friends.

"He finds them normal," she told me with a chuckle. "He always wonders what they see in you." Having known Ross for so long I decided not to be insulted and laughed.

Presents were exchanged and conversation flowed as we caught up with gossip about the people I used to see.

"Do you remember Graham Woods? The smarmy looking guy who lived on the ground floor, always thought he was funny?" Lizzie was a huge one for talk, she enjoyed making us squirm as she had another tale to tell, one she should no doubt have kept to herself. We all looked at each other, vaguely recalling the name. I nodded. "It turns out he had an affair with that dolly bird from the hair dressers on Bridge Street, and, they have a baby together." The guy Lizzie spoke about had been everyone's idea of a nightmare partner, his constant stream of bad jokes was a complete turn off for any potential relationship.

"I don't believe you," I laughed. "Where did you hear that?"

"I bumped into her the other week when she was out pushing the pram. Thought I hadn't seen her in the salon for a while and that was why. When I asked her about the baby's dad she told me it was him."

"Do they live together?" I asked.

Hamish joined in the conversation. "No," he said, "Graham won't leave the flat and she doesn't want to live with him. It's a strange set up."

I was quite pleased with my tree, cut down from a nearby wood and Lizzie couldn't resist telling me about hers, a much smaller, artificial version, suitable for her rather modern apartment. Nothing had changed. I knew we would remain friends all our lives even though we had little in common. It was most likely the glue that kept us together. Sitting by the tree I reached for the presents, reading the tags before passing them round. Richard had spared no expense and bought me a bottle of perfume, obviously remembering it was my favourite. I'd got him a scarf and gloves set and sewn his name inside the gloves. When he saw the tag he screwed up his face before releasing an embarrassed grin.

"I thought you couldn't sew?" he said.

"I taught myself," I laughed, as he threw the gloves at me in a playful gesture.

Lunch was ready at one-thirty and we gathered in the dining room to enjoy the feast Lucy and I had managed to rustle up.

"This table could be used for a séance." Ross couldn't resist.

"This table has been used many times for a séance," I replied.

"How about when we've eaten?" Richard asked. I sat up, stiffened and glared at him. He rarely showed an interest in the paranormal, even though he respected my mediumship.

"Are you drunk?" asked Lizzie.

"Pissed as a fart," he replied. "But by the time I've eaten all this I'll be sober and in the right frame of mind to bring in the spirits."

"It's not a game," I said.

"Why don't you show us how it's done then?" Richard was testing my patience. I decided to eat my food and ignore his suggestion.

"Well?" he continued. "I'm interested to know what my future holds."

"I don't want to tell your future," I insisted. "It's Christmas Day. My day off."

"Ah, but is it a day off for the spirits?" asked Lizzie.

This time I glared at her. I didn't want to conduct a séance. I didn't want to even talk about my gift whilst dining with friends. I could sense Lucy shifting in her seat, recognising my discomfort.

"Great turkey," Ross tried to change the subject.

"I wonder if there's a soul above us with evil intent!" Richard was over stepping the mark but I felt unable to tell him what I thought of his ignorance. I was quite sure an angry soul did indeed hover above him, scowling with red eyes and perhaps, as he so arrogantly put it, evil intent.

"Guys, I really don't want to do a séance today."

"Just leave it, Rich?" Lizzie said, putting down her knife and fork as she reached for the sprouts. "Anyone?" she asked.

"Not for me, thanks," replied Lucy, "I have so much turkey here." I noticed she didn't have as much as she usually would but decided not to question it. She seemed a lot better than she had done in the last few days. Ross helped himself to more vegetables whilst Hamish and Lizzie pulled the crackers I had set by their plates.

"What the hell was all that about?" asked Lizzie after the meal. The others were relaxing in the lounge whilst she helped me clear the plates away. "I know he's had a few but he was deliberately making you feel uncomfortable, Cam. Have you done something to upset him?"

"I haven't seen him for months. I spoke to him on the phone last week to make sure he was coming today and he was fine. He hasn't changed, has he? Still can't take his drink!"

Our laughter brought Hamish into the kitchen. "Glad to hear you two laughing," he pointed out. "Any ideas what's wrong with Rich?"

"What's he doing now?" I asked.

"Slouched on the sofa, talking to Ross. I think there's some kind of competition thing going on."

"What do you mean?" I asked.

"You, with you I mean, woman." Hamish put his arms around his wife, kissing the back of her neck. It reminded me of the way Marcus had kissed me, those shivers which travelled down my spine just before we went up to my bed.

"Oh don't tell me they both want Cam!" Lizzie was quick to jump to conclusions.

"Afraid so, old girl. Looks like you have two hungry guys in there, both wanting a piece of you."

My feelings of discomfort at the table had just escalated, tenfold. I didn't believe either of them felt that way. Perhaps a séance would be a good idea after all. Take their minds off me for a while. It was a new feeling for me to cope with.

Charades took over the afternoon at Lucy's request which ended with me making a complete fool of myself whilst acting out "Star Trek". I was quite relieved when Lizzie and Hamish announced they had to leave because they wanted to call on Hamish's parents before night fall.

"You look happy, Cam," Lizzie said, as she walked through the back door. "What's your secret?"

I shrugged, my innocence failing me. "I'm always happy, you know me!"

"Thanks for having us, it's been a great laugh, and the house is gorgeous. I'm so envious."

"Next time you come we'll have a walk round the farm, I'll show you the grounds. And don't leave it too long till you visit again." I hugged her then kissed her cheek. As they were taking Richard with them it felt like a weight had been lifted from my shoulders.

"Thanks, Cam," he said, before getting into the car. He was struggling to manoeuvre into the seat, obviously the amount of alcohol he had consumed weighing heavily. He blew me a kiss then said, "might see you soon."

I closed the door and returned to the lounge where Lucy and Ross were sat watching television, I noticed Lucy looking particularly tired and I offered them both to stay the night. I was thrilled when they accepted and found myself in two guest rooms, turning down beds and making sure they had fresh towels.

"I'm glad we're staying." Ross surprised me as he stood in the doorway with hands in his pockets. "I've been wanting to ask you all day, have you had your hair done, it really suits you." The smirk on his face told me he had followed me upstairs intentionally. My thoughts were confirmed as he approached me, positioning himself to place his arms around me.

"I said you could stay in the guest rooms. My room is in the west wing." For some reason I felt it important that I pointed this out, although at the time I thought it made no difference to Ross's state of mind after the huge glasses of Scotch he had drunk.

"Why don't you join me in here tonight? You know I've never been able to forget you, Cam. It's only a matter of time before something was bound to happen between us." He had definitely had too much to drink.

"Why don't you take a shower? A cold one." I moved away, making my way back to the door, leaving him standing in the middle of the room.

His head now facing the floor, he tutted. Perhaps this was the way he treated women; expected them to sleep with him upon his lurid suggestions. I left the room, aware that he was following me.

"Ross, I can't sleep with you." I so wanted to tell Lucy about Marcus but I felt mysteriously worried about how she would take it.

"Are you sleeping with someone else?" he asked suddenly, and to my surprise.

"Yes, for heaven's sake, yes I am."

"Who?"

"None of your damn business." I quickened my pace towards the stairs having said too much already.

I knew Lucy would keep my secret once I told her but I had to be careful. I was sure Marcus wouldn't have wanted people to know about our one night of passion. Not yet anyway.

Making my way into the lounge I poured myself a drink, unable to look at Ross who now stood in the doorway. I just wanted to tell him to leave. Lucy looked peaceful. She had fallen asleep against my silk cushion.

"I've decided to go back to LA," Ross announced, eyeing my reaction.

"When?" I wasn't sure if I had sounded relieved. I sank back into the sofa, taking a sip of the brandy Ross poured for me earlier.

"As soon as I can get a flight. I might as well go back to the life I've got used to."

"Lucy will be terribly upset. She enjoys having you here."

"I know, but she knew it wouldn't be forever." He joined me on the sofa, a little too close for comfort. "I doubt I shall ever come back."

"Of course you will, what about Lucy?" He shocked me.

"She won't miss me. If she wants to see me she can come over to LA. I've realised during this visit that I just don't belong here anymore. You know about belonging, don't you, Cam?"

The brandy warmed me. It also made me feel differently towards the man whom had insulted me with his philandering ways yet now appealed to my good nature. It was as though someone was putting thoughts into my head, taking my heart away from Marcus.

As Ross drank his Scotch I realised my hunch was right. A female spirit stood near the fireplace, a smile lifting her lips slightly while her eyes fixed themselves upon mine. It was Jane. "Your second chance," she said. It meant nothing.

Ross looked at me again. I wondered if he had seen her also or if he simply questioned my sudden movement.

"Is there a ghost here?" A sceptical tone, Ross turned my head with his voice.

"Yes. She stands by the fireplace," I replied, with a little regret. "She's called Jane, someone I used to know." The words left my mouth without me understanding why. I didn't recall knowing anyone called Jane, not in my current life.

"What does she look like?" he asked.

"Right now, she has a golden aura around her. She has brown, shoulder length hair and beautiful eyes."

She turned away, gliding towards the lounge door, wanting me to follow her. Leading me to my reading room, her manifested spirit waited for me at the door. I opened it and went in. Ross came too, somewhat nervous at the potential outcome of her request. The room was naturally dark though a small amount of artificial light shining from the hallway guided us to a small bookshelf. I had filled it with books, yet individually, each one had been taken off the shelf and put neatly onto the floor. Stacked up in exactly the same order they had been placed on the shelves I knew Jane had been responsible for this action. She turned to me, her delicate face aglow with the most beautiful aura of sunshine yellow. I wondered if she was trying to give me a message concerning books, or maybe one book in particular.

Her voice echoed in my head as she said, "touch the fireplace." I moved closer to it, examining the mantle. Inquisition beckoned me to put my hand to the space she was so determined I touched. I could feel Ross stood behind me, his mood having changed to fear.

"What is it?" he asked, still standing behind me, his breath blowing onto my neck.

"There's something inside the fireplace, I'm sure there is," I said.

"Bloody hell. Are you going to put your hand up the chimney?"

"I might," I tried to hold onto the assertiveness I had suddenly found.

I was tired. My head was beginning to hurt from the long day of Christmas. Jane's spirit was fading; she obviously felt she had done the task she needed to do for that day and I was sure she would come back. She seemed determined to have me discover the secret in my reading room, one which was beginning to leave me in a state of confusion. I turned to Ross. He walked quickly towards the door, encouraging me to leave with him.

"I don't know what's going on here, but I'm not staying," he said, as I turned thoughts over in my head. I replaced the books on the shelves, not really taking much notice as to the order they had originally been arranged. What was I supposed to find hiding in the fireplace? Apart from the endless amount of nests built by the jackdaws, I couldn't think of anything else.

Chapter Sixteen

We all slept soundly that Christmas night. Fortunately, Ross stayed in his own bed and I was able to retire to my room without having to fend him off. I got the impression he had been somewhat perturbed by Jane's presence, not to mention my tuning into the message she had given me. I was grateful to her. I hoped she understood.

I knew it would only be a matter of time before she visited again but I was prepared to wait until she did before doing anything more about searching the fireplace. There was no rush. It was on my mind but my priority lay with Lucy. I couldn't stop thinking about the old man's message to his grandson, a message which been clearer than I cared to admit to Ross. Lucy had been impressed upon me and I knew communication focused around her. She was sick. I didn't know how bad she was but I had to find out. Meditation opened up to me as I positioned myself, feet resting firmly on the floor, eyes closed and mind a-blank. I would try and persuade the old man to come through, if not then, perhaps he would visit me later. I needed an answer that even I could not work out. But he didn't come.

Lucy and Ross left on Boxing Day, wanting to spend the day on their own. I hoped he would tell her about his intentions to leave. Once more I sat alone, my thoughts still with the old man and Lucy. But a knock on the door at lunch time took me away from the world of spirit as I took my guest into the kitchen.

"I had a free day," Marcus said, "wondered if you wanted some company?"

"Yes, I hadn't made any plans." He took his coat off, hanging it over a chair.

"How was yesterday?" he asked. "And how's Lucy?"

"Yesterday was good, it was lovely to catch up with everyone. Lucy's okay but she was very tired." I made us some coffee. "Ross wants to go back to America but I think he should stay a while. He obviously doesn't think Lucy's that bad."

"Are they close as brother and sister?"

"They certainly used to be but since he moved away I guess they've grown apart. I tried to talk to him but he was drunk." I decided not to tell Marcus about Jane's visit.

"That's a shame. He hasn't been here long, has he?"

"Just a few weeks. She'll be very disappointed." Marcus touched my face, running his fingers down my cheek.

"I really enjoyed Christmas Eve," he said.

"Me too. Did you enjoy your day with your sister?"

"My sister?" he seemed a little confused before adding, "oh, yes, of course. We had a nice day, quiet but always a pleasure to spend time together." He lent towards me, his lips gently sweeping against mine. I kissed him back.

Unable to contain ourselves any longer, we pushed aside the newspaper and magazines which lay on the table. His touch was sensual, intensity pouring from every inch of his body, taking me away from the world I had been so wrapped up in during the last twenty four hours. The way he held me, his strong arms protecting me against the solid surface whilst his gentle moans of pleasure satisfied my mind. We kissed, tenderly, in between claims of wanting more. My only regret was that it had to come to an end. We sat on the sofa for the rest of the afternoon, laughing at the television and eating the high calories that sat looking rather forlorn beneath the Christmas tree.

"I wish you could stay the night?" I asked him.

"I'd much rather be here."

"Are you going to stay?" I was hopeful.

"If you'll have me," he replied. I felt a blast of cold air brush past my leg.

He must have felt me shiver as he backed away, questions in his eyes and a slight look of concern overwhelming his handsome features.

"Kiss me again," I requested, a part of me wanting to know if we had been joined by a jealous entity. The other part hoping we were alone.

A female spirit stood with her arms folded, her back to the fireplace looking straight at me. Her face seemed kind yet she seemed to disapprove. My mind began to race as I realised it was Anne. She had no right being in the lounge. She had interrupted an intimate moment and I was reluctant to tune into her energy.

Marcus, unsuspecting, rose from the sofa. "Shall I make us a coffee?" he asked, much to my relief.

"That would be lovely. You know where everything is, don't you?"

"I'll find it." Anne's gaze followed him to the door, before she turned back to me and faded from sight.

***

It was late, about 11.15. We lay in bed. Myself unable to sleep for a mind of racing thoughts as I tossed and turned, listening to the owl by my window announce the darkness. I was emotional. Having no reason for my sudden grief I could feel myself getting hotter, yet a light breeze blew beside my face, perhaps a bid to cool me. It was then that the sheets on my bed were tugged; gently pulled as though a child's hand requested my attention. I lay on my side still feeling the gentle air surrounding my skin. Marcus breathed softly as the sheets continued to move, a little more forceful. I called out the name Jane, as my heart raced faster when I realised she had joined me.

I knew she wanted me to follow her again. My mind was relaying her message in frantic state. I felt I had no choice but to follow. Attiring myself with dressing gown and slippers I made my way to the door, a little apprehensive at what I was about to find, if anything at all.

The mirror on the stairs gave reflection to a shadowy figure; that of a man in still pose whilst footsteps trod by its gilt framed glass. I sat on a step for a moment, watching in wonder, talking to a space filled with fact. It was sometimes difficult to work out on which staircase my spirit visitors stood, until they settled beside me, exhilaration sprinting through my body. My neck became stiff as I tried to turn my head towards the energy that brushed against my clothes.

The distant sound of the servants' bell rang from the ground floor of the house. I suspected it was coming from my reading room, where Jane was so keen to take me.

Still unable to see any spirit manifestation I continued on until I reached the room to where I felt I was being led. Before my hands reached the handle, the door opened, slowly; creaking hinges haunting noisily through the house.

A candle stood in the middle of the table, its small flame flickering. The books had once more been taken from the shelves and placed onto the floor in neat piles. Jane didn't need to tell me to touch the fireplace again, I moved briskly towards where I felt the reading room may open up to reveal a hidden secret.

Having no idea what I would discover I sat down and began to tune into the spirit world.

"Jane? Are you here with me?"

The flame gently flickered.

"Jane, if you're here please show yourself."

My hand felt icy cold. As the flame danced I was sure I'd been joined by a spirit determined to make contact. But as I looked around the room, the shock that I got startled me from communication I had managed to summon. The manifested spirit of a man stood in the room. He stared at the fireplace, his eyes tearful while his lips curled in readiness to speak. I gripped the arms of the chair, wondering why I felt the entity looked familiar. His profile reminded me of a visiting spirit which I had not seen for a few months, that of Harold Baxter. For a reason I couldn't understand he made me feel protected, there to ensure no harm came to me. Maybe he felt Jane would have inflicted harm or maybe there was a more sinister reason for his presence, but I knew he had no intention to cause me any fear.

As I turned towards the corner in which the male spirit looked, it was clear that a second manifestation was about to emerge. A bright, white light shone by the fireplace, becoming larger with every blink until, eventually, I recognised the outline. A smaller figure of a woman stood with her hands on her hips looking directly at her opposer.

An authoritative grin revealed her identity to me. My grandmother had joined us together with the spirit of Harold Baxter.

Chapter Seventeen

O ne of them knew something. Maybe all of them knew the same, an event that had occurred leaving me to solve the mystery. My new found occupation as a detective was soon to prove me capable of more than my mediumship yet unbeknown to me, I was to learn something of great importance. A fact of my life that only a handful of people knew, all of whom had passed over.

I had been sat in the reading room for two hours, most of which were spent sleeping and was woken by Marcus as he prodded me quite sharply.

"I wondered where you were. I turned over, reached out to you and you'd gone." He looked concerned. "I've been through the house. I tried this door but it was locked, then I came back after hearing a noise in here and it was open again."

"I'm sorry, I'll come back to bed now." My eyes were struggling to stay open as Marcus helped me out of the chair, his strong arm supporting me up the stairs.

Sleep came easily once my head touched the pillow. The next thing I remember was waking up in my bed, alone. I lay a while, recalling the events during the night, desperately hoping I hadn't ruined things for Marcus and me, even though our relationship had only just begun and I felt determined to make it work.

My thoughts wandered to Jane and her whereabouts after seeing my grandmother and Harold Baxter in the reading room. Where had she gone? I needed to find out the reason for her leading me their again. It was at that moment of thought when my bedroom door opened having been nudged gently from the base.

I sat up quickly. A rush of excitement thrown in my direction as my thoughts raced around the world of spirit.

"Breakfast is served." I saw the tray first, laden with a feast of morning tucker. Marcus brought me breakfast in bed, a total surprise and a warm welcome after a somewhat unusual night.

My heart melted. Was it possible to fall in love so soon into a relationship? Yet I had. I wanted him to accept me for being me; to forget about our spiritual differences, our lives led by another world. But more than anything, right at that very moment, I wanted him. I needed to feel him inside me again, teasing me and caressing my aroused body. It was like we had entered the honeymoon period of our relationship, when all is well with each other. I ached for his touch, for that sensual tongue to explore every part of my body.

I took the tray from his hands and placed it on the table beside me before holding out my arms for his embrace.

"You spoil me," I said, and kissed him softly on his lips. "Come back to bed, breakfast can wait."

He bent down towards me, taking me in his arms, capturing my mouth against his. That same tingling shot through my body, arousing me like before. I wanted him more than anything at that very moment. Letting his tongue stroke my neck I threw my head back in readiness, the only thoughts in my mind being Marcus.

He pulled me out of the bed, separating my legs. Penetration felt incredible as I drowned in his lust, completely at ease by his luxurious touch. Right there and then, he was everything I wanted in a man.

"That was wonderful," I said, as he rolled away from me.

"You were wonderful," he smiled, a satisfied glow shining from his eyes. "Aren't you going to eat your breakfast now?"

"I think I've just had it," I replied, snuggling into him, tucking myself under his outstretched arm.

"I have an appointment at half-nine," he announced, much to my disappointment. "I'd better take a shower." He leant over to kiss me before getting up. For a man of fifty-eight he was in remarkably good shape.

I sat up, taking the breakfast tray from the table and leaning it on my lap. Even though the tea had gone cold, Marcus has left a glass of fresh orange. He returned to my bedroom after ten minutes, his hair wet, a towel hiding his modesty. He quickly got dressed then sat on the bed, holding my hand in his.

"I'll call you." He lifted my hand to his mouth.

"Don't leave it too long," I said, as he stood up and left the room.

A part of me was still unsure about our relationship. Our differences were hugely focal, our lives perhaps incompatible. Not knowing when I would see him next left me wanting him again. But I made the decision not to phone him and wait for him to ring me, like he said he would. Instead I phoned Lucy. I wanted to tell her about my liaison and my new found romance. I wanted her to give me an opinion, to advise me on whether she thought I had made a fool of myself. Ross sounded quite worried about her for a change, answering the phone after it had rung just once.

"She hasn't eaten anything since being at your place."

"I'll come over. You should have phoned me, Ross, I knew she wasn't right."

Speeding along the country roads to Lucy's house I arrived to find Ross looking out of the window. My thoughts of it being just a virus became thwarted as a vision came into my head, one which I tried desperately to banish. But upon seeing my good friend lying in her bed I realised that the vision had been more accurate than I cared to admit. It was obvious that Lucy needed a doctor even though she refused help. Ross had tried several times to encourage her, causing a slight rift between them. I sat on the end of the bed and held her hand. She was too weak to even grip my fingers, the colour having drained from her skin. I wanted to cry for her, hold her and persuade her to get medical help. But it was as though she knew how sick she was, almost telling me that help would do no good.

"Let me get the doctor for you." I prayed my words wouldn't fall on deaf ears.

Her quietly spoken tones ate into my heart. "Okay, the number's in the book." She could hardly speak the words and I had to listen intently. "I've been ill for a long time." Her announcement came as no surprise. The earlier vision had told me the same, showing me a terrifying scene portraying a woman in hospital robes.

"I want you to go into hospital, Lucy. You need help. They can make you better."

"No." Somehow she found the strength for a stern answer.

"Have Jacob and Rebecca been to see you?" If it was as serious as I was beginning to suspect it was important they were told.

"I don't want them here," she said. But I wasn't happy. I was nervous; frightened that I was being left in the dark about something I felt I had a right to know.

I left her alone while I went to find Ross. In the kitchen he rose to his feet upon my entry. He too had no colour. He was worried, his eyes questioning whether I could help in some way.

"We need to contact Jacob and Rebecca," I said, "and a doctor. Where's the phone book?"

"Jacob and Rebecca know she's ill, they just don't know how ill. I told them yesterday that she has a virus and could do without visitors for a few days. I'll phone Doctor Philips, he'll come round I'm sure." He made his way to the sideboard.

"Ring him first then I'll phone Jacob and Rebecca after we hear what he has to say." A part of me already knew what the doctor was going to say.

Ross dialled the number of the surgery. Within ten minutes Doctor Philips arrived at the front door, his medical bag in hand, a solemn look on his face. He knew something, too. Ross led him to Lucy, both of us quite sure it wouldn't have been a waste of his time. She lay still, her eyes closed, both arms falling loosely by her sides.

The doctor approached her, speaking softly, trying to coax her from sleep. Unable to sit up she slowly opened her eyes and looked at each of us in turn. I curled my mouth up, a guilty smile forming on my lips. Ross stood by the door, probably ready to run at the first sign of hostility.

But Lucy managed the weakest smile before closing her eyes once more, allowing the doctor to examine her. Ross and I waited in the kitchen for him to come downstairs.

"Could I use the phone, we need to get her into hospital. She's very dehydrated."

"What's wrong with her?" Ross asked.

"We need to do tests, I can't confirm until we get her into hospital."

"Shall I go too?" I asked, looking at Ross who was passing the phone to the doctor.

"There's no need for that just yet," he said. "I'm sure Ross will phone you, once we've run the tests."

I waited for the ambulance to arrive, watching as Lucy was wheeled into it. I felt helpless and decided to go back to Rosehill, taking a detour to the vicarage on my way.

Marcus preferred to stay in during the afternoon, his door always open to parishioners. I was one myself, someone in need of a friend and a shoulder. Whether the vicarage was the right place to go was something I felt unsure about but as my vicar, I felt he owed it to me to offer support, if nothing else. I got out of the car wondering why this man continued to make me feel nervous. I was in love with him, I knew that in my heart, yet I was wary of his ways, apprehensive of his approach.

The lady I had seen a few weeks ago walked by, Verity, the friend who was new to the village. I smiled at her, glad that she reciprocated. But her smile was odd, sly somehow, an indication that she might be hiding something. I wondered if my disbelief in coincidences ought to be forgotten just this one time, for I felt it strange that this woman had once again appeared near the vicarage just as I was arriving. But I had more important things to think about. I needed Marcus's support.

Before I reached the front door Marcus opened it, his smile caused my legs to almost buckle beneath me. I had to compose myself, remember why I had come to his house, so I returned the smile. His hand touched my arm as I walked through the door and I sensed his concern at my unexpected visit.

"Are you okay," he asked, as he closed the door. "I'm sorry I haven't been in touch, were you expecting me to?"

"I could do with a friend, Marcus."

"Why? What's the matter?" A concerned expression covered his face.

"It's Lucy again; she's been admitted to hospital."

"Oh heck, I'm sorry I had no idea she was so ill. What is it, do they know?" He went over to the drinks cabinet and removed two tumblers from the glass cupboard. "Drink?"

"Not for me," I replied.

"Which hospital?"

"The General. She's in a bad way, I don't know what to do." It was then that the tears came, pouring down my cheeks. He put the glasses down and walked over to me, placing his arms around me.

"Hey, don't cry." He stroked my hair. "Shall I take you to see her?"

I was grateful for his offer. "The doctor said he preferred me to wait by the phone. He said Ross would ring me to let me know what's happening." I lifted my head, wiping tears from Marcus' jumper as I looked into his eyes.

"Do you want me to come home with you? Just in case Ross rings?"

"No, I'd better go back on my own. I'll be fine. I'll ring you when I know what's happening."

"I don't like you leaving like this. Why don't you let me stay with you?"

I couldn't think straight. My mind was overwhelmed with thoughts of Lucy lying in a hospital bed, whilst Ross stood impatiently at a pay phone, trying desperately to contact me. I kissed him before turning round to walk towards the door. The words were clear in my head, "go to her," softly spoken by the spirit I knew so well, my grandmother. I moved briskly to the front door, opening it clumsily, trying too hard to exit the house. Marcus followed me to car, his voice hardly legible in my state of confusion.

"Drive safely," he said, "and ring me when you know something." I nodded, forcing a smile as he backed away, leaving me to drive my car along the country road.

Upon reaching the main road I saw a vision, a woman who turned to look at me, her eyes glaring through my windscreen. I knew I needed to get to the hospital. Fast. There was no time to lose.

Chapter Eighteen

*T*he car park was full and I wasted valuable time finding a space. My legs somehow carried me to the main entrance where I stood in a fluster, examining the signs to the correct corridor. It was a long and lonely place, and for some, never ending. Voices emitted around my head, screams of pain, crying and the sounds of desperate pleas. Many a life had passed over to the next world as an empty carcass would have been wheeled to the next phase. The sign had directed me to the end of a desolate corridor, to a nurse's station which stood bare. I cleansed my hands. The door to my left led to a small ward with four beds, two either side. Two of the beds were occupied, one of them by Lucy. She lay, motionless, hooked up to wires and machines, way beyond my comprehension. I didn't know what to say to her, wondering if she could hear me anyway. I pulled up a nearby chair and sat on the edge of it, holding her hand, desperately hoping for movement.

There were a few nurses mooching about the ward, adjusting wires and checking drips, pens being drawn upon clip boards, frantically noting little or no change. I smiled at one nurse. She seemed friendly, ready to speak to me and so I asked her the inevitable question.

"How is she?"

She placed the clip board back against Lucy's bed and came towards me, sympathy emblazoned on her face. She didn't need to speak, her mind was open and her thoughts were filtering in to mine.

"We're doing all we can," she said.

"Have you found out what's wrong with her?"

"We're still running tests." She began to walk away, then turned to face me. "Are you a relative?"

"As good as," I began. "She's my best friend, has been most of my life." The nurse continued to move away. "You must have some idea what's wrong?"

"I'm sorry, I can't discuss it with you unless you're a relative." I looked down at Lucy, her expression peaceful. It was obvious she was in a serious condition and I thought it would have made no difference if the nurse gave me some indication.

I held Lucy's hand, watching as she seemed to be cheated out of the future she so wanted to have. We were like sisters. I recalled the day when she went into labour with Jacob, and Paul was away on business. I was there for her then, holding her hand, stroking her face as her skin creased beneath the pressure of childbirth. We'd been through so much together. I knew her inside out as she did me, and I felt like I had the right to know what was going on with her body as she continued to rely on a machine to help her breathe.

"Lucy?" I stroked her forehead. "I have something to tell you." Unsure as to whether she could hear or not, I decided to tell her about Marcus, hoping it might wake her, encourage her to sit up and fight. "I've met someone. He's a lovely man from the village." The machines carried on bleeping. "He's called Marcus Calloway. Reverend Marcus Calloway. I know you won't believe it but it's true. I'm really fond of him, Luce. And I want you to meet him."

The nurse glanced over in my direction, probably wondering who I was talking to. She smiled when she realised it was Lucy. I wondered if she thought it was hopeless, but perhaps worth a try. I smiled back before turning my attention back to Lucy.

"He's older than me but that's doesn't matter. You know me, I like the older man. You'll love him, Luce. He's so gentle and kind. He respects me. I thought we'd have a problem at first when I realised he told me his opinion of my work but I've since realised that it doesn't matter. I'm happy." My face was lighting up as I thought about the closeness Marcus and I were starting to experience. "I think Lizzie picked up on it on Christmas Day; she told me I looked happy and asked what the secret was. I'm surprised she didn't say anything to you. He's stayed over at Rosehill. I've been dying to tell you but I didn't know whether he would rather it was kept quiet." I gripped her hand tighter. "You won't tell anyone, will you?"

My eyes became filled with tears as I thought about what I was asking. I was shaking, listening to the rhythmical noises from the monitor, desperately trying to hear the sound of Lucy's breathing amidst bleeps and telephones ringing.

He couldn't have chosen a better time, I thought, as Ross burst through the doors to the ward. He flung himself towards Lucy's bedside, taking her other hand in his grasp after dropping a small hold-all onto the floor. He was flustered.

"I'm glad you're here," I said. "The nurse won't tell me what's going because I'm not a relative." He took her other hand in his. "Can you ask her?"

"Where is she?" he asked, looking around the ward. "I'd have been here sooner if I hadn't got stuck in traffic. I've brought her a few things from home."

"She's over there," I pointed to the nurse who now stood by a desk on the far side of the ward. "There's been no change since I've been here but they must know something by now." I touched his arm gently.

He walked briskly over towards the nurse and she turned round to face him. They both looked towards Lucy and me, a conversation taking place that I couldn't hear. The nurse was shaking her head while Ross put his hand to his mouth, hiding an anxious expression. I stood up and began to walk over to them.

"What?" I said. "Tell me." The nurse looked at Ross having no intention of breaking hospital rules. Ross came towards me, placing his hand on my arm before leading me back to Lucy. "What's wrong with her, Ross?"

"She said it's leukaemia." He put his hand to his face, rubbing his forehead as though in disbelief. "Why didn't we know?"

"Did Lucy know?"

"I don't think so. I want a second opinion. They can't be right." Ross's tears began to flow and I noticed him shaking. "I'm going to find a doctor."

"Ross, wait. Let's just stay with Lucy. The doctor will be here soon, I'm sure." He had gone terribly pale as I held onto him, trying hard to stop him from collapsing. I reached for a chair. "Here, sit down."

We sat on opposite sides of the bed, our hands each clasping one of Lucy's, when Jacob and Rebecca arrived. It was pitiful to see them. They were just starting out in their adult lives, and witnessing their mother as she breathed through tubes was the last thing they needed to see.

Ross stood up. "Thanks for coming."

"How is she?" Rebecca asked.

"She's not good, sweetheart." Ross held his niece. "I rang you from the car, I wasn't sure you'd heard me."

"What's the matter with her?" Jacob sat on the bed and stroked Lucy's hair. "Why is she hooked up to this machine?" I looked at Ross. I felt it wasn't my place to tell them and visually encouraged him to do it instead.

"Your mum has leukaemia."

"No!" Rebecca covered her mouth before sitting next to Jacob on the bed. "She can't have."

"Darling," he began, "she's very poorly." The devastation had hit us all as we sat around the bed, wondering how long it would be before caring for Lucy would become a full time job. Rebecca cried, as I had cried earlier with Marcus.

Wiping tears from my face I looked around the sea of distressed souls. "I'll go and get us a drink. Who wants one?" I asked, feeling it necessary to leave them on their own for a while. Ross asked for a coffee so I left the ward, praying that Lucy would wake up before I returned.

The coffee machine was along the corridor. It seemed a mountain climb away but I continued, the smell of disinfectant reaching out to my senses. An elderly couple walked towards me, engrossed in conversation. A doctor came out of a side ward, his stethoscope hanging around his neck like an opened noose. He lifted his head for a second, just to acknowledge me. I reached the machine and fumbled for change in my pocket. Trying to make sense of the correct buttons to press I finally made the choice. The machine was achingly slow as the coffee trickled from a long stainless steel tap, just about reaching my plastic cup. I removed the cup and pressed the button again. Another agonising wait as more coffee made its way reluctantly to its destination.

The doctor I had seen earlier was coming back the other way, another brief smile hiding an otherwise arrogant expression. A young man was walking towards me, red faced and sad, not of this world. His feet glided along the immaculate floor, and I could see his heart resting peacefully through his clothes. I smiled to him. He knew I had seen him and stopped for a moment, perhaps wanting me to talk to him, find his loved ones to pass on a message. But my time was precious. I needed to get back with the coffees.

I walked past the restful heart, his smile continuing to bore through me, the sadness in his eyes almost changing my mind about stopping for a chat. As I turned from him, passing him along the corridor, I realised a woman stood at the door to the ward in which Lucy lay. She was dressed in white muslin, her hands reaching out towards me. My heart raced. All the years of friendship with Lucy ran by me, a flash of memories grating in my head; I desperately tried to banish them, knowing the only explanation for such thoughts.

The woman didn't move. She was waiting for me to get closer. The coffees were beginning to burn my hands as I approached the fresh spirit, a soul having no option but to continue. Tears stung in the back of my eyes, I knew what I was seeing but I didn't want to believe it was true. The soul smiled, unfazed by her sudden passing. Screams tried to escape but I remained silent. It couldn't have happened whilst I was gone, that short time I had chosen to leave her bedside in order to find a coffee machine. But Lucy was there, now stood within three feet, wanting me to accept her passing.

I pushed open the door to the ward. Ross, Rebecca and Jacob sat by Lucy, still hooked up as if no change. As I reached the group I placed the coffees on the bedside table, relief for my hands. All three looked up at me as though asking if I knew anything. Lucy's spirit stood at the foot of the bed.

Within seconds, one of the machines started to bleep continuously, indicating Lucy had stopped breathing. Two nurses ran over, shooing us away, insisting that we stood by the door of the ward as they started to pull the curtain round her bed. I stood next to Lucy's spirit on the other side of the curtains as we heard the nurses try hopelessly to resuscitate the body which had already passed over.

"What's happened," screamed Rebecca, as she started to shake uncontrollably. I held her, trying hard to shield her from the sound of her mother losing the battle of life.

"I want to know what they're doing in there. She's my mum." Jacob started to walk towards the closed curtains.

"Let's just wait here," Ross said, before taking hold of his nephew, placing his arm around his shoulder. I sensed Ross was being strong for the sake of Jacob and Rebecca as I noticed him discreetly wipe away tears from his eyes.

I wanted to stay strong too, let Lucy see that I could look after her babies and perhaps offer support to her brother. I went over to Rebecca and held her. We had always been close but she needed to know that she would need someone to support her, now more than ever. And then there was Ross, a tall and broad shouldered man, probably breaking up inside. I so wished he could have seen Lucy like I did, a beautiful woman dressed in white muslin, standing with us, a sparkle in her eyes and a vibrant smile.

A doctor came to the bed also trying to give life back to Lucy. Silence suddenly encased the ward before Rebecca's cries turned into howls and Jacob joined her with sobs of his own. I went over to Ross, allowing the distraught siblings to hold each other. I held his hand and looked at him. Tears were falling gently down his cheeks; he was trying so hard to maintain composure until he turned to face me, his arms stretching around my shoulders. I held him and let him cry against me whilst I watched Lucy fade from sight. She had to go; she had to leave me to grieve without being able to see her.

The doctor appeared from behind the curtains. A solemn expression painted on his face, he walked over to Ross who now stood by himself. "I'm sorry."

"No," Ross replied, before his legs buckled beneath him. The doctor reached out to steady him.

"Come and sit down," he said, leading him by the arm to the nearest chair.

"Why didn't you save her?"

"We tried everything. Her heart was too weak and we couldn't resuscitate her. I'm so sorry."

Jacob and Rebecca held each other, sobbing. "Can we see her?" I asked.

"Just give the nurses a little time to disconnect the machine then you can go in." The doctor put his hand on Ross's shoulder before turning to walk away.

"How long has she been ill?" Ross asked.

The doctor turned round to face the question. "A few months," he said. "Didn't you know?"

Ross turned round and looked at me, raising his hands, questioning whether I was aware. "I had no idea. She didn't say anything." He glanced back at the doctor before approaching me. "Did you know?"

"Well, I thought she was ill, but I didn't know it was so serious." I suddenly thought back to the reading I had done for Ross and the visit from his grandfather. "Oh, my God!"

"What?" he asked.

"Your grandfather. He was telling me but neither of us wanted to listen." I started to cry. "I'm so sorry, Ross. I knew there was a reason why he visited us and told us what he did."

Ross put his arms around me. "Neither of us could have known, Camilla. Lucy didn't want us to know, did she?"

"But I always listen to the spirits. I knew something; I couldn't confirm it though because Lucy didn't want to talk about it. Oh, God, the poor woman. She knew all along and she's lived with this on her own."

The nurses came out from behind the closed curtains. "She's ready now," one of them said, before touching my arm. "I'm so sorry we couldn't help her."

Jacob and Rebecca went first, walking cautiously towards Lucy as she lay motionless in the bed. She looked calm. One could have been forgiven for thinking she was just sleeping. I stood at the foot of the bed, trying hard to stay focused on the beautiful woman who's empty shell remained in tranquillity. I watched Rebecca and Jacob as they held their mother, their desperate pleas echoing around the ward. They had hardly seen her in the last twelve months; university had taken their time yet Lucy always understood, giving them space whilst supporting them financially.

Ross released his grip on me and moved towards the bed. He held Rebecca whilst I moved to support Jacob. He turned towards me and moved aside on the bed, allowing me room to sit down and be part of the closeness of their family unit.

Chapter Nineteen

*T*hree days had passed since Lucy's death and she had chosen not to contact me. Perhaps she had spent her time with her children, discreetly watching over them as they continued to weep in her absence. I noticed a tiny light danced above my dressing table, shining through the darkened room, almost beckoning me to watch. I sat on the edge of my bed to find out who wished to be known. The light continued to shine; a tiny spectacle hovering as if searching for its next destination. My eyes became transfixed on it whilst my mind's eye was telling me a spirit manifestation was about to take place, yet I couldn't work out who it was. I felt confused. Emotions were flooding to the surface with no available answers. I wanted it to be Lucy. But, for some reason I felt anxious.

The temperature dropped, my breath became visible in the dim light of the room. I wanted to ask out for communication but my voice seemed to drown in the silence of a deathly echo. I heard the dull tones of a man, speaking as though unaware of me. My heart pounded heavily, I could feel myself becoming a little scared at what I thought was about to take place. I listened intently, his voice was clearer now and I was quite sure it was that of the unsettling spirit male. His face began to form, a shadow surrounding the area where his body would be. Yet all I could see was a face, red eyes, a smile which froze me. He held something in his right hand, long, silver in colour; a knife. He knew I was there. He had deliberately confused me again, making me believe he was just a passing soul. The light I had seen in the corner of my room had been a warning sign, not from my grandmother, and not from Lucy. But from a man I needed to learn more about, a man I had only just found out existed after reading for his wife, Alice Baxter.

A second spirit appeared, that of his brother, Harold. Their cries rang in my ears as Harold's last moments were being re-enacted. An explanation was forming in my head as I watched William Baxter plunge the knife into his brother's back, the smile still present on his evil lips. I could only watch in horror; a scene hopelessly portrayed like a theatre production on stage. What still confused me was why William had chosen my bedroom to relay this tragedy. And in particular, why show it to me.

The funeral was naturally melancholy. Many of Lucy's friends, including Lizzie, Hamish and Richard, gathered in her local village church, eager to pay their last respects to a wonderful woman of their community. Jacob, Rebecca and Ross walked behind the coffin as four pall-bearers lifted her above their heads and placed her gently upon a brass stand. The altar seemed an apt place for one so loved. I could feel her beside me as her perfume lingered in the air. I wanted to reach out to her children and tell them that their mother was right there, watching the grief take place at her own funeral. But it was neither the time nor the place. Too many tears flowed and Ross was the rock he needed to be. Rebecca spoke beautifully, a poem she had written, personal and appropriate to their family alone. I realised Paul was in the church with us too, it had been five years since his passing. He stood by her coffin, looking down with immense sadness. When Rebecca read her poem, his eyes scanned the church in a desperate search for Jacob who cried whilst leaning against his uncle. I felt Paul's regret in my heart, a longing to turn back the clock and revisit a time he impaired. He had ruined his own life and only had himself to blame for his own death. I struggled to muster up sympathy for him, yet now I knew he had nothing. I hoped he wouldn't pressure her in the other world. Perhaps he would ask for my help; and I would choose not to give it.

Rebecca words were said with trembling voice, tears filled her eyes as she tried to compose herself. Her eyes lifted from the paper she held and scanned the throng of emotional mourners who sat, listening intently. I knew Lucy would be proud of her; I also knew Lucy was stood beside her, being the support she had always been. She smiled at her daughter. My heart ached for another moment with my best friend. Facing a future without her seemed so incredibly daunting. Neither of us thought about dying in our forties, even though we knew one day our lives would take a new path. But Lucy had only lived half her life, she wasn't ready to become an astral, and I wasn't ready to see her as one. Thinking about the wonderful times we had shared, I realised how much I wanted to live my life to the full; cherish each day.

I preferred to think of the wake as a celebration of Lucy's life. She had led a wonderful existence and I wanted people to acknowledge her for being the incredible woman that she was. It was a quiet affair, some of the friends who had attended the service turned up at Rosehill where I arranged for caterers to supply a buffet. We drank champagne, Lucy's favourite drink, and those older family members had a glass of sherry, their traditions perhaps not stretching to the modern ways of life. Jacob and Rebecca seemed better after the service had finished; they hugged me in turn.

"Mum would have loved all this champagne," Rebecca said.

"Her favourite drink," I agreed. "I'm sure she won't miss out." She laughed. I noticed Lucy had turned up. She stood in the corner of the drawing room, scanning the dessert of faces, smiling at some as she impressed thoughts upon me of 'I haven't seen them in years'.

"Do you think she came to the service?"

"Of course she did, Jacob, she wouldn't have missed it for the world." I hugged him again before turning to Rebecca. "Your poem was beautiful, darling."

"It felt good to speak in front of everyone. I think mum would have been proud of me."

"She's always proud of you, both. I'm just going to say hello to Lizzie." I walked away, making my way towards where Lizzie, Hamish and Richard stood, chatting.

"How are you?" Richard asked, as I approached him. He kissed my cheek.

"Okay, under the circumstances. It's hard to believe isn't it?" I said.

"You're not kidding. It doesn't seem five minutes since Christmas day. She seemed fine to me," Lizzie said, Hamish nodding in response.

"She was tired, but she did put on a good front, I admit."

"Did you know she was ill?" Lizzie asked.

"Only at the end. She had us all believe that she was suffering with a bad cold. I knew it was more than that but even Ross was fooled."

"It must have been hard for you at the hospital." Hamish put his arm round me.

"It was. But it was harder for them." I turned round to look at Jacob and Rebecca who were now talking to Ross.

"I wish we'd have known. We could have said goodbye properly." Lizzie started to cry as Hamish put his arms around her, leaving me standing opposite Richard. He looked at me.

"We miss you in the city," he said. "Do you think you'll ever come back?"

I shook my head. "No, Richard. I'll never come back. I've made my home here."

"And what about friends?" he asked. "Have you made many of those since moving to the country?" He glanced over at Marcus.

"One or two," I replied. I noticed Ross making his way towards me, a half-smile etched on his lips as he saw me talking to Richard.

"Thanks for all this," he said, as he stood beside me. He turned to Richard and shook his hand. "Good to see you again."

"You, too, Ross." Richard looked back at me. "I'll just get myself another drink. See you later." I watched him walk away, Hamish still holding Lizzie as she cried softly on his shoulder. My eyes desperately searched for Marcus in a bid to commend him on a beautiful service.

"It was all for Lucy," I said, turning back to Ross. We smiled at each other. "Would you excuse me," I asked. "I need to speak to Marcus." I left Ross with Lizzie and Hamish as I wandered into the kitchen, believing Marcus to be in there. He was stood looking out of the window.

"That was beautiful," I said, approaching him, intending to put my arms around him and reach for a kiss.

He turned round to face me. "I expect he'll stay now." Marcus wasn't asking.

"Who?"

"Ross."

"I shouldn't think so. He has a life in California. He was only here for a few months." I recalled seeing Marcus talking to Ross earlier. "Did he tell you that?"

"He told me a lot of things. He wants to stay and look after you. Said he thinks you're going to need him around for a while." I stared at Marcus, unsure as to what I should say. "He also said you two go back a long way."

"We do. I've known him for years. He probably just wants to make sure I'll be okay before he makes plans to go home."

"I got the impression this is his home now." I could tell he was jealous but it was so unnecessary. I slipped my arms around his waist, gripping him in my frustration. How could he think such a thing? "I'd better go, I have a sermon to write for Sunday." He pulled away from me, briskly walking towards the door without looking back.

"Marcus, don't be ridiculous. You're blowing this out of proportion."

"If there's something going on between you and Ross, I'd prefer to know." He stopped at the door, once more turning to face me.

"There's nothing going on. What's wrong with you? I've just buried my best friend. Don't be so cantankerous."

"I get the impression Ross thinks you have some kind of relationship going on."

"Is that what he said?"

"Not exactly, but I'm not stupid, Camilla. I've seen the way he looks at you, the way he talks to you. He never left your side at the church." I became angry at his accusations, turning my back on him as he continued through the door.

"He was being a friend. He knows how close I was to Lucy. He's hurting just as much as me, you know."

"I'll ring you," he said, whilst turning the handle. "Take care."

""Bye, Marcus," I closed the door after him. Jealously was something I loathed.

I spent all evening thinking about Ross wondering why Marcus had been so sharp with me and why he suddenly thought Ross would want to stay in the Scottish Borders. It had been his home, many years ago, but he had nothing to keep him here. Jacob and Rebecca were capable of looking after themselves and had family to help out, not to mention me.

I sat in silence, my mind was awash with confusion. I had known Ross for many years and wondered if a flame still burned in my heart for him, and if Marcus had recognised a moment of nostalgia in my eyes. Ross looked incredible that afternoon.

In our youth, Ross had always stuck up for me. He had been like my big brother, forever around when I needed someone to rid me of unwanted attention. There had been many times when I thought about a future with him, during the nights we shared together.

It was 11.30. The night was drawing to a close as I continued to contemplate my life. I could feel no spirit presence, just a hole in the fabric of life. I was once more alone with my thoughts and I wasn't sure it was a place I wanted to be. I had been here so many times before, desperately trying to ignore the sadness that I always felt. A part of me hated it. Another part of me knew no different. I had spent twenty years living alone wondering about my mother, about her discovery into another world. She so seldom visited me. To be here, in this place with only me to think about was proving difficult since I had met Marcus. Spending time with him had given my life a new perspective.

I knew she loved me; she had been the main love of my life. It wasn't as if I needed her now, but I did need to remember her. Photographs were all I had and memories were beginning to fade.

I decided to sit in the reading room, not because I wanted spirit to join me, but because it was such a tranquil place, a place where dawn didn't break and night didn't end; a place of hope when I was feeling low, a place of explanation when my mind raced with thoughts. I opened the door listening to the hinges creak with age. The dim light from the hallway guided me into the room and I closed the door, before standing by the small table and chairs. The velvet curtains were closed; I made a point of closing them earlier in the evening. I went over to the arm chair and rested myself upon its leather cushion, sighing as comfort overwhelmed me; I loved being in that room.

The sorrow I felt earlier in the day at Lucy's funeral remained as a light entered my heart, trying to drown the images of sadness to a forgotten dimension. It had been such an emotionally draining day, highly charged sensations surging through my body as I remembered my past with Lucy. Why had I never accepted a marriage proposal, loved the way I wished to, had a child even? Did I regret my life so far? Did I feel so sad towards myself that I wanted to go back and change what I had already experienced? But it was too late. Surely, I couldn't revisit my past without feeling regret. When I found Rosehill I thought I had found my life. I thought I was complete. The jigsaw I had been trying to accomplish was within my reach and I thought I was able to tidy it up, put it away and start living the life I had always wanted to live.

The only problem was someone had taken away my hopes and dreams. I stared into the darkness, shadows vying for my attention, searching for a place to rest. I could feel my body seizing, my limbs rigid, and my mind knowing that another soul now stood within my space. The room remained in darkness, a glimmer of light trying aimlessly to filter in. The spirit which now hovered before me was male. My first suspicion of it being Lucy was dashed when I realised the aroma of aftershave invading my senses. The smell was familiar, not one I had experienced often but one I had only recently discovered. I couldn't see his face but I felt love; an overpowering sense of adoration pouring from the mysterious soul.

I called out, requesting that spirit moved an object or knocked on the table, perhaps even touched me. Somehow, I knew I was safe. I knew this was a visiting soul, yet one that seemed familiar with the surroundings of Rosehill. It was a comforting feeling, as though we were meant to be there. There was a bond between us; not just a feeling of being together but something stronger. Spirit moved passed me, making its way to the fireplace.

The manifested soul turned its back on me but within seconds turned to face me again and for a brief moment I saw a face; that I thought was Harold Baxter. Taken aback, I stood away from my chair, asking spirit to communicate with me, tell me why it surrounded me with love. But no sooner had the words left my mouth, spirit began to fade into the fireplace.

Chapter Twenty

*L*ucy was still fresh in my mind and I wondered if she would visit me soon, tell me what it was like in her new home. She had promised me years ago that if she were to die first, she would come back and give me a full account of what death was like. I was looking forward to hearing from her.

The next day, Marcus called round. Hearing his car draw up, I stood at the door, waiting for him to approach me. I smiled briefly.

"I didn't expect to see you so soon."

"I've been worried about you. I'm sorry if I upset you yesterday, it wasn't my intention." He stroked my cheek.

"Have you had any breakfast?" I asked, still a little angry at his jealousy but hoping to put it behind us.

"I had something at Julia's. That's where I've been," he announced. "She's been fired."

Julia Henderson, the journalist who threatened to expose me as a liar. If she had written an article, it had never been published for I scoured the papers for weeks after and didn't find any reference to our meeting. I think the events must have frightened her enough to stop her making a fool of herself. I hadn't seen her in the village. I heard she worked away during the week at a newspaper office in Edinburgh but even at weekends she never seemed to be around. So, perhaps she had overstepped the mark and lost out to one in authority. I felt a sly smile resting on my lips. Looking at Marcus I couldn't work out whether it was work or pleasure that had encouraged him to visit her.

"How did you hear about her losing her job?"

"She rang me, late last night. We've been friends for a while."

"So you're her knight in shining armour," I joked, trying to make light of what seemed a tense situation.

"I wouldn't go that far," he replied, shaking his head and managing a slight smile. "She just needed someone. Journalism is all she knows and I don't think she has many friends in the village." I could have predicted that after my meeting with her at Rosehill.

"Shall we go for a walk? It's a beautiful morning." The sun was bursting through an array of scattered clouds, even though coldness warranted coats. I gathered the dogs as they sniffed their way along grassy tracks and abandoned puddles. Marcus seemed serious. I felt there was some urgency in his pace as he walked beside me towards the drive gate and into the fields.

"Is there something you want to tell me?" My voice raised at least two octaves at the end of the question, hoping his mood might lift and we could perhaps find a little romance along the gravel path.

"Yes, I have something I want to talk to you about."

"Go on." My nerves were a little on edge as I invited him to continue.

"Ross!" I looked at him, my pace slowing a little in surprise at his sudden exclamation.

"What about Ross?"

"Is he in love with you?"

That stopped me in my tracks. "I doubt it," I said, sniggering in the hope that Marcus would realise how mad he sounded. "What makes you ask that?"

"I can't get it out of my head. It was as if nothing could come between the two of you." He paused. "Not even me."

"Don't you trust me?"

"Of course I do," he replied. He smiled, weakly. "I'm not sure I trust him though. If he stays here because of you then the poor guy's deluded."

"But we don't know if he's staying yet do we? It's just something you seem to have cooked up and he probably has every intention of going back to his life in California. I think he has a girl friend over there, not to mention a job and an apartment."

Our walk took us to the far hill of the first field. It was one of my favourite places to stop and gather my thoughts. The dog's obediently stopped and sat down to wait for us, a habit of being told to stay having been instilled within them. It was only January and the wind continued in her determination to beat the clouds away. My hands were cold even though I wore gloves. I would have asked Marcus to hold me, warm my body with his own, but his words were ringing through me, making me determined to protect myself from his strange behaviour.

We stopped on the hill. An ancient tree stump served as a small seat, just big enough for two adults to sit upon. I sat down but Marcus continued to stand. He hovered around me, waiting for me to speak, probably wondering if I was prepared to ask Ross when he planned to return to America. But still, a part of me held back; how nice it would be should Ross decide to stay in the area. And how complicated it could become.

"I can't believe you haven't seen it," Marcus continued. "You've known him a long time. Haven't you seen that twinkle in his eye when he looks at you?" He forced a smile.

"No, I haven't seen it." I lied. "I don't know how you could say such a thing when you don't know him. We're just friends, Marcus. That's all."

The conversation was going nowhere. He shook his head, the smile still straining to change his mind. I stood up, called the dogs to me and began the walk back. At that point I wasn't sure I wanted him to walk beside me. It was times like these that I needed spirit guidance and on this occasion it wasn't there. I was alone again, my thoughts eating into the love I so wanted to feel for this man. I had spent the last few weeks believing that Marcus and I could be together, fight against the odds of a spiritual clash in our relationship. And now the wall was beginning to crumble. Such a big part of me wanted Ross to stay nearby but I couldn't understand why. And what really concerned me was the feeling of guilt I had. My friendship with Ross could have gone further if I had allowed, but I stopped it happening.

"So what will Julia do now?" I decided to change the subject.

"She said she'll try freelance."

"Did you know she came to see me once?" He looked at me, raising his eyebrows in surprise. "She said she was going to write an article about me but I never read it."

"I didn't know she knew you. What was the article about?"

"My mediumship," I replied. "She said I was a fake."

"She's very straight with people. I've had a few disagreements with her. I shouldn't imagine she meant to upset you though."

"You weren't there. She was pretty rude to say the least." I whistled for Ben, my collie, before he zoomed off into the distance after a terrified rabbit. "She asked me to do a reading for her."

"Oh, I see," he said. "I'm quite surprised."

"I assume she never wrote the article, unless I missed it."

"She didn't say anything. You shouldn't worry, she's a nice enough person." I wondered if Marcus and I were actually talking about the same Julia.

The walk back to the house was a little more pleasant when he put his arm around my shoulder, pulling me into him after noticing how cold I was. No more mention of Julia was what I preferred; another complication to our relationship was something we didn't need.

As we reached the back door, I turned to him. "Would you like a hot drink, I'm having one?"

"I'd love a cup of tea."

"So, where do we go from here?" I stirred the tea and waited for an answer.

"I've upset you again, haven't I?"

"I don't like to think you're jealous." I placed his tea before him on the table. "What we have is special. Let's not spoil it." He looked up at me, his eyes struggling to make contact with mine.

"I know it's special. I'm glad I found you. But you have to tell me if something happens between you and Ross."

"Marcus," I leant towards him, my lips almost meeting with his. "There's nothing going on between Ross and me. I'm with you." I kissed him, glad that he responded.

"If you need to talk about Lucy, you know where I am. I know it must be hard for you."

"I miss her. I'll always miss her. My life won't be the same now but I know she'll be here, somewhere." I moved in for another kiss before sitting down on the seat next to him. "Forget about Ross, let's concentrate on us."

I wrapped my arms around his neck, sealing my lips passionately against his. "Have you got time?" I asked, planting lazy kisses around his cleanly shaven face.

"I haven't got long."

I wanted to show him how much he meant to me and how wrong he was about my feelings for Ross. Perhaps I wanted to show myself, too, as I let Marcus lead me into the drawing room, gently persuading me onto the sofa before confirming a burning desire within both our hearts.

The house was quiet after he'd gone, restful as I went from room to room, hoping to feel spirit presence beside me. It seemed I was alone. I wanted Marcus in my life yet I couldn't stop thinking that I didn't want Ross to leave. In all my adult years, I had never felt such confusion. But I kept wondering if Marcus really wanted me the way I yearned to be wanted. He would never understand that spirit found me and that I didn't go in search. He couldn't understand that my communication with the other world was a precious gift, bestowed on me by the spirits themselves. I couldn't refuse it; I couldn't take it back; my life was filled with spirit presence. However, this day they didn't seem to wish to correspond.

Chapter Twenty-One

*A*s the day drew to a close the television beckoned, anything to take my mind off Marcus and stop the confusion that was mounting about Ross. I got to the lounge and was just about to sink into my recliner when I heard a car draw up in the drive way, gravel crunching beneath tyres. I looked out of the window to find Ross, parking up his shiny new Jaguar, on loan whilst in the Borders. He got out, his debonair smile boring into my heart like a forbidden lust. I went to the front door and opened it.

"I haven't caught you at a bad time, have I?"

"It's never a bad time," I replied honestly. "Come in; I was just about to sit in the lounge and switch the television on. I'll make us a coffee. You okay?" I led him into the kitchen.

"Yes, I'm fine, I just wanted to see you. Make sure you were all right after everything that's happened."

"I'm tired, but I'm fine." I smiled at his thoughtful mind. "I thought the funeral went well, as far as funerals go. How are Jacob and Rebecca?"

"They're going back to Edinburgh in the next few days. I think Jacob's eager to get back to normal, get the impression Rebecca needs a bit more time but she knows I'm here for her."

"I hope she knows I'm here, too. It won't be easy." I remembered the passing of my own mother, the feelings flooding back in the same way they were bound to do for Rebecca.

"I've made a decision, Camilla. I wanted to tell you first." He looked at me as he sat down at the kitchen table. From the expression on his face it was serious and whatever I said wasn't going to change his mind.

"I've decided to stay." His words hit me like a bolt of lightning.

"But I thought you liked California. You've made a life there, haven't you?"

"Yes I did, but since Lucy died I've realised I need to be here."

"Where will you live?" My stomach was in knots. I felt a childish sense of excitement galloping through my body.

"I'll live in Lucy's house for now. I'm sure the kids won't mind." He seemed to have it all worked out. "You're okay with that, aren't you?"

"Of course I am," I said, wondering why he thought it necessary to ask.

"I'll have to go back to LA at some point, to collect my stuff. Haven't decided yet whether to market the apartment or rent it out. What do you think?"

Why was he asking my opinion? And why was I feeling like an over enthusiastic teenager whilst sat at the table with him, a man I had known for thirty five years. I was seeing a softer side to him; it was as though he'd mellowed almost overnight, helping me recollect the way my heart used to beat for him. The guilt rushed to the surface and I imagined Marcus when I told him the news, information that he had almost assumed to me earlier.

"I don't know, Ross. What's the market like over there? If it's anything like ours, perhaps you'd be better renting it out for now."

"I'm not sure to be honest. I'll have to go back and sort through my things, have a chat with an estate agent perhaps."

"Why don't you go through to the lounge and I'll bring the drinks in."

I followed him and sat down on one of the sofas. He stood by the window and surprised me as he sat down beside me, smiling as he looked into my eyes.

"How's Marcus?" Ross couldn't have been interested.

"He's fine, he was this morning at any rate." I drank my coffee. This changed side to Ross was interesting me; it was quite nostalgic in fact.

"He seemed a bit fraught yesterday." I didn't want to agree so I looked in my cup, preferring to avert his eyes. "I can't weigh him up, sometimes I think he's a great guy and then I wonder what you see in him. Guess it's just me. He's obviously a hit with the ladies."

"A hit with the ladies? What's that supposed to mean?"

"Just meant he seems to have a lot of lady friends. He's a vicar. I suppose it's only to be expected."

"And to which lady friends are you referring?" Ross looked at me as I noticed a sly smile developing on his lips. He knew something and was determined to make sure I did too.

"Oh, you know, that woman from the village, the journalist. Think I must be in the wrong job."

I could feel my defences rising. "Who have you been talking to?" I asked.

"I was talking to the guy who lives next door to the pub." I thought for a moment. "He came to the funeral?"

I suddenly remembered him. "Of course, sorry, it's been a long day. So, you and him were discussing Marcus, were you?"

"I said how nice the service was and how well Marcus did. The guy just put me right on a few things."

"A few things? Like what exactly?"

"Well, I wouldn't trust him." Ross re-positioned himself. He crossed one leg over the other throwing his arm along the back quite close to my shoulder. He was making me nervous. I shuffled along a fraction, wondering what he intended to do. "Do you love him?" he asked.

"Yes," I was quick to answer, and he was quick to snigger. He didn't believe me and I didn't blame him.

"We've known each other long enough, Camilla. You must know how I feel about you?" I wasn't sure what he expected me to say so I didn't speak. "I mean who does this guy think he is anyway? He spends the night with that journalist then expects you to come running when he clicks his fingers."

"What do you mean, spends the night?"

"Last night, he was there, didn't you know?"

"Well yes, I knew he'd been to see her. She lost her job and he went to console her."

"Console her, you can say that again."

"How do you know he was at Julia's over night?"

"I saw him."

I stared at Ross, utterly baffled. He continued. "I came to see you this morning and when I drove through the village he was just leaving her house. She was stood at the front door in what looked like a dressing gown, seemed to be waving him off."

"Why didn't you come here?"

"I called at the village shop and by the time I got back to the car I noticed him driving past me, then he turned into your driveway. I thought you might want some privacy so I went home."

"That doesn't mean to say he spent the night though. She lost her job yesterday and he said he'd been to see her. They've known each other a while." I was desperately trying to make excuses for Marcus having been at Julia's but I was running out of options. I wondered if he intended to tell me about it and how he had the audacity to accuse Ross of being in love with me.

"Are you jealous of Marcus and me?" I asked.

"I'm not jealous. Well, maybe a little," he laughed, "but I think you deserve the truth. I won't let him treat you like shit. I'm not prepared to stand by and let him do that to you." The Ross I knew so well seemed to have returned, his protective arm reaching out.

"Marcus is good to me. He isn't having an affair." But I wanted to phone him, have it out with him. Hope it was he who answered the phone.

But it wasn't just Marcus who I didn't trust. It was me. My feelings for Ross had increased so much recently. As he stood up to leave I saw it; my future, grabbing me in spectacular fashion and reminding me that I had wanted Ross for many years. I looked up at him, staring into his soft brown eyes. He knew. He had always known. We moved towards each other, our eyes in a continuous lock, our bodies almost touching. He cupped my face in his hands, lifting my head towards his lips.

"We can't," I whispered, quickly backing away from him. "I'm with Marcus."

"I'm sorry. I shouldn't have done that." He turned round and started to walk towards the door.

"We're both to blame. Let's not spoil a friendship."

"I'll see you soon," he said, before reaching the front door, and gently closing it behind him.

I stood in the hall for a few minutes, asking myself what had just happened, too big a part of me wishing he had stayed.

Chapter Twenty-Two

I had a reading booked at 11am the next day, meditation and tranquillity were needed. I couldn't stop thinking about Marcus and him being with Julia. I was hoping for spirit guidance during the reading for it was deemed to be an intense time. The reading room was its usual peaceful environment; waiting, enriched with hope to discover life from beyond. I sat at the table; cup of tea to my right, a lit candle in the centre.

During my youth I had spent years thinking about Ross, wondering why he chose to turn his back on me. And in my twenties, when he came back to stay for a brief visit with his family, I silently begged him to see me, to hold me in his arms and tell me he would stay, just for me. But he didn't.

He did hold me in his arms as we danced together at Lucy's wedding. His face was so near to mine, close enough I wanted to whisper in his ear that I loved him. That I would always love him no matter what. I wanted to thank him the following morning for staying with me on Lucy's wedding night, for making my dream come true. And then I wanted to hate him for packing his bags and leaving, hurrying back to California without an explanation.

I was twenty-five. My best friend had found love with Paul, excitedly driving off into the sunset to start her new life, and I stayed. I was quite happy in my apartment in Edinburgh but there was always something missing, always some great gaping hole in my heart that I could never fill. I was a popular medium in those days but when I gave news to my clients of their impending loves and romantic paths it left me feeling lonely. I would hibernate for days afterwards, yearning to pick up the phone and dial Lucy, asking her for Ross's phone number. But I couldn't bring myself to do it. I always felt I would have been troubling him. I wanted him to love me, not pity me.

As I sat in the chair that morning, waiting for my eleven o'clock, I heard a woman's cry. My mind was being taken back to a time when my heart screamed out for something that was always missing. The woman cried louder as each time I concentrated harder. I then knew that my own mother was with me.

"Mum?"

"I'm here," she confirmed, her voice gentle and as clear as if she had been on our earth plane.

"Why are you crying, mum?"

"I'm worried about you."

I immediately thought about Ross. "You don't have to worry about me."

"It's up to you, Camilla, but you'll have to make a choice. Don't let Ross break your heart again."

"I'm not going to." I was overwhelmed by emotion at realising her presence.

"You deserve better. Make a choice and stick with it." I could feel her hand brushing against my face as the warm glow of her aura shone, my heart longing for her to stay. "I'll protect you, my darling. But you have to protect yourself too."

I started to cry as she stood by my side, hushing me like a baby. The sensation tingled through my whole body as her protective hands stroked my skin.

"Stay with me," I requested. "Help me make the decision."

"I can't. You have to do that yourself. And you will." The room suddenly became cold. My mother withdrew her hand from my face, moving away towards the book shelf. "You'll work it out," she said, before fading from my view. I barely had time to compose myself as my client rang the door bell, making the dogs bark. My mother had gone, leaving me devastated once more as I felt I had lost her.

I ate a light lunch then lay down, eager to recharge my batteries. I took myself back to a time when I thought I was happy. A time when being on my own didn't matter so much. My mind was open as my body lay sleeping, allowing dreams to take over and remind me of the childhood days I shared with my mother.

Somehow, I knew the phone would be silent that night. My wishful thinking had been more towards hoping Marcus would phone but my senses indicated a quietness surrounding me as I sat in front of the television. I was a little fidgety, nothing of interest was shown and I resorted to reading. I glanced at the phone so many times, urging myself to call him then stopping before temptation took over. I wasn't sure I wanted to know the truth; I thought I was happy with him. The day had been a tiring one, energy found from within yet seemingly taken from me in a moment's notice. My bed beckoned as I wondered what Marcus was doing, and if he was alone.

It was still quite early as I lay awake, unable to get comfortable. I switched on the lamp and looked at the clock which read 9.45. It was no use, I had to speak to Marcus. I got dressed and quickly brushed my hair, grabbing a coat and running downstairs to get the car keys. The dogs looked up in surprise, three faces questioning my haste. During the drive to his house, I hoped I would find him in, praying he would be on his own. I wanted so much for Ross to have been wrong.

He was in, the lights were still on in the lounge. I knocked on the door and waited, my heart racing at the prospect of having to face an answer I didn't want to hear.

"Camilla, what's up?" Marcus opened the door and reached in for a kiss but I gently brushed against him, trying to stay focused on the reason for my visit. "Come on through." We walked into the lounge and he turned off the television.

"I need to talk to you," I said, sitting down on the armchair.

"Sure, what's on your mind?"

"You are, Marcus." I stared at him as his lips curved. "Ross saw you yesterday." His eyes suddenly stopped twinkling.

"Saw me where?"

"Leaving Julia's. He said she was stood on her doorstep in her dressing gown."

"And?"

"He also said you were there all night, consoling her."

"Is he spying on me, or something?" He shifted on the sofa. "So what are you saying?"

"I just want to know. Did you spend the night with Julia?"

He sighed heavily and lifted his arms up in defence. "I stayed at her place, yes. But we didn't do anything. She's a good friend of mine, she needed company." He stood up and walked towards me. "Come on, Camilla, you don't honestly think there's something going on between me and Julia, do you?"

I rose from the chair, unable to look into his eyes. "I'd like to think not. But why stay with her all night? I find that a little strange if I'm honest."

"I stayed with her because she needed a friend and she doesn't have anyone else."

"Have you stayed with her before?"

"Once or twice, yes, but in separate bedrooms." He reached out to touch my arm. "Don't do this. Ross got the wrong end of the stick, and he had no right jumping to conclusions, putting these ideas into your head." But something was stopping me from believing Marcus. I wanted to, I really did, but I couldn't help thinking how little I knew about him. I thought we were lovers. I wiped away the tears that were forming, making the hurt obvious as I couldn't stop thinking about him being with someone else. I'd only ever loved one other man in my life, Ross, who now seemed to be coming between Marcus and me. The tears wouldn't stop, they were preventing me from making sense of the situation I faced. Marcus continued to stand before me, a worried expression on his face as though begging me to believe him. But something didn't feel right.

"Camilla!"

I stopped, the anger causing my voice to rise. "You're not being honest with me. Something's going on between you two. You had a nerve coming to Rosehill yesterday, accusing Ross of being in love with me, when all along you're going behind my back?"

"I'm not going behind your back. I'm a vicar, I'm here for all my parishioners. Julia just happens to be one of them who needed me."

I opened the front door. "I'll see you," I said, as I made my way to my car. I didn't look back. Eager to get back to Rosehill, I sped along the country road, narrowly missing a deer as it bounded from behind the hedge. I was trembling, hoping I didn't meet any cars on my way home, relieved to be back inside my familiar surroundings as I turned into the driveway.

It was too late to phone Ross even though I yearned to. I waited until the next morning before dialling his number.

"I've been to see Marcus," I said, upon hearing his voice. "I asked him about being with Julia."

"Oh, Cam, I'm sorry, was I right, did he spend the night?"

"Yes," I said, getting upset again.

"Did he tell you?"

"He told me he'd stayed there but said it was because she needed a friend. He didn't admit to them sleeping together."

"Shall I come over?"

I needed a friend too. I also needed a change of scenery. "I'll come to you, if that's okay. Are you busy?"

"I'm just sorting out a few of Lucy's things, it'd be great if you could come and help."

I arrived at Ross's to find him in the drive next to a pile of boxes. He came over and opened the car door for me.

"Lucy's things," he said, nodding towards the boxes. "It's stuff the kids don't want so I thought I'd give it to the charity shop. You can have a look through if you like. There's more in the house." He hugged me; it was an unexpected but welcome gesture. "Let's go in," he said, taking my hand and leading me into the house. "We can do it later."

The hall still smelt of Lucy's perfume. Everything looked the same, but the atmosphere was different somehow, the life had been sucked away from magnolia walls as pictures hung in silence. We went into the front room, Ross beckoning me to sit down as he pointed to the sofa. He sat next to me.

"I don't know how he could do that to you. He doesn't deserve you caring about him." He put his hand on my leg, his voice sympathetic.

"I don't know whether I believe him. He says they're just friends. But it seems strange that he spent the night when they live in the same village."

"Maybe you should ask her?"

"I don't want to see her," I replied. "She's not a nice person, or at least she didn't seem to be when I read for her."

"She came to you for a reading?" he asked, seeming a little confused.

"Yes. She said she was going to write an article about me being a fake then something happened when a spirit communicated." I stopped and remembered something else she had said. "Oh, God, Ross!" I raised my hand to my mouth.

"What?"

I told him how she advised me to stay away from Marcus before she left. He turned away, shaking his head. "I wonder why," he said.

"You don't think they've been seeing each other all this time and I never knew?"

He turned back to face me. "Who knows? You haven't been together long, have you?"

"Not really, but long enough that I thought we had something special between us. I can't believe he's done this." Now it was my turn to shake my head. I desperately wanted Ross to offer an explanation but I knew in my heart that I wouldn't have listened. It was all stacking up too neatly.

Ross's eyes were sparkling into mine as he seemed to move closer towards me. I wanted him to comfort me, reassure me that everything would be okay and that Marcus and Julia's relationship was platonic. But he didn't. He continued to bewitch me, confusing me further as I was reminded of the depth of my feelings. His hand still rested on my leg and I looked down at it, wondering why I didn't mind it being there. As I glanced back into his eyes I felt his lips caress mine, softly, making me tremble once more. I responded, the firmness of our kiss increased and we finally embraced, holding each other like long lost lovers. My eyes closed tightly as his hand moved towards my thigh, causing my legs to part. I almost encouraged him to continue. His other hand stroked my shoulder, moving down before resting on my breast with anticipation.

I was aroused. But I suddenly remembered where I was. I pulled away from him, standing up and making my way to the door.

"I don't need another complication in my life, Ross," I said. "I'm sorry."

He stood up, too and joined me at the door. "You don't need to say you're sorry, Cam. I just want to be here for you."

"I know." I touched his face, gently stroking his cheek. "And I'm glad you are. But we're just friends, that's all we can ever be. I need to sort this out with Marcus."

He smiled as we walked to the front door. "What are we like?" he laughed. "I can't stop thinking about you. It's like I've gone back twenty-odd years."

I laughed with him, glad to make light of the situation. "It's called a mid-life crisis. I'll call you soon." But I knew it wasn't a mid-life crisis. It was far more than that only I didn't want to admit it to myself. Marcus had hurt me. But I knew two wrongs didn't make a right and having a relationship with Ross would have been something I might have regretted.

⁘

That night I was visited by a male spirit. He wanted to sit beside me, causing my arms to shake and my body to feel cold. He knew me by name; Milly, the nick name my mother had given me when I was a child.

The spirit began to manifest, the vague shape of a man presenting himself in my lounge. I wasn't shocked at his presence, nor was I afraid. It seemed my heart wanted him to be there, that there was a purpose for his visit, a purpose only I should know. Yet I didn't know. I couldn't understand why I felt so calm, so full of adoration for the entity that had prevented me from a scheduled past time, it never occurred to me that he had appeared out of love. The manifested shape disappeared as quickly as it had come, leaving a sense of tranquillity in the room, a feeling of contentment. The next spirit to visit me that night was my grandmother. It was to be a busy one as she presented in full manifestation, her expression slightly worried. I asked her to bring the male back, to let me see his face once more. But she refused. Said I wasn't ready. It seemed she was reluctant however, to tell me who the male was. It was another mystery, perhaps connected to Rosehill.

Chapter Twenty-Three

*T*he next day I picked up the phone and dialled the vicarage. After a few rings Marcus answered, much to my relief.

"Are you doing anything?" I asked.

"Nothing important." I sensed a little hostility in his tone.

"Can I come over?"

"Sure."

I dashed upstairs to apply some fresh make-up and comb my hair. I thought about what I would say to him, how I should approach the subject of him and Julia. It wasn't long before I arrived in the village, and I noticed him knelt down in his front garden. I stopped the car, seeing him walk towards me as I glanced over at him. He took off his gloves before opening the car door.

"I didn't know whether you'd come to see me again," he said, a hint of pity in his voice.

His hair was ruffled and I noticed a rip in his jeans. I was tempted to wipe a small area of soil from his cheek but I refrained and got out of the car.

"We need to talk, Marcus."

"Let's go inside," he said, smiling at me as he gestured for me to walk ahead.

He closed the front door and I turned to him. "Tell me the truth; did you sleep with Julia?"

He shook his head and replied, "No, I didn't and I never have done. I don't know what else to say to you."

"Why did she warn me to stay away from you?"

"When did she do that?"

"Before she left, after the reading I gave her."

He shrugged. "I haven't a clue. Perhaps she was just protecting me. I really don't know. What I do know is that I don't fancy her, never have and never will." I followed him into the kitchen. He pulled a chair out from under the table before parking himself on it and crossing his legs.

I loved him and I so wanted to believe him. Perhaps Ross had jumped to conclusions; seeing Marcus at Julia's had put ideas into his head, probably making him think there was some kind of future for him and me. But it was Marcus I wanted to be with. I sat down opposite him.

"I don't understand why she would say something like that. You have to admit, it's looking pretty suspicious."

"There's nothing suspicious about it. Ross saw me, thought he would tell you and the whole thing's been blown out of proportion." He stood up and went to the kettle. "Drink?"

"No thanks."

"Look, Camilla. We've been seeing each other a while now. I'm not going to spoil it by sleeping with someone else. It's you I want to be with."

"But there's so much I don't know about you. I want to be more involved in your life."

"And there's quite a lot I don't know about you, too." He turned to face me. "You've only had these doubts about us since Ross came back, haven't you?" I thought about that for a moment.

"Well, yes. But I guess if Ross hadn't seen you at Julia's I'd never have known you'd stayed all night. You obviously weren't going to tell me."

"Because it's not important. I was there to support her, just like I'd support you if you needed me to." He came towards me, leant against the table and folded his arms. "How many times do I need to say it; it's you I want, no one else. I'd like to think we have a future together. Maybe turn these last few months into something that'll be, oh, I don't know, incredible, something neither of us have ever experienced before." He cupped my face in his hands. "I love you, Camilla." The sparkle in his eyes returned as I looked into them.

"I want that, too," I said.

"Have you spoken to Ross?" he asked, pulling away.

"Yes, I saw him yesterday."

He lifted his eyebrows. "How come?"

"I needed a friend." I smiled, hoping Marcus would see my point. Fortunately, he did.

"And you still don't believe he's come back for you?"

"No, of course he's not." I didn't want to lie to him. "But he is staying. He'll live at Lucy's for a while."

"You're okay with that?" He asked the question with a surprised voice.

"It's not up to me. I'm sure Lucy would have wanted him to stay. He still has friends over here, and there's Lucy's children too."

"And you..."

"Yes, and me, I'm a friend, just like Julia's your friend."

"Maybe we need to start trusting each other more." He kissed me.

"I guess I've learnt these last few days that having friends of the opposite sex is perfectly normal." We both laughed.

"Talking about sex," he began, before pulling me onto his knees, caressing my neck with his tongue. "Can you stay a while?" he whispered into my ear. "I could do with a back massage after all the bending down I've done in the garden." I couldn't resist him. We seemed to understand each other again, our differences having been put aside. Right then, nothing could have mattered more to me than having Marcus in my life.

Chapter Twenty-Four

A few days later I heard noises in the cellars and decided to investigate. As I reached the bottom of the stairs, I looked around in the dim light, one lamp illuminating a forgotten place. Plaster peeled from ancient walls, once applied with a loving hand, perhaps admired by proud eyes. A small heap lay upon concrete floor; damp, forgotten. Visible patches of stone greeted me as I touched its crumbling walls, my fingers excavating years of standing decay. Tiny paws scurried beside my feet, a desperate wish for freedom and a life still to live. Cobwebs wrapped around my hair, tearing strands whilst I trailed a long ago creature from sleep. Steps almost gave way beneath me; clear danger looming should I have lost control. My hand needed to grasp for safety, a rail of aged wood and early craftsmanship. Descent to darkened rooms in trepidation, the unknown as was always my existence. I had learnt not to fear, to look forward with challenging mind, embrace with anticipation. With a flickering candle I made my journey, a short wait before the unknown would be familiar territory. From days gone by I could feel my thoughts drowning in residual energy, a possession becoming too close for comfort, spirits vying for my attention. I wanted only one yet I wasn't sure which one. My frustration played on my ever potent mind but I was drawn, beckoned by a force that I couldn't resist. My destination would soon become clear, light would shine upon perishing rooms and my eyes would see the love which continued to overwhelm me. There were just a few more steps to take, more deterioration from an occupied space. I wanted to know who sought me from the depths of Rosehill; which soul still lived to protect me in my home, and why.

I arrived in the first room, a large pantry, shelved and mouldy. The open door clung to a hinge, determined not to fall to plaster-ridden floor; two square sheets of glass at the top, thick with dust, dark brown wood flaking, woodworm having lived within for too many years.

Old and murky bottles stood on a top shelf, cobwebs encased around them. Putrid tins with lid intact, broken glass, rusty pans, all shared space upon shelves, memories recorded by servants' hands. The candle continued to flicker so I cupped my hand around its flame, the darkness would have been too thick for me to wander these desperate rooms. More scurrying, orbs, perhaps dust, whispers from another world. I made my way into the next room, a large space filled with a debris littered floor. The room was staggeringly cold, my cardigan unable to warm me. A small light shone in one corner, alerting me to a possible presence and my potential find. I transfixed to the light as it grew, a steadfast glow increasing in intensity whilst performing before my eyes. A shape began to appear, a body first, legs following. The light became the figure of a man, to which I felt I had been invited to witness. My breath was evident; my hands were frozen to the bone. I didn't feel afraid though I was cautious, the atmosphere adding to my apprehension.

The light now shone against the head of the figure that stood before me, seemingly unwilling to show a face. It was the same outline as the spirit man I had seen often around the house, still shy of allowing me sight of his identity. "Who are you?"

I shuffled amongst the debris, my shoes causing a crunching row to break the silence. Spirit whispered, so difficult to hear, my ears couldn't pick up what the entity tried to convey.

"What do you want from me?" I tried another tactic, perhaps spirit didn't want me to know who he was.

Another whisper, yet this time clearer, this time legible. The name, Hal, came to me. I knew of no one with this name yet I continued to feel familiarity when faced with this soul, as though I should have known this man, perhaps in a previous life.

"Grandma, if you're here, please help me understand who this spirit is."

"You're not ready," my grandmother spoke. Ready for what, I wondered. Nothing made sense. Spirit seemed to have encouraged me to approach him, communicate in the way only he could, yet I was being reminded once again that he wasn't ready. I watched as spirit began to fade, the light dimmed as the shape of a male was no longer visible. The flame on my candle almost diminished as I moved closer to the area in which spirit had presented. I cupped my hands around the weak, orange glow, feeling the warmth against my ice cold skin. I felt urged to reach out and touch an empty space; a lost soul trying in vain to make contact with someone who no longer resided on our earth plane.

It was time for me to leave that place. I had to leave the decaying rooms as they were, undisturbed and unloved. But I would return; I would wait for a signal from the spirit who needed me. And in the meantime, I would seek answers from my grandmother. She owed me an explanation at least.

❦

I allowed myself some peace and quiet over the next few days. Marcus had to go on a course for a few days which took him to Newcastle, but he rang my mobile several times, telling me how much he missed me and how he wished I'd have gone with him. It was during that time of thought and restfulness that I was once more visited by the strange spirit of a man. The spirit seemed only to appear when I felt sad. I had noticed a pattern during the last few months, whereas if ever I was anxious or feeling a little down about something, the faceless spirit would manifest before me, unwilling to show an identity. This made it difficult to work out who it was. To see a spirit face was obviously the best clue to recognition and some spirits gave me thoughts and allowed me to hear a voice, occasionally not always their own. But this spirit male didn't do anything to help me understand a reason for his visits. The only thing I felt was a deep sense of love; a wonderful contentment in my heart where a light shone bright enough to illuminate the world. I asked spirit to communicate with me, but he wouldn't. And once more, the manifestation vanished as quickly as it had arrived. Followed swiftly by my grandmother, almost demanding that I do not trouble the spirit male, but I give him time to make contact, whenever he is ready. However much I respected my grandmother as my spirit guide, I often found myself feeling frustrated at her demands, desperately looking for a reason behind them. But I never seemed to find one.

"He's not ready," my grandmother would say. Then she too, would vanish.

I arranged to meet Marcus at an Italian restaurant in Kingsway when he got back. I'd missed him and I could tell he'd missed me by the way he almost begged me to join him. He was doing a speech in the town hall beforehand. He sat at a table for two by the window, a lit candle burning in a small lantern decorating the centre. When I walked through the door he appeared to be studying the menu, maybe averting his eyes from my entrance. He rose, quickly pulling out the opposite chair, a gentleman indeed.

"Have you been waiting long?" I asked, returning the kiss he softly planted on my lips.

"No, not at all. I've been looked after." He nodded towards a pretty brunette waitress, clad in uniform, looking particularly Italian. "How are you? I've really missed you these last few days."

"I'm fine. I've been busy, stayed at home to be honest, catching up on stuff."

"Stuff?"

"Paperwork, bills, estate admin, you know how it is. I couldn't take on Rosehill without understanding that it came with hours of forms to fill in and cheques to sign."

"I thought you left that to accountants and managers?"

"I do, mostly. But I like to know what's going on. I do own it after all." The brunette came over, poised with note pad and pen.

"Can I get you anything to drink?" Her focus rested on Marcus, who looked incredible dressed in a silver-grey suit with tie.

We both ordered a white wine, sending her away with a slight twinkle in her eyes. Marcus turned his attention back to me.

"You look fabulous. I feel so proud taking you out in public."

I smiled and looked down at the table, my cheeks flushed as a surge of embarrassment flowed through me upon the arrival of the brunette.

"Have you chosen?" she asked.

I looked at the menu again. "I'll have the Brassato 'all Amarone, please.

"Spaghetti Carbonarra for me, thanks," said Marcus, as he closed the menu and passed it back to her waiting hands. She gave him a flirtatious grin before turning on her heels.

"I think she fancies you," I sniggered, as she walked away.

"Can you blame her?" We both laughed as he lifted his arms up, admiring himself.

"So, what's all this about then?" I asked.

"I haven't seen you for a while. I wanted to show you how much I love you."

"That's nice of you. And bringing me here, too. No expense spared."

"Of course not. Only the best for you." He reached over the table and took hold of my hand, stroking it softly with his finger.

"Are you coming back to Rosehill tonight?"

"If you'll have me."

"You can show me how much you love me." I was almost whispering.

"I think you already know that." His eyes were twinkling as I remained transfixed. It was like we sat amongst a crowd of strangers where nothing else mattered apart from the feelings we had for each other. I'd never felt that way in all my life. Not even with Ross.

"We have something really special, don't we?" he asked.

"Definitely. I'm a little out of practice, I've never had so much attention."

"You deserve it." The food arrived and we both sat back against our chairs, giving the waiter some space to put the plates down.

I placed a napkin on my lap. "This looks delicious," I said. "I wish I could cook like this."

"I'm sure you can. Cooking for one isn't that much fun is it."

"We should eat together more often; these Italians are wonderful in the kitchen."

"You're wonderful in the kitchen," he said, a cheeky grin on his lips. "As I recall."

"You're terrible tonight," I said.

"I've missed you. These last few days have felt like weeks."

"Was the course useful?"

"It was okay, I suppose. I met some nice people. The hotel was beautiful. My bed was far too big for just me, though." He took a sip of his wine and looked at me. "Maybe next year you could come with me?"

"I'd like that." I hadn't been away for a long time, holidays were something I tended to miss out on. But a short break in a romantic hotel with Marcus sounded perfect. "What did you do while you were there?"

"We had to write sermons, give speeches, tell each other a little about our parishes. I just talked about the village church, not a great deal to say because it's a small community, but the vicars who came from larger parishes seemed interested. I think I was one of the older ones actually. The course seemed more for a younger generation of clergy, ones just finding their feet."

"Were there any women vicars there?"

"One or two; I didn't notice many though."

"It seems to be a shame to me that not many vicars are women." I took the last mouthful of beef, replacing my knife and fork on the plate.

"Arh, well," he said, "I guess it's just not so popular for women to take on the role of a vicar. They're better at other things."

"Like what?"

"Looking after the men, cooking, cleaning, washing, bringing up kids, you know, that sort of thing." I stared at him for a moment before noticing the twinkle in his eye getting brighter and his smile becoming more prominent.

"You'll pay for that," I said, picking up my wine glass.

"You can punish me later."

Marcus paid for the meal before helping me with my coat. "Thank you," I said. "Now, are you following me?"

"Why don't you come back to mine for a change," he said, as we walked to our cars. I agreed, deciding to follow him back to the vicarage.

When I arrived, I noticed he had thoughtfully left the front door open. I went in, closing it gently behind me. The hallway was lit together with the landing at the top of the stairs but there was no sign of him.

"Hello," I shouted, looking upstairs.

"I'm up here," he replied. "In my bedroom."

I switched off the hallway light and went to join him, finding him lying in bed, a bottle of wine and two glasses on his bedside table. As always, my heart leapt when I noticed his bare chest, silver hair showing above the duvet.

"Come on in, I've kept the bed warm." He pulled back the duvet, revealing his magnificent body to me, giving me no time to think about anything other than lying by his side. I slipped out of my clothes whilst he poured the wine and passed me a glass as I made myself cosy in the bed.

"Cheers," he said, clinking our glasses together. "Here's to us."

"You're so good to me." We took a sip of wine before he took the glass from my hand, placing his also, on the table.

"I love you," he said, then kissed me.

I pulled away from him, our lips just centimetres apart. "I love you, too."

Chapter Twenty-Five

I lay awake that night, Marcus breathing softly with his face near to mine. I was tired but I couldn't sleep, my heart was still racing with the excitement of being in love. Darkness infiltrated the atmosphere and the only light which shone in my mind was a tiny flicker of hope burning for the visiting soul to witness. My eyes were open, yet I saw no evidence of life. Death however, played its hand, revealing something I hadn't yet experienced in my own existence. It wasn't a dream but a scene of a past life, an old and tired energy which circled around a dark and dreary place. I could smell perfume, sweet and feminine; the faint sound of footsteps coming towards me, unnerving me from the comfort I had previously enjoyed. The energy which presented to me was female, a young woman in her thirties, seemingly unsure as to her whereabouts. I suspected she didn't realise she had passed over, always a sad occurrence for me to deal with, a difficult passing which would have happened unexpectedly. But I wasn't sure whether she was here to see me or Marcus. She had come for a reason. My job was to decipher her message and maybe help her in her quest to find peace. But I was confused. She didn't look at me; she stared only at Marcus who lay beside me, still sleeping soundly. I asked her if she was connected to him in some way, but she didn't reply. It was as though she saw only him.

My vision wasn't improving and my eyes weren't adjusting to the darkness. Yet my mind's eye saw the woman whilst I continued to smell her perfume and hear her movements in the room. Marcus couldn't help her, he would only have disbelieved in her presence. I encouraged her to leave but she was clearly only interested in him. I whispered his name, assuring myself that he was definitely asleep. He turned over, now facing towards his guest. She smiled, averting her eyes to mine, and then she disappeared. The light in my mind diminished. Darkness once more surrounded even my mind's eye and my sight began to adjust to the blackness. Marcus continued to sleep by my side, fortunately unaware of his visitor's sudden appearance.

The bed was warm but my inquisitive mind got the better of me as I pulled back the duvet, slowly getting up, desperate not to disturb him. I went downstairs not really sure why, but when I found myself in the lounge I knew there was a reason for my curiosity.

I went to the sideboard, a huge ancient piece of furniture, having been lovingly restored, dark brown and pampered. I switched on the lamp and was instantly drawn to the right hand drawer, gently opening it with a little apprehension. It would have been terribly humiliating should Marcus have caught me snooping through his things but I knew there was something in that drawer that I had to see. A collection of papers, receipts and business cards, some photographs, black and white, old, containing possible family members; a few colour photographs were beneath them which were, I felt, what I needed to find. They would show me a side of Marcus I didn't know existed. They were wedding photographs, a line up of the wedding party obviously happy and enjoying their day. Familiar faces leapt at me as I realised who they were. Marcus, looking much younger, was dressed in a morning suit, a cream carnation decorating his button hole. He stood next to a woman whom I knew instantly to be Julia Henderson, even though she too, looked much younger than when I previously met her.

She wore an ivory suit consisting of knee length pencil skirt, her hair styled in curls falling loosely at each side of her face. She carried a small bouquet of ivory roses, green foliage surrounding her hands. And on the other side of Marcus stood a woman I had seen a few times, presented as an astral. It was the beauty who had shared our walk and our meal, the same spirit woman who had since stood by Marcus as he slept.

My stomach turned over. I was tired and unable to focus yet I continued to rummage through the drawer, frantically trying to find more evidence of something I knew little about. I had so many questions now to answer, perhaps finding a reason behind too many lies. I wanted to hope my love for Marcus had not been wasted, yet he had to explain to me what was going on. I would wait a while, get my head around the find, and then I would begin my inquisition.

The atmosphere seemed flat, even though I thought I'd heard noises from upstairs, the room directly above the one in which I stood, frozen by suspicion. It sounded like someone walked about in the room, footsteps frantically made their way across the wooden floorboards. It wasn't Marcus's bedroom, that room was at the back of the house and I was at the front. I knew it wasn't Marcus, but who was it? I replaced the photographs and decided to seek evidence of an astral at the vicarage. I gently closed the drawer, lifting it slightly as it struggled to fit back into place, then switched off the lamp. As I approached the stairs I realised the noises of footsteps were nearer, as though someone stood at the top, hovering about on the landing. My heart was racing again. I couldn't see anything as I fumbled about for the stairs, not wanting to switch on the light for fear of waking Marcus.

As I reached the top I failed to notice the footsteps, as though the astral was either standing still or had left Marcus and me to it. He hadn't moved in the bed, still lying with his back to my side as I quietly got in beside him. He sighed heavily and I assumed he was asleep. I was quite sure the spirit had left as I settled myself against the pillow, my heart calming down and my eyes beckoning rest.

I must have eventually got to sleep for the next thing I remember was Marcus's body against mine. I awoke and looked at the clock on the bedside table. It was six-thirty and I had to leave, get back to Rosehill to tend to the dogs.

"Good morning," he said, kissing my bare shoulder.

I thought about the events through the night, wanting to choose my words carefully before I asked him to explain the photographs. I wasn't sure he would appreciate me going through his personal things.

"Good morning. You slept well."

"I did," he answered. "Didn't you?"

"Not too bad. I got to sleep eventually. I'm much better in my own bed." I snuggled into him, reluctant to get up and face the day.

"I'll go and make us some breakfast. You wait here." He moved away, getting out of bed and reaching for his clothes.

"No, that's okay. I need to get back home."

He turned to me. "Are you coming back?"

"I have a few things to do, but I'll see you later if you're not busy?"

"I'll be in all day today. Having a day off from duties, probably clean the car, do a bit of house work. Unless....."

"No way." I laughed, pushing him away as he moved towards me, almost collapsing onto the bed. "I'll come back later, probably this afternoon." I got up and dressed, leaving him to compose himself and start the day.

Chapter Twenty-Six

I arrived back home to three excited dogs in their outside kennel, tails wagging at the prospect of a run on the garden and a bowl of dried food. I stroked them in turn before closing the back door. But as I turned to walk into the kitchen, a negative atmosphere almost winded me. Something had entered my space, and it had no intention of a friendly union. Trying to ignore the coldness which lingered in the kitchen I made myself some tea, leaning to switch the morning news on the television whilst I sat and drank. It didn't surprise me that in the light of the negative energy the television wouldn't switch on. I knew I would have to give in eventually, succumb to the force which appeared stronger than my own.

"Please show yourself." I showed irritation in my voice; I had things to do, apart from wanting to get back to Marcus. But my guest had other ideas. Spirit was angry as proof came from a scattering of papers, thrown to the floor like a bad-tempered child. I froze. Throwing items was something I abhorred in my own home, I didn't welcome malevolent spirit nor did I welcome anger.

"Who are you?"

"He belongs to me." The angry soul now hovered beside me; its energy encased my left side, paralysing my arm with the feeling of pins and needles.

"Who does?"

"You need to know the truth about Marcus." A blast of cold air swept past my face; spirit energy drew my attention to a picture I had recently taken of Rosehill.

"Please present yourself, show me your face."

An artificial breeze blew amongst the littered papers which still lay on the floor.

"Ask him about the photograph you found," the spirit said, a woman's voice ringing in my ears. But within moments of the breeze, calmness rested within the atmosphere. She had gone. The photograph; a picture of the man I loved stood in between two women, one I had met and another who seemed familiar. Her face kept appearing in my mind, the smile etched with happiness as she seemed to revel in the attention of a photographer. And then there was Julia Henderson; the rude and arrogant journalist. Should she have been involved with Marcus romantically, I was sure he would have admitted. I no longer wished to believe there was something between them, but the photograph was telling me otherwise. His closeness to her in the image indicated they had a bond, one far deeper than a simple friendship.

<hr />

That afternoon after I arrived back at the vicarage I decided the time was right to approach Marcus about the photograph. I wanted to pretend it had been psychic intuition, my mind having seen a picture of him stood with Julia Henderson and the spirit woman. But I wanted our relationship to be based on truth.

"I don't want you to be annoyed with me," I began, "but I couldn't sleep last night and found myself in your front room." I looked towards the window before turning back to face him and continue. "Something was in the house, other than you and me, I mean. I know you don't believe it, Marcus, but I was encouraged to open a drawer in your sideboard. I wouldn't normally go through your things but I couldn't seem to stop myself."

He looked puzzled. "What have you done?"

I walked to the sideboard and opened the drawer, then stood back whilst pointing to the photograph. He took it out and looked at it before passing it to me.

"I know Julia Henderson," I said, "but who is the other woman?" I pointed to her as though more interested than curious.

He sat down on the sofa and sighed. "She was my wife."

I stared at him. "What?"

The shock on my face must have been obvious to him as he beckoned me to sit down. I had only seen this one photograph of her, yet I was suddenly aware of the spirit woman who had been with us the previous night. Words were failing me.

"Why haven't you mentioned her?" I asked, as I gave him back the photograph.

"Because she killed herself." He replaced it, gently closing the drawer as I found myself having to come to terms with another shock. "I hated her for what she did; I was totally unaware of how unhappy she was, but she made sure I found her body, writing a note, asking me to meet her."

I sat down next to him, looking deeply into his eyes. He held my hand. My annoyance at being unable to realise the fate of this woman was overwhelming me.

"Meet you where?" I asked.

"In a disused building, not far from where we lived in London. We used to go there in the early days, when we were courting." His voice was wavering and I noticed a tear escape from his saddened eyes.

"Why haven't you told me about her?"

"I never want to talk about it," he answered. "It happened a long time ago. We were young and I was selfish. I had no idea how she felt."

"What was her name?" I was quite sure I already knew the answer.

"Anne. She was beautiful. I was attracted to her as soon as we met in college. We were both studying to be teachers, me in physical education and her in science, so some of our classes were together. It was more or less love at first sight. For me anyway."

"And her?"

"I asked her to marry me when we were just twenty-one. She said yes straight away and we were so happy. We got married a couple of years later and after ten years we decided we wanted to start a family. We'd both qualified to teach but she'd struggled and wasn't sure she wanted to continue. It would have meant her taking more exams and she wasn't committed enough."

"You've got children?" I asked, wondering if I was expected to accept any more secrets.

"No. She couldn't have them. We tried for three years until she..." he paused, turning away from me and wiping his face with his hand.

"You can tell me, it won't go any further." I continued to hold his hand.

"She couldn't take it anymore and that's when she did it. I didn't know she was so desperate." He turned back to face me. "I would have told you. I wasn't going to keep it from you."

"I wish you'd told me sooner. You can trust me, you know. I'm not going to tell anyone if you want to keep it a secret."

"People don't know about it round here."

Then I remembered Julia. "Why was Julia with you on your wedding day?"

"She's Anne's sister. She moved up here years ago and we always kept in touch. She was the one who told me about the parish looking for a new vicar. I guess she helped me get the job."

"So she's your sister-in-law?"

"Yes." He stroked my face. "I'm sorry, Camilla. I know I should've been honest with you."

"Why didn't you tell me the truth when I asked you about Julia?"

"Because I would have had to tell you about Anne, and I didn't want to. Not yet. And besides, Julia is a friend now. She's a good friend and she always will be."

"I realise that now."

"I'll tell her that you know."

"Is that why she warned me to stay away from you?"

"Most probably. She's been so protective towards me. It's been her and me for the past few years, since I moved here. I guess she felt our friendship might be threatened. She still misses Anne."

It all made sense. "Do you still miss Anne?"

"I think about her sometimes. But it's been over twenty years now since she died. I stayed in London for eighteen years, living on my own."

I now started to realise it was her who I had seen in my television screen when I first moved into the farm house. I felt sorry for her, knowing how deeply unhappy she must have been to have committed suicide and now to see the only man she ever loved in the arms of another woman. It wasn't surprising she visited me, making me feel uncomfortable in my own home. It was then that I felt I could at last move on. The relationship I had with Marcus was more open than it had ever been, and even though I wished he had felt confident enough to explain it all to me sooner, I was still grateful to him for making me feel a valued part of his life.

I decided to tell him about Anne's visits, knowing I was risking another disagreement between our spiritual opinions.

"I've met her," I said.

"Who, Julia? I know, you said."

"No, I'm talking about Anne." He stared at me.

"Has she visited you?"

"Yes, a few times. I didn't realise who she was." He nodded. "It doesn't matter if you don't believe me. I can accept that. But she was the one who beckoned me to look in the drawer last night."

He turned towards the sideboard. "I believe you," he said, turning back to me, his eyes unable to look into mine. He stared down at the sofa. "She's visited me, too."

That was a shock, a revelation I never thought I'd hear Marcus admit to. I sat back against the cushions.

"When?" I asked.

"The first time was when I lived in London. I didn't want to believe it was her. I made up my mind to go into the priesthood after she died, and I knew it was wrong if I believed in her spirit."

"It wasn't wrong, Marcus. She was there, she wanted to connect with you, tell you she was okay, probably that she loved you and that she was sorry for what she'd done."

"I was angry with her for what she'd done. Taking her own life like that turned my world upside down. She should have talked to me about being so unhappy. We could have worked through it, maybe even adopted a child, but she just gave up and ruined both our lives." His tears were now prominent, making their way down his cheeks. I lifted my hand to his face and tried to wipe them away.

"She wouldn't have left you alone though," I said. "She obviously followed you here."

"Yes, I know." He held my hand again. "I wondered whether she'd contact you. When you never said anything I assumed she hadn't done."

"I didn't want to say anything; knowing how much you disapprove I thought best not to it."

"It's not that I disapprove. I just don't want to believe that our souls are taken from us only to communicate with total strangers. God is who we communicate with, that's all that matters to me." He stood up. "I need a drink."

"I'll make us some tea," I suggested, following him into the kitchen.

"No, I mean a proper drink." He opened the cupboard and reached for a bottle of Scotch. "Are you having one?"

"No thanks. I'll have a coffee."

"I'm a vicar, Camilla. I can't believe in ghosts."

"But you do, don't you?" I watched him get a glass down from the shelf. He poured some whisky into it then took a sip.

"Yes, I do. I know Anne's been here."

"What about Julia? Does she know? Has she seen Anne, too?" I put the kettle on to boil, before getting a cup out of the cupboard.

"No. And I want to keep it that way. She doesn't believe."

"I wouldn't be so sure," I said. "After what happened at Rosehill after her reading she might have changed her mind."

"What do you mean?"

"Books fell from the shelves; she was really shaken up. I'm surprised she didn't say anything."

"She didn't. Do you think it was Anne?"

"I can't say. The spirit seemed angry. I thought it was someone protecting me, to be honest. Julia was quite rude towards me."

"Anne was never angry. She was just so very unhappy." He managed a weak smile.

I sat with Marcus in his kitchen for a further hour, talking about Anne and the marriage they had. He was happy back then and I realised how she probably saw me as competition. But she needed to be set free from the torment she was obviously still facing. She had to accept that Marcus was with me now, that she could no longer prevent him from moving on with his life.

I held him close to me, grateful that I finally knew the truth about Anne and that I could perhaps concentrate on releasing her spirit from our earth plane. After twenty years it was time she moved on too.

Chapter Twenty-Seven

Spring was upon us as daffodils presented themselves, vibrantly changing the colour of my otherwise bland garden. A new dawn in our lives, where one could either start afresh or face the next challenge, imminently lay ahead. Rosehill bloomed as the brightness of petals danced in the breeze, drawing ones eye in fascination, whilst the days once more lasted past an evening shade. I enjoyed sitting on the terrace, soaking up a view which would capture my heart till it no longer beat. The sound of lambs in the fields and their frantic mothers suddenly started to drown out the silence of winter. Every window offered new life to view, a family making their way in the world, oblivious to their destination. Tiny buds appeared on the branches of hedges whilst a little green could be spotted discreetly finding its way to the trees which continued to stand and overwhelm the drive way.

Night fell. I knew my home entertained from far and wide, the voices beckoned me to their part of a never ending world. There were footsteps on the stairs, doors opening and closing, lights being switched on and off. I was needed, by many. Returning to my reading room, lighting the candle which faithfully stood in wait, I sat at the table, the Crystal by my hands. Knocking came once more, from the fireplace, the velvet curtains blew in an artificial breeze as a manifestation began to appear. It was a female spirit, a dark silhouette standing before me eager to convey her message.

"Show yourself," I requested, my voice a little shaky. The energy moved towards me, an arm reaching out to mine in order to take hold of my hand. I reached out in return, unsure as to where spirit wanted to take me. Her space was cold; my breath was visible. I moved slowly towards the waiting soul, before she turned to face the fireplace. She hadn't manifested completely but I was certain the spirit was Jane.

"The chimney," she whispered, pointing towards it. It was cold, so very cold. But I knew something was behind the bricks, perhaps inside the chimney stack, something which bore significance in my life.

The flame on the candle instantly went out. "You need to find the truth behind Rosehill." I could see a golden aura surrounding her body

"Then I shall," I replied.

"You need to do it soon, Camilla. This can't wait any longer."

I stared at the original features of the beautiful eighteenth century fireplace, realising how serious her words sounded. The room suddenly went completely dark. Unable to see my hand in front of my face I panicked, needing to find the light switch. But my body was frozen, paralysed by the spirit which wanted to be a part of me, who now wanted to possess me. This had happened to me a few times before, an uncomfortable feeling where energy had become connected to my aura. But on this occasion, the energy caught me by surprise, knocking me off my feet as it entered my space and became a part of my thoughts, channelling my mind and overwhelming my whole being. The energy was much stronger than mine and I knew there was no escape. Lifting myself from the floor I managed to crawl to the nearest chair, trying desperately to force myself to stand. But the force threw me back, eager to get its own way, hell bent on taking over my mind. I knocked my head on something I suspected was a table leg.

I was scared, a fear I had seldom experienced with spirit presence. But I also thought another energy had entered our space, perhaps that of a strong male, as Jane would have been unable to apply such force. I shouted for my grandmother for if ever there was a time I needed her, it was then. But she didn't come forward; instead I remained in the room, unable to work out who the malevolent force was that threatened either me or Jane. The atmosphere was heavy, an invisible cloud hanging above me as though waiting to pounce. My heart was racing and I was perspiring, fear instilled within me as I wiped my forehead, a light headed feeling enveloping me. I reached for the chair, an overwhelming urge to sit down. More books were thrown to the floor, but this time by the hands of an angry soul. I sensed Jane was still with us but her energy was weak, she was obviously desperate to leave.

"Help me, Jane." I managed to scramble onto the chair, leaving my arms on the table in front of me. "Who else is in the room?"

"I can't stay," she said, fright evident in her tone. "Get out of here, while you can."

The next thing I remember was waking up on the reading room floor, dim light surrounding me, yet calmness within my heart. The possession had at last left. The candle was lit again and I noticed my grandmother stood over me, smiling. She held out her hand. I placed my hand near hers, an opaque outline of an old lady's limb. She lifted me from the floor, allowing me time to stand and compose myself. I went towards the light switch, illuminating the room once more, only to find a scene of devastation. The hearth rug had been torn, too many places to mend; the Crystal lay on the floor near the book shelves. But what upset me the most was how my red velvet curtains had been torn from their rail, left in a pitiful heap. I went to them, gathering one up in my arms, wondering who could do such a thing. Whoever it had been was quite keen to destroy my sacred room. Perhaps even destroy me.

I worried that Rosehill would become a place of anger rather than the peaceful surroundings I was used to. Morning came round eventually and I forced myself from my bed. I was now a medium on a mission; a woman with a challenge to find out if she had an enemy.

***

It took a couple of hours to clean up the mess. I decided to throw away the rug and buy a new one, it was too badly damaged. I was deeply upset about the curtains and even though I was reluctant to get rid of them I didn't want to become a hoarder. Marcus joined me that afternoon, holding my hand as we walked through fields containing new life. The sun shone. Birds sang whilst sheep gathered together, making the all familiar sound of mother and offspring. A train hurried past a few fields away. The smell of spring lingered in the air as fresh daffodils continued to brighten the grasses along the path. A field of oil seed rape grew at our feet. The day seemed bright; no clouds threatened us, or the stillness in the air. I loved my walks in the fields, shouting after the dogs as they raced ahead, hopeful that I would never want to turn and go back. A rabbit caught my attention in the distance, its eyes staring towards us. Unfortunately the dogs had seen it too.

"It's so beautiful up here," he said, looking around as he appreciated the tranquillity that was my home. "You're very lucky."

"I know. I never want to live anywhere else."

"And why would you? I'd be proud to live at Rosehill, too." I looked at him, a brief thought running through my head, before I looked away, hoping he didn't think I had misinterpreted.

"I think spring is such a lovely time; new life, bright colours." I pointed towards a hill in one of the fields. "We have a gorgeous array of bluebells over there."

"You can see them from the back bedroom window in the vicarage."

I stopped. "Shall we sit down here? It's one of my favourite spots." He agreed, taking off his coat and placing it on the grass.

"There you are, use that." I sat down on the coat, leaving a small amount of space for him to join me.

"It's okay," he said, "I don't think the grass is wet."

It was then that he put his arm around me and pulled me into him, as I rested my head on his shoulder. The view which held our gaze mesmerised us both, miles of countryside at our finger tips, yellow fields blowing in the gentle breeze. Young lambs ran after their mothers, trying hard to keep up, worried they would miss out on lunch. Everything felt perfect; the peace, the view, and Marcus. I turned to face him, once more drowning in his beautiful blue eyes. He put his hand under my chin, gently lifting my face towards his. The kiss he offered massaged my mouth and we sank together against the coat, him ensuring my head didn't touch the grass. Even though the field was open I felt as though we were completely alone. It was our world of a continuous journey which only we could ever take.

Marcus stayed at Rosehill that night. I lay in his arms until he went to sleep, then I turned over and stared into the darkness. Once more a light shone inside my mind, showing me a vision of Anne. This time, she appeared in front of me, her eyes transfixed on Marcus. I sat up in bed, more perturbed than I had been for a while. There was something about the way she looked at him, something in her eyes; it was obvious the love she felt for him would never end. She ignored me as though she had no interest in me. It was quite unusual for a spirit to present before me should it not wish to communicate.

She continued to stare at him and I turned to look at him too. Even though he had admitted to knowing about Anne's presence I hadn't pushed the conversation further, realising he would rather not talk about her as if she were a spirit.

It was then that Anne turned to me and whispered, "he will always be my first and only love."

As Marcus was asleep I decided to get out of bed, psychically encouraging Anne to follow me. She did, the gentle patter of her footsteps walking behind. I took her into one the guest bedrooms at the other side of the house, not wanting to wake Marcus as I spoke to her.

I sat on the bed, feeling her energy in the room, sensing she stood near the window. "Show yourself to me, Anne." She slowly began to manifest again, her face with an aura of golden light surrounding it. "Why have you come here?"

She was certainly very beautiful. The room was cold but not as cold as I had known it. Yet I could still feel a slight breeze, catching it occasionally as she moved around the room.

"I love Marcus," she said. Her eyes were sad now.

"I know you do. But that was a long time ago. Marcus needs to move on with his life. You need to let him go."

"I'll never let him go," she replied. "He loves me, not you." I was taken aback with her words, they ate into my heart as I realised that unless I insisted she left, she would never be able to move forward. Twenty years had been a long time; I had to think about my relationship with Marcus, knowing that if Anne continued to haunt our lives, there wouldn't be a future for us.

"Of course he loves you, he'll always love you. But he also loves me." I lowered my voice. "You have to let go. He's with me now."

"Never," she said.

"You're not being fair on Marcus. You must realise that."

"I'm not leaving him."

"But you already did that, Anne. You hurt him terribly when you...." I stopped.

"Killed myself?" she said. "I did it; I shouldn't have done but I couldn't see a way out of the depression I felt. Marcus wasn't bothered about having children. It was me who wanted a family."

"Marcus said he wanted a family too." The room got colder. I wrapped my arms around myself.

"He did, once. But it didn't affect him the way it affected me. I tried to make him see how hurt I was feeling but he chose to block it out."

"Perhaps that's because he was hurting, too. In his own way. He's a private man, I've realised that since we've been together. He wouldn't have meant for you to go through it by yourself. Your death left him devastated."

She started to cry. "I won't leave him again. He's my husband."

There seemed to be no reasoning with her. The room fell silent and the breeze ceased leaving me feeling a little warmer. She had gone. I made my way back to Marcus who still slept. I got in and snuggled into him, not wanting to wake him but wishing he would hold me, reassure me that it was me he wanted now. Not Anne.

Chapter Twenty-Eight

*I*t rained the next morning, large, heavy drops knocking against the window like desperate tears falling from the sky. Marcus and I laid together, staring at the ceiling which seemed to hypnotise our thoughts. I could have lay there forever, knowing it was a place we both wanted to be. He was the first to move, lifting my head carefully from his chest. I watched him as he dressed, his beauty overwhelming my thoughts once more. He was graceful, refined in the way he moved, the way he leant over and kissed me. I turned over, now facing the wardrobe, somewhat saddened when he announced he needed to get home. I heard his car leave the drive and I got up, putting on my dressing gown whilst recollecting the events of Anne's visit.

I couldn't sense her in the house anymore, but I knew she would return. I was a little scared at the way she had been adamant in her decision to stay, grounded amongst human souls. I wanted to tell Marcus of the conversation I'd had with her during the night and I wanted to ask him if he wanted her more than me. But, even after his revelation about his conflicting beliefs, I knew it would be best not to force him to make a choice. He had me and I was sure I was all he wanted. Losing Anne was something he had come to terms with but her continuous presence and communication with me had to be stopped.

Later that day, Ross rang, inviting me to his place to help him sort through the remainder of Lucy's things. I was thrilled he'd asked me, glad of a distraction to my worries concerning Anne. Marcus had to make a few visits in the parish and as we hadn't arranged to meet up I decided a day with Ross would make a nice change to my otherwise empty schedule. I arrived at his house just after lunch.

"Have you eaten?" he asked, as he came to the car to greet me.

"No, are you making something?"

"Sure. I've got some ham, I'll make us a sandwich. How are you?"

I followed him into the house. "I'm very well. Thanks for asking me over."

"You look well," he said, kissing my cheek gently as we stood in the hallway. "It'll be better to have a woman's opinion with Lucy's clothes. I don't know what to do with some of them." He looked at me, his eyes scanned my body. "Were you the same size?"

"I think she was slimmer than me," I laughed and patted my stomach.

"Oh, I don't know. She lost weight near the end but I'd say you were more or less the same." We went into the kitchen and he took out the ham from the fridge. "Brown or white bread?"

"Brown for me. No, I think you'll find that Lucy was smaller."

"I was wondering if there was anything you might like to keep of hers, not just clothes, but jewellery too?"

"I'm sure there will be. Have the kids been through her stuff?" I watched as he carefully buttered four slices of bread.

"Rebecca took some of her jewellery, the expensive stuff, you know what she's like. Jacob took her mobile phone and laptop."

"That's Rebecca, alright," I laughed, taking a plate of sandwiches from him.

"Eat those first, then I'll take you to her room where I've left everything out."

"I'll have a look. If there are clothes that I can wear then I'll take them. Otherwise you could give them to the charity shops in town."

"I've done that with lots of things already," he said, making us a drink then joining me at the table.

We ate lunch before going upstairs to Lucy's bedroom. Ross had put piles of clothes on the bed and left a couple of boxes under the bay window. I noticed they contained ornaments and packets of photographs. Lucy's life had been condensed into a cardboard container. I sifted through the clothes first.

"You're right, there's some my size here. Are you sure you don't mind me having them?"

"Of course not. She'd have wanted you to have them."

I found a pair of red trousers that I remembered Lucy buying on a trip to Glasgow one Christmas. It had been a lovely weekend break spent shopping, and later drinking till the early hours. I lifted them up and put them against my legs.

"I'll take these," I said. "I remember when she tried them on in the shop. She went out of the changing rooms to find me and ask my opinion but I was looking at something else and she was almost accused of stealing them. It was so embarrassing." I stroked them. "That was a lovely weekend though. I'm going to miss our shopping trips at Christmas."

"I remember her wearing those," Ross said.

I continued to look through the clothes, putting aside the ones I knew were too small. Some I didn't care for, but quite a few jumpers were suitable so I put them on a pile on the floor. Ross was going through the boxes, picking out ornaments and holding them up for me to look at. I didn't have many ornaments at Rosehill so I agreed to take some home.

"I'm going to dedicate a shelf in the drawing room at Rosehill, to Lucy's memory. She'd like that," I said, seeing a small figurine of a mother and child in Ross's hands. "Where did you find that?"

"It was in a box under the stairs. I know she was planning a car boot sale not long before she died and I think it was meant for that." His eyes scanned it carefully. "I've never liked it. I think Paul bought it for her when Rebecca was born." He moved over to the bed and sat down. "Can I ask you something?"

"Of course."

"Do you think she can see us doing this?"

I couldn't sense her with us but I was sure she'd have visited Ross many times. Although I hadn't yet communicated with her at Rosehill I hoped the day would come when she found enough energy to talk about her journey on the astral plane. I felt Ross was asking for my reassurance. His gentle side showed as tears welled up in his eyes.

"I'm sure she can see us. She'll be very happy that you've asked me to help."

"Is she here now?" He looked around the room.

"I don't think so." I touched his arm. "But she isn't far away. I know you miss her."

"I do. Living here on my own has given me a lot of time to think about things. All those years living in America put too much distance between us, in more ways than one. I wished I'd have been here for her when Paul died."

"That's in the past now, Ross. I was here for her. She needed female company, I think. Anyway, she came to see you not long after his death, didn't she?"

"Yes, she did. But she was so angry with him. I think if he hadn't have killed himself, I would have done it for him." I thought about Anne, and the way she had killed herself, too. I wondered if Lucy had met up with her in the spirit world.

I looked at him and wiped away his tears with my hand. "I'm here for you now. You can always ring me if you need a friend."

He looked into my eyes. The closeness we had once felt came rushing back to me as I remembered how much I had once loved this man. It was a moment of weakness as he lent towards me, almost touching my lips with his. I drew away, clumsily knocking his hand as I stood up, causing the figurine to fall to the floor.

"Oh, shit!" he exclaimed. "I'm sorry, I should have..."

"It's all right, nothing happened. I bent over to pick up the ornament. It had broken in two.

He turned to face me. "I know there's no chance for us but sometimes I just think about the old days, remembering what we had. Being here, in Lucy's house, well, it brings back all those memories." He lent over one of the boxes, taking out a packet of photographs before opening it up and pulling some of them out. "Look," he said, passing me one of the pictures.

It was one of him and me, taken at the reception of Lucy's wedding. We were sat together, his arm around me, smiling into the camera, our faces almost touching.

"I remember that night like it was yesterday," he said.

I looked at the photograph, overwhelmed by memories. "Me too. But it wasn't yesterday, Ross. It was a long time ago." I handed back the photograph. "It was a good night, wasn't it?"

"One I'll never forget."

We finished looking through Lucy's things and I chose a few more clothing items together with some ornaments and pieces of jewellery. Ross wrapped the broken ornament up for me; he didn't have any super-glue so I offered to take it home and fix it myself. It had been such a nostalgic afternoon and I felt bad leaving him on his own when I left at five o'clock.

"Why don't you come over tomorrow for supper," I said. "I'll ask Marcus, too. You can get to know him a little better."

"I'd like that. Thanks, Camilla." He hugged me, kissing me softly, but this time without the romantic feeling I had sensed earlier.

"Thanks for what?" I asked, as I pulled away and walked towards the front door.

"For being here. For being you. I know what we had is in the past but you'll always be special in my life. You'll always be the girl I fell in love with.

I smiled, not really knowing what to say. "Bye, Ross. See you tomorrow night. Seven o'clock. And if you want to stay over, you're very welcome." I had a feeling he might do just that.

Chapter Twenty-Nine

*M*arcus called the following morning, fresh from a visit to a grieving parishioner. When I went to greet him at his car, I noticed his notes on the seat beside him, handwritten, no doubt concerning the impending funeral. His mood was quite solemn as he got out and walked with me to the back door, a struggling smile when I kissed him, before entering the house.

The mournful parishioner was Alice Baxter. Her sister had suffered with dementia for many years and lost her battle with life the previous day. She was a sweet old lady, without a care in the world, having nothing else to live for and now having given up on life, waiting patiently to be taken onto her next journey. I had admired her on the few occasions we had met, hoping that I would perhaps feel the way she did when I was old and had done everything I wanted to do. But Alice was naturally sorrowful. Marcus said she had expressed anger for the way her sister had been taken, unsure as to whether a religious service was appropriate. He obviously had to listen to Alice's anger, trying his best to help her make sense of life. It was my guess that she still grieved for her husband. But there was something Marcus wasn't telling me. He seemed different that morning, holding darkness within his soul. He didn't want me to see, he couldn't have allowed me into his mind, and I became a little frustrated at being unable to work out why.

"You seem upset," I said, wrapping my arms around his neck.

"It wasn't a nice meeting with Alice. She's very bitter."

"I can understand that. Why don't you sit in the lounge. I'll make us a drink and bring it through."

"I can't stay long," he said, sitting down at the kitchen table. "Don't make me a drink, I've just had one at Alice's. I just came to ask you what you're doing tonight."

"I wanted to ask you the same thing," I replied. "I've invited Ross round for dinner. Thought it might be nice for you two to get to know each other."

He looked thoughtful for a moment. "Yes, I'd like that. I have another meeting this afternoon but I can get back here by six, if that's okay?"

"Of course. I told Ross seven o'clock. He might stay the night then he can have a few drinks."

"Oh?"

"He was really upset yesterday. I went over to help him sort though the rest of Lucy's things. I didn't realise how much he missed her."

"I see. You think a change of scenery might do him good?"

"Yes, I do. I hate seeing him so distraught."

"You really care about him, don't you?"

"Of course I do. He needs a friend right now." I hoped Marcus wasn't jealous again.

"We all need a friend. You're a good person, Camilla. I hope he doesn't take advantage of your kindness."

I shook my head, remembering the romantic encounters I had recently experienced with Ross, trying desperately not to give too much away. "He won't. You don't have to worry."

"So what have you done with Lucy's things?"

"I've kept some of the clothes and a few ornaments." I picked up the figurine of the mother and child which I had recently repaired. "This was something that Lucy's late husband bought for her. She always loved it. I think she'll be glad I have it now." He took it from my hands, looking at it underneath.

"Royal Doulton. It's beautiful. Where will you put it?" he asked, handing it back to me.

"I'm going to put it in the drawing room. There's a shelf in there that I can use for her things."

"That's a nice idea." He stood up and walked towards the back door. "Sorry I can't stay longer," he said, reaching towards me for a kiss.

I kissed him back, once more wrapping my arms around him. "See you later," I said, as he went to his car.

That afternoon I decided to sit in the reading room for a while, try a little meditation and see if I could contact Lucy. The atmosphere in there was heavy, oppression hammering into my mind. I heard a noise coming from the fireplace, as though something had fallen from inside the chimney. As I looked over, a book fell from the shelf next to it, seemingly forced by invisible strength. I went to pick it up before watching another, hardbound, fall to the floor. I stood back, expecting the rest to be moved, a little excited at having eventually been in the presence of the poltergeist that insisted in stacking my books on the floor. I closed the shutters, the windows still bare from curtain material. The light immediately faded as darkness embraced me. More books fell from the shelves, each one carefully stacked on top of each other, in front of my eyes. It was a wonderful moment of poltergeist activity, one any medium would have been enthralled to experience. At that stage I couldn't see who was responsible for the act, but I could feel a presence. It wasn't Lucy but that of a male, someone who I felt was in need. I had an incline of what came next, once the books had been removed. A new light began to shine, just a pin prick to begin with, becoming a manifestation in its wake. It was a man indeed. A tall, broad man, presenting in his fifties I assumed, kind eyes yet sadness surrounding his heart. He kept turning towards the fireplace, his attention occasionally diverting to me. I had seen him before, it was Harold Baxter. But I couldn't understand why I felt so strongly towards a man whom I didn't think I knew on a personal level. I was still confused as to why Alice Baxter had brought Harold into my life, and whether she knew we had connections. I hated to feel frustrated, as though I was missing something vital. I wanted to know about the spirits which visited me, it had always been important to learn about them. My grandmother had helped since I discovered my gift, but recently I noticed her absence.

I felt that she knew something about this man, about his reason for appearing before me. Yet I also felt she thought it best not to be around when he was. He had unfinished business, and to think it was with me made it all the more mysterious. But why all the secrecy? Why choose me to connect with? Had it simply been a co-incidence that Alice had chosen me to read for her, or, as my disbelief in co-incidence dictated, was all this meant to happen? Was Harold meant to be in my reading room, removing books from my shelves?

Adrenalin ran through me, I was firing on all cylinders, eager to find out what was going on at Rosehill. This wasn't only my life that had significance to Harold's presence, it was the house too. The spirit of Jane seemed to be wanting to tell me something that focused on books, and now Harold seemed to encourage me to find out.

I nodded to the entity which continued to entice me towards a mystery. I reached out and touched the fireplace. My outstretched arm was icy cold, almost numb to the bone. The voices started shouting as though to each other; angry, desperate pleas, from one man to another. I couldn't hear anything other than the voices, evil laughter, screams and wails ringing in my ears, piercing my soul. It was the most horrendous sound I had ever heard; in all my years of mediumship I had never encountered such ferocity. I didn't recognise the voices even though I could clearly hear them to be male.

My arm remained cold as my fingers caressed the wall. Harold stood still even though I sensed he was becoming agitated. Getting to the bottom of the mystery was all I wanted to do. I was even prepared to invite a friend of mine to the house, a medium who could cleanse the room, free the tormented soul. Having already witnessed the scene of murderous activity many months before, I was prepared for this to be so. I couldn't have been prepared however, for the truth.

<hr />

Marcus arrived at Rosehill on time. The chimes on the grandfather clock in the hallway sounded six times as his car drew up in the driveway. He let himself in, petting the dogs as they greeted him like a master. He found me, plumping up cushions on the lounge sofas, and pulled me towards him.

"How was your meeting?" I asked, after he had kissed me.

"It's been a long day," he replied. "First Alice then Mrs Thompson. She's burying her husband next week, too."

"Sounds like you've had a tough day of it." I made my way to the kitchen and he followed me.

"I've had better days." He went to the drinks cabinet, taking out the decanter of Scotch. "Do you mind?" he said, reaching for a glass.

"Help yourself. You don't have to ask."

"Are you having one?"

"No, I have a few bottles of wine in the fridge. Don't want to be drunk before Ross arrives."

I was cooking a chicken in the Aga, together with roast potatoes. It smelt divine as I opened the oven door to peel back the tin foil.

"You can set the table if you like. I thought we'd eat in the dining room tonight." Marcus went to the cutlery drawer and took out knives and forks. "Get a few wine glasses, too," I said.

"Is it okay if I stay tonight? Or would you rather just have Ross here?"

"Of course you can stay. I expected you would anyway. And why would I just want Ross here?" I smiled at him.

"I didn't know whether you wanted to talk about old times."

"We can do that with you here, can't we?" I based the chicken before returning it to the Aga. "Are you okay?"

"I think I've had another visit. From Anne." I stared at him, it explained his mood.

"What makes you say that?"

"I thought I heard her speak to me, when I got back home after being here this morning. I opened the front door, went inside then heard her. She said, 'Marcus, it's me'. I recognised her voice straight away. I ignored it at first, thought it was my mind playing tricks on me, then the television switched on in the lounge and when I went in there I could have sworn I saw her, standing by the fireplace. It was weird, Camilla, really weird."

"Sit down," I said. "I need to tell you something." I sat next to him at the kitchen table. "She came to see me the other night, when you stayed. She was in one of the guest bedrooms and she spoke to me. She's quite adamant that she isn't going to leave you again. She doesn't want us to be together. I'm not sure what she's planning to do, Marcus, but I got the impression that she'll do anything to split us up."

"Why didn't you tell me?"

"I didn't want to."

"She can't stop us seeing each other," he said, holding my hands in his.

"I know, but knowing that she's here, trying her best to stop you moving on is really bad news. I need to help her. I'm not sure I can do it on my own."

"What do you want me to do?"

"I want you to tell her that she has to let you go. She needs to be sure that you're happy again, that you've already let her go and you've moved on with your life."

"How do I do that?"

"Perhaps with my help," I suggested. "We might need to do a séance, connect with her."

He pulled away from me, standing up and walking towards the drinks cabinet. "I can't do that. You know I can't."

"I know this is difficult for you, Marcus. But you've already acknowledged that she's here. You've already said you believe her spirit is around you. No one needs to know about this, just you and me."

"I'm not sure I can. I'd be betraying the vows I took, making a mockery of the church." He refilled his glass. "Can't you do it by yourself?"

"I could try. But it would be better if you tried with me. I know it's against everything you believe in."

"Let me think about it," he said, joining me again at the table. "But if anyone finds out I'm even thinking about it I'll lose my status as a vicar."

I stood up and lifted the Aga plates before putting pans on them. I didn't want to pressure him, but the choice had to be his. He had already broken his vows, though I didn't want to say anything. I knew it would only be a matter of time before Anne visited again.

Chapter Thirty

oss arrived at seven o'clock. He brought a small hold-all with him and passed me a bottle of white wine. He shook hands with Marcus before kissing me on my cheek.

"I take it you're staying over?" I asked, looking at the bag. He nodded. "You can sleep in the room you used at Christmas."

"Shall I open the wine?" Marcus asked, seeming a little uneasy. I glanced at him, hoping this wasn't going to be a bad idea.

"Go ahead," I said, opening the drawer and taking out the corkscrew. "Pour me one, too."

"Is that one of Lucy's jumpers?" Ross looked at me.

"Yes, does it suit me?"

"It looks better on you than it did on Lucy," he said, making us both laugh. Marcus poured the wine and passed a glass to Ross.

"Did you know I bought her that one?"

"No. When did you give it to her?"

"I brought it with me last year. It always looked too big on her but it fits you perfectly." He brushed his hand down my arm. I glanced over at Marcus who pretended not to notice.

"I remember seeing her in it once, probably not long after you arrived." I got plates out of the cupboard and passed the oven gloves to Marcus. "Can you get the chicken out, please?"

"Shall I carve it?" he asked.

"Yes, please."

"Can I do anything?" Ross asked, hovering about with a glass of wine in his hand.

"No, you can sit down and enjoy the meal," I said. "Leg or breast? Or both?"

Ross laughed. "You know me, Cam, I'm a breast man." I realised how it sounded and I once again glanced at Marcus, hoping he hadn't taken it the wrong way.

"Go and sit down in the dining room," I told Ross. "Marcus and I will bring it through."

Marcus came over to me and put his face close to mine. "A breast man, eh? Man after my own heart." I was relieved, even if I did pick up on a brief hint of jealousy.

We joined Ross in the dining room. "I love this room," he said. "You've made it beautiful, Cam."

"It's one of my favourite rooms. I don't use it often enough."

"More wine, Ross?" Marcus picked up the bottle which Ross had placed on the table.

"Yes please," he replied. "It's been a while since I've been out somewhere and not had to drive home."

"What are you doing with yourself these days?" Marcus filled up the glasses before sitting down.

"Not very much, if I'm honest. I went to see Jacob and Rebecca last week but they're studying and don't really need me around. I've been thinking about going back to America."

I looked up from my plate. "I thought you'd decided to stay here," I said.

"I did." He looked at his food. "But there's nothing for me here anymore. I'm at the wrong age to find a job, not that there is anything in my line of work."

"Well, that's true. But I'm sure there's work somewhere. What about farming?"

"Nah, not my style. I haven't sold the condo and the tenants I found are moving out in a few weeks. At least I've still got somewhere to live over there."

"What's your line of work?" Marcus asked.

"I'm a beach life guard. Have been for years. I've also worked at hotels in Beverley Hills but it was too demanding. People expected too much. In the end I moved to the sand, found work there."

"I imagine you've met a lot of famous people?" Marcus seemed interested.

"One or two.

"What will you do when you go back?" I asked.

"I'll probably work in a club or something like that. I've been thinking about opening a bar with my friend, Tommy. He already has a couple and was asking around if anyone wanted to go into business with him, open another. But then I came over here and never made the decision."

"I wouldn't mind working in a bar," Marcus said, much to our surprise.

"You?" I exclaimed.

"Yes, me. I like being with people; I'm good at socialising."

"But can you add up?" I asked, making Ross laugh. "It's not like counting out the collection plate on a Sunday morning."

Marcus reached for the chicken, taking two slices with his fork. "How long have you two known each other?" he asked.

"A long time," Ross laughed. "And yes, she has always been a sarcastic sod."

Marcus smiled. "I guess you know what you want, Ross. No point staying somewhere if you don't feel settled." I glanced at him, wondering if there was a bit of relief in his tone.

"You're right, mate. I lived in America for a lot of years, too many to count. I guess the life I made over there needs me to go back. I'll miss the UK but I have a lot of friends in Santa Barbara."

"Girlfriend?" Marcus asked.

"An ex. We were more casual than you guys, though. I wasn't sure about where it was all heading. And when I came back here last year she didn't seem to care. Mind you, I'll probably look her up when I go back."

"I didn't know you had a girlfriend," I said, taking a mouthful of chicken.

"Like I say, it was nothing serious."

"So when are you planning to return?" I noticed Marcus's mood had lifted considerably.

"Next month. I'll put Lucy's house on the market first. The kids said they'll sort it out. She left it to them in the will so I'll let them deal with it."

"Is that why you've been getting rid of so many of her things? I wondered if you'd keep anything for yourself," I asked.

"Yes. I thought if I sorted through everything now it would be something the kids wouldn't need to do. I'm glad you took those ornaments, Cam."

"Oh, I haven't shown you, have I. I've put them in the drawing room, they look perfect in there. The figurine glued together nicely. It looks like new, you'd never know it was broken."

"I'll have a look later," he said, finishing off his wine before picking up the bottle and refilling his glass.

"I'll go and get another bottle." I got up and went into the kitchen. I could hear the men talking but wasn't able to make out what they were saying.

When I returned they were laughing, Ross having obviously said something amusing to which Marcus thought was hilarious. It was good to see them laugh together. It was also good to know that even though Marcus and I were lovers, my relationship with Ross was still strong, a friendship which would always remain.

After dinner we went into the lounge. Ross sat in the armchair whilst Marcus and I made ourselves comfortably on the sofa. He was sat quite close to me, his leg touching mine and I noticed Ross look over a few times, glancing down as he must have realised how intimate Marcus and I were.

"How long have you been a vicar, Marcus?" Ross asked.

"Twenty years now. The church I had before this one was huge. So different to the village community."

"Which do you prefer?"

"This one, without a doubt." Marcus put his hand on my leg. "I wouldn't have met Camilla if I hadn't come up here."

"Why did you move up here?" Ross asked, prompting Marcus to remove his hand and look at me.

"My wife died. Her sister moved up here not after it happened and five years ago she told me about the parish needing a new vicar."

"Your wife? Heck, I'm sorry, mate. I had no idea you were married."

Marcus looked at me again. "I've only just told Camilla. I don't talk about it, it was a long time ago."

"Still, it must have been hard, losing your wife. How long were you married?"

I sensed Marcus wanted to change the subject but he politely answered Ross. "Twelve years."

"Have you got kids?"

"No, we couldn't have children." I stood up, hoping it might tempt Ross to think about something else, another drink perhaps.

"How did she....?" Ross began, before Marcus interrupted him.

"She killed herself. She took it very badly when she realised she couldn't have children."

Ross stared at me, then looked back at Marcus. "Oh, I'm sorry, I shouldn't have asked."

"That's okay. It's just not something I like to talk about."

"Well, I can imagine it isn't, you being a vicar and all." Ross shifted in his chair.

"Right, who wants a coffee?" I asked, clapping my hands together.

"Not for me," Marcus said. "I'll have a Scotch."

"Me too. Shall I get them?" Ross stood up.

"Okay, help yourself. I'll make myself a coffee." I left the room, praying that Ross wouldn't ask any more awkward questions about Anne. Fortunately, I hadn't sensed any spirit presence during the evening but I was sure she wouldn't be far away if she realised she was being discussed.

I couldn't make out whether Marcus was jealous of my friendship with Ross even though both men got on so well. I decided to leave the washing up until the next day and made my way back to the lounge. The atmosphere seemed a lot lighter as I sat next to Marcus.

It was midnight when we finished our drinks and I announced that I was going to bed. My eyes were struggling to stay open. Marcus got up and held out his hand to me, waiting until I took it in mine. I looked over at Ross as he too got up.

"Thanks for a great evening, Cam," he said. "That meal was superb."

"You're welcome. I hope it's cheered you up a bit."

"Being with you always cheers me up," he said, walking over to me and gently brushing the side of my face. "Thank you," he whispered in my ear, before going towards to the door.

"Sleep well, Ross," I said. I turned to face Marcus who was looking at me with his eyebrows raised.

"Just friends?" he said.

"Just friends," I answered.

"What did he whisper in your ear?"

"Thank you. That's all." I kissed his lips. "Come on, let's go to bed."

The following morning, Ross left first, leaving Marcus and I to clean away the previous nights pots.

"I enjoyed last night," Marcus said. "He's a nice guy, but I still think he fancies you."

I laughed and gave him a friendly punch. "You're mad. So long as you fancy me, I'm not bothered about anyone else."

"I do fancy you," he replied, then looked at his watch. "But right now I need to dash. Got a few things to do today." He kissed me. "See you later," he said, before leaving the house.

I took a duster out of the cupboard and went into the reading room. My sudden decision to clean it surprised me as I opened the door and looked towards the fireplace. Everything seemed in order. The books remained on their shelves and the candle stood, proud and dignified on the mantel piece. But once again, I heard the noise from the fireplace, the sound of possible twigs falling down the chimney. I wondered if I should have got a chimney sweep in to clean it out properly. I picked up the candle sticks and dusted the mantle, replaced them then dusted round the hearth. As I sat on the floor, I glanced up towards the chimney stack.

Without realising what I was doing, I placed my hand inside the chimney and started to feel around. I didn't have a clue why the sudden urge had taken me, but I knew there was something I needed to find. I could sense a faint energy in the room, but was unable to decipher who it could have been. I suspected it was Harold at one point, when a distant aroma of aftershave drifted past me.

I moved my hand around inside the stack, feeling a ledge a few inches upwards. I positioned myself on the hearth so I could put my hand further inside. The bricks felt cold and dusty and I hoped desperately that I didn't disturb a spider from its rest, I'm not sure I could have continued.

But my mission to carry on overwhelmed me as I began to realise that there was indeed something I had to discover. As my hand felt around the ledge I suddenly touched something. I reached further in, my neck now craning to see. Protruding a little, I grabbed the item and pulled my hand from the chimney stack. I looked down at my hand. The item was a hard-backed book, almost white in an ancient bed of dust. I blew it and brushed my hand across it, sending the dust in all directions, spoiling my newly dusted hearth.

I could just about see some words on the front, but they were illegible. The writing looked italic at a glance, and I was able to make out the word 'Diary' in the top left hand corner.

Chapter Thirty-One

I took the book to the table and carefully opened it, afraid crisp and delicate papers may escape. The writing on the first page was only just legible, I struggled to make it out, but it seemed as though the words 'Harold Baxter' protruded their way from paper to my mind. The more I looked at it, the more adrenalin ran through my veins and I could see my hands physically shaking in readiness to learn about my new found mystery. I turned to the next page to find words scrawled across a yellow background before deciding to move into the kitchen in order to try and work out what they said. It was warmer in there as the Aga gave off its usual welcome, always drawing me in. I placed the book on the table.

The light did indeed shine in my favour, the words were easier to see and therefore I was more able to read what looked like a diary. It was Harold Baxter's diary, to be precise.

"Rosehill; I found this place, unable to understand why, yet here I am, once more alone and able to gather my thoughts."

I read on:

"Alice came to see me today, we made love. She wanted to go too soon, I wanted her to stay forever. I can't imagine her going back to that house, living with a man she no longer

*loves. He leaves for overseas on Thursday, perhaps we will
spend more time together."*

The confirmation I needed that Alice and Harold did have an affair.
The date read 29th January 1964.

There were more entries, mainly focusing on Harold's building
work of which he clearly enjoyed doing around the house. To know
that he had lived at Rosehill was a find in itself. An interesting yet
ordinary man, that morning, Harold became someone I felt I knew
well. I could only feel warmth towards him, not really understanding
why this was. Arriving on the page titled, 13th August 1964, I decided
it was time to close the book, continue my reading after lunch. I found
my bookmarker. Fortunately, I had no clients until the following week
leaving me free time, perhaps enough time to finish Harold's diary.

Clouds began to drown out the beauty of the clear, blue sky,
threatening rain fall against what had become a particularly pleasant
day. I was keen to get back to the diary, eating what little food I had
prepared quickly, hoping to learn more about a man whom had once
resided in my home and perhaps still did. I knew I would soon want to
see Alice again, ask her about Harold, she would surely have known
the answers to the questions which were swimming around my head.
But I would read a little more before ringing her; I would satisfy my
impatience and calm the nerves I now felt. That was when Marcus
arrived.

It was always good to see him even though I would have preferred
to be alone and continue reading the diary.

"I've got an hour spare," he said, noticing the diary on the table.
"What's this?" He picked it up.

"Please don't," I almost snapped at him, my rudeness quickly
turning into a smile.

"What is it?" he asked again. "Where did you find it?" His eyes
seemed to pierce through its pages, his thoughts burning with
curiosity.

"It's a diary. It belongs to a man who used to live here. I found it
inside the chimney in the reading room." How much was I supposed to
tell Marcus? Was it okay to tell him how Jane had lead me to it; or how
Harold himself had encouraged me to look inside, perhaps in order to
find it? Surely Marcus's scepticism wouldn't have accepted my
explanation. There were many things about my mediumship that I
couldn't discuss with him and I thought this would be one of them.

"Have you had contact with the owner of the diary?"

I stared at him. "Yes."

"Harold Baxter. Is that him?"

I looked deep into Marcus's eyes, unsure what they told me. Seeing the name on the front of the diary had obviously told him who it belonged to, but I was afraid he was being sarcastic, making fun of my beliefs.

"Yes, that's him. I've read some of it, it's very ordinary so far, just the diary of a middle-aged man who worked as a local builder."

"Does he have anything to do with Alice Baxter?"

"Yes, he was her brother-in-law. William, her husband, was Harold's brother."

"And do you know what happened to him?"

"I'm not sure, but I don't think it was a natural death. Why are you interested?" I asked, surprised at his questions.

"Because I heard that he was murdered." I joined Marcus at the kitchen table.

"I know he was murdered." I struggled to look Marcus in the eye. But he seemed concerned for me.

"So Harold Baxter has contacted you? What did he say?" Marcus was incredibly serious.

"He hasn't said much, it's the way he makes me feel, the things he's shown me. I assume he was stabbed whilst in an altercation, but I couldn't tell you who did it. Do you know?"

"Rumour has it that the brother did it." Marcus shrugged.

"Do you want to see where I found it?" I knew I was taking a chance, but Marcus seemed unusually interested. We stood up and he outstretched his arm in typical gentleman fashion.

Marcus went over to the fireplace.

"Have you got a torch?" he asked, turning to face me. I went to get one from the kitchen, realising he wouldn't have been satisfied with my love for candlelight.

He shone the torch up the chimney. "Can you see anything?" I asked.

"No, but there's and awful lot of twigs, probably from the jackdaws. You should have this cleaned out." He switched off the torch. "Did you think there was something up there in the first place?"

It was my opportunity to tell the truth, take a chance and hope he believed me. I would face the laughing and the patronising comments if and when they came, which I was sure they would.

"I'm not sure you will believe me if I tell you."

"Try me." He was serious. I wondered if Anne had visited him again, made him realise that there was some truth in what I said. We moved to sit at the table, both determined to get to the truth.

"Alice came for a reading not long after I moved in. Her husband, William, came through to me. I could tell he was totally in love with her as he never took his eyes from her. Then he showed me a photograph, it was a black and white picture of a baby. Their child I assumed." We both sat down at the table. I hoped Marcus wasn't laughing at me, that his expression was genuine. "After the reading, Alice told me that she had an affair with Harold and as a result of that affair, the child was born. She had allowed her husband to believe the child was his. She said he still believed it to be the truth when he passed."

"And that would have been around the mid sixties. Am I right?"

"Yes, I think you are," I replied, quite excited at the thought that Marcus did believe me after all. "According to the diary, it was during 1964 when they were lovers. Which means the child will now be around the same age as me. The only child I thought Alice had lives in Aberdeen; she told me about how proud she is of her, becoming a doctor and marrying a consultant. I've never seen her in the village though. Have you?"

"She talks about her daughter occasionally, she has photographs of her too, but I've never met her. So what made you look for the book?"

"The spirit of Harold Baxter mainly, together with another spirit that visits me often. Her name is Jane. She seems to appear for no reason. She's led me to this room many times."

"But you don't know who she is?" Marcus's eyes searched deep into my soul. Jane's identity was becoming known to me as I suddenly thought she could have been the baby in the photograph of which William Baxter had produced during Alice's reading.

"You don't think....." I sat, bewildered at my own theory.

"It's possible. I've never met Alice's daughter. How old does she appear when she visits you?"

"I've always thought she looks around mid-forties."

"Do you think Alice asked you to read for her to see if Jane would come through?"

"It's possible."

"Or did you feel it was only her husband she sought confirmation from?"

"I don't know. She was pleased to know William was with us, she didn't mention Harold during the reading, and she certainly didn't mention Jane. When I told her about the photograph she began to cry."

"I think you need to talk to her, get to the bottom of it. This is your home now, not Harold's. They have no right putting this kind of pressure on you." So Marcus did believe me. He was every bit sympathetic towards me and I was relieved to say the least.

"I'll phone her, ask her to come to the house, you too if you'd like to hear what she has to say."

"I'd appreciate that. It's very mysterious isn't it? Quite exciting really, to think that we could be uncovering a deep and dark secret." He stood up, looking at the clock on the mantle. "I need to go, said I'd be at the church meeting by two. We're discussing flowers for summer." He rolled his eyes. "I can't wait!"

"All part of being a vicar, I suppose." I followed him into the kitchen, accepting his kiss before he left, agreeing to meet up that night for dinner.

I felt I had made a breakthrough so far as Jane was concerned and particularly as Marcus seemed to believe me. What I wanted to know was when she passed, and if indeed she was the love child of Harold and Alice. And who was the daughter who lived in Aberdeen. If indeed there was another daughter in Aberdeen.

My head was beginning to hurt as more questions appeared before me. I knew I wouldn't have been able to rest until I found the answers. I hoped Alice would be able to give me those answers and we could move forward, making it possible for the spirits of Harold and Jane to finally be laid to rest. And then there was the issue of William Baxter. Had he murdered his brother? The re-enactment which had taken place in my bedroom some months previously told me he had. I always had faith in my visions, and I was determined to continue believing in myself.

I went back to the reading room, wondering if I would find out anything else. But so far I had only found out what I already knew, about Harold having an affair with Alice. I needed to read on, perhaps discover when a child was born to them. If the love-child was Jane, she would have been forty-five, maybe forty-six.

I heard the sound of twigs falling again before Jane appeared once more. She stood in front of me, smiling, a beautiful expression of which I had never seen. She looked happy, contented, her eyes exuding kindness whilst she looked into mine, passing her thoughts to me.

"Everything will be alright now," she said. At that stage I didn't know what she meant. But I had a feeling Alice would be able to tell me.

Chapter Thirty-Two

*D*arkness began to overwhelm the skies; the rain had stopped at least, leaving an intense starry night. The lights at Rosehill started to flicker, a sign of astral presence as I walked the corridors in order to find and connect with my guest. Significant noise emitted from a guest room, the one where a child's rocking horse stood from years ago. The hinges of its door menaced my thoughts as I entered the room, laid out for visitors who wished to use it. My offers of hospitality had often been extended to those of another plane, knowing it was the most comfortable for their needs. I was sure it was used regularly. Being in the east wing of the house, it was furthest away from my own bedroom and therefore often forgotten about by me, until my astral guests became a little too noisy.

I realised as I walked into the room that a car had drawn up in the driveway, its door closed as I heard footsteps on the gravel. I looked out of the window and saw Marcus making his way round to the back. It was quite early and, even though I was about to welcome spirit communication, I was glad of his company. I left the room and went downstairs to greet him, meeting him in the kitchen.

"This is a surprise," I said. "I didn't think you were coming tonight." I kissed him.

"I wasn't going to but I've been sat thinking about poor Alice all day."

"What about Alice?"

"I'd like to find out more about this diary that seemed to belong to her brother-in-law. Have you read anymore?"

"Not yet, I was thinking of doing before you arrived." I kissed him again. "But I'd rather you were here."

He wrapped his arms around me. "Can I stay tonight?"

"You don't have to ask that, Marcus," I said. "I don't mind sharing Rosehill with you."

⁂

He left early the next morning, urging me to phone Alice before he got in the car. "She might like to see the diary," he said. "Let me know what she says."

"I'll speak to her, ask her round for supper or something, maybe tomorrow night?"

"That would be fine with me. I'll talk to you later." I watched as he drove away before going back inside.

I spent the day shopping in Kingsway. I didn't tend to go often but when I did I would make a day of it. By the time I got home it was approaching supper time for the dogs which I made before noticing the diary still sat upon my kitchen table, a country-scene marking the page in which I had reached. I thought I'd put it away before I left the house but I wasn't so sure, having Marcus there seemed to send my head into a spin half the time. Nothing of much interest had grabbed my attention so far, apart from the confirmation of his affair with Alice and the love child possibly being Jane, but that was something I could have worked out myself, with the help of spirit guidance. No more light shone through the window, for darkness was now upon me. False light above from the chandelier was hopeful but I decided to shine my torch upon the words.

> *13th August 1964*
> *Words cannot describe the elation I feel, yet I know I have no right to feel this way. I respect her honesty. I'm finding it hard to write down the words but I want to look back on this day and remember when it was that Alice told me she is pregnant with our child. I have questioned her, unfortunately upsetting her when she thought I didn't believe the child could be mine. But she assures me it is. A part of me wants*

to help, offer support, but I don't think she'll accept my gesture.

I don't want to be angry for thinking she will tell William the child is his. She won't leave him, even though I've suggested it. The child is due in February; she wanted to be sure it was mine before she told me the news. I feel she has betrayed me somewhat. Has she slept with William? But I have no right to feel betrayed for he is her husband. I am only her lover.

I felt sad for Harold. He had obviously loved this woman so much that he was willing to sacrifice his relationship with her together with his child, because she had vowed she would never leave her husband. He seemed like an amazing man. A man of whom I felt I ought to have known.

5th September 1964
I wonder every minute of every day about my child. I haven't seen Alice for almost four weeks and I miss her. She doesn't want to visit me at Rosehill and I can't understand why. My love for her will never end and she must know this. I desperately want to see her. William is still away at sea, as far as I am aware he will not be back for another month.

I heard a voice last night whilst I lay in my bed. It was that of a woman; well spoken, perhaps well educated. She kept saying, "I am alone," but I couldn't make out any more words. I felt she was talking to me. I hope to hear the voice again tonight.

6th September 1964
The voice of the ghost woman didn't appear. If she did visit me, I couldn't hear her. I'm going to visit Alice later. I can no longer sit and wonder about our child, about the love I have for this woman. I'm going to declare my love to her and hope she will reciprocate.

I wondered who the ghost woman was of whom Harold wrote about. When I first took occupancy of Rosehill, that room had obvious signs of having previously been used on a regular basis, I thought by the previous owner. Of course, the house was in a very tired state and in desperate need of renovation, but wall paper still clung to the walls, there were remnants of chintz curtains hanging at both windows and a bed still stood against a wall, its mattress having been feasted upon by desperate mice and insects. For me to be able to understand Harold better I realised that if this were the case, it would be appropriate for me to continue reading the diary from this room, perhaps being able to connect with his spirit and learn what the lady had meant earlier.

The room was once more cold, as though unheated unlike the rest of the house. I sat upon the bed, a new king size mattress on a four-poster. Even though my skin felt cold, my heart was feeling signs of warmth, the common indication that a loving and positive energy was within my space. I was eager to make contact. It seemed the energy was too. I held the diary in my hand, the torch in my other. It was particularly dark underneath the canopy and so I moved to the chaise longue which stood at the foot. Floorboards creaked, the familiar sound of someone moving alerted me, making me turn my head towards an antique wardrobe that stood against a wall. There, a shadow appeared, a still figure trying to manifest. I looked at the diary of which I needed to continue reading.

7th September 1964
I went to see Alice yesterday evening. She answered the door looking more beautiful than I have ever seen her. I noticed the bump, our child growing inside her remarkably tiny frame. I wanted to hold her as soon as she looked at me but I stood back, unsure as to why she seemed displeased to see me. I asked if I could go inside and she agreed, saying not for long. We stood in the hallway, unable to find the right words to break the ice. I told her I loved her. She told me I had to leave.

I am heartbroken but I did leave her, I didn't want to upset her by outstaying my welcome. Rosehill felt cold upon my return and I drank myself to sleep, devastated, and perhaps a little angry.

I could understand Harold's anger; having been disallowed from having anything to do with his unborn child and being rejected by his lover, I was starting to feel incredibly sorry for this man. And I started to see Alice in a new light.

The diary continued but with no mention of Alice. That was until February 1965 when I suspected I would read further of this somewhat tragic love story. William seemed to be under no illusion that the child was his yet his work took him away when it was born. According to Harold's words, he didn't want to be around when his wife gave birth to their child, for he felt his wife was beneath him, child birth was a woman's thing, of less importance to that of a man's work.

15th February 1965
Went to the Brannington Arms to meet George. He congratulated me on becoming an uncle. Alice had a girl, yesterday. I'm going to call her my Valentine Baby. Alice has called her, Jane. I like that name. I drank too much at the pub and almost told George that I'm the father but I stopped myself when Arnold offered me a cigar and asked me to join him in a toast for the proud father, William.

I can't believe this is happening. I feel as though I'm telling lies to my friends in the village. How could anyone not know I'm the father? Every time I think of Alice with our daughter, my heart aches to be with them. William doesn't deserve either of them; deserting her the way he did. I'm always here for her. I just wish I could tell her and insist that she understood once and for all.

It was at that point in the diary where a number of pages had been torn out. I had no idea why of course, but I wanted to assume it was because Harold had written about visiting Alice and his daughter, only to destroy the evidence at a later date. My mind was buzzing with possible facts. But the hour was late and my eyes were straining to continue reading.

<hr>

"You haven't reached the best bit." A voice awoke me from my rest. I had collapsed with fatigue upon the four-poster, comfortable yet now incredibly cold, my limbs shivering as I sat up to establish who was making contact at three in the morning.

"Who are you?" I asked.

Having woken me, the voice could no longer be heard. Perhaps I had been dreaming; it happened often when I would suddenly wake to the sound of voices, only to assume it had been a vivid dream. Still dressed, I got beneath the sheets, covering my freezing body, making a mental note to check the radiator once the heating was back on in the morning.

Chapter Thirty-Three

The following day, I phoned Alice and invited her for supper. We agreed a day so I phoned Marcus to make sure he was able to join us too. I didn't want to read any more of the diary until I had spoken to Alice, feeling I needed to know more about the man whose life I was discovering by his own admissions.

Marcus arrived late afternoon, looking particularly dashing. I made him a drink and he asked to go into the reading room.

"Have you found anything else?" he asked.

"I have to be honest with you, Marcus, I'm surprised that you seem to believe me."

He looked at me and smiled. "I'm surprised myself," he said. "Part of me doesn't want to believe it but I know that Anne's here, so I guess I have no reason not to believe in Harold."

"But doesn't it go against your faith?"

"Of course it does. I'm angry with myself for letting it go this far." He sighed. "But I can't deny what I think is happening." He held me in his arms. "What time is Alice due?" he asked.

"I told her seven o'clock."

He looked at his watch. "It's only four thirty. Any ideas what we can do to kill the time?"

I kissed him before pulling away and walking towards the door. "I need to be ready when Alice gets here. I need to keep a clear head, make sure I ask the right questions." I turned back to face him and stroked his face. "There's always tonight, after she's gone. You are staying aren't you?"

"If you'll have me. I don't have any plans tomorrow so we could have a lie in." That sounded good.

"There we are then, that's settled. Now make yourself comfy in the lounge and I'll make us a coffee."

The television was on in the kitchen. I had thought I could hear voices as I approached the door until I realised it was the sound of the news channel, being watched by an unseen force. I felt the evening was going to be fascinating; I also felt that Alice was not to be our only guest.

She arrived at seven o'clock. The kettle had already boiled on the Aga, cups and saucers waiting. I thought she seemed a little nervous as she wandered into the kitchen, probably eager to ask me why I had invited her for supper. Marcus stood to greet her, gently taking hold of her hands.

"Sit down, Alice," I beckoned, pointing at a chair.

"It's a cold night," she said, rubbing her hands together, cupping them around her mouth as she warmed them with her breath. "I expect it takes a lot of heat to warm this old place?"

"It does," I replied. "But I don't have heating in all the rooms, mainly the ones which are used." I passed her the tea. "I've made a beef stew. Marcus's idea, he's more expert in the kitchen than I am." He laughed.

"It smells delicious. I've hardly eaten anything today. Been suffering with a sore throat for a while."

"Oh? Have you seen the doctor?" I asked.

"Oh yes, I've been on antibiotics but they're finished now. He said to see how I am in a few days and if I'm no better he'll give me another prescription."

"I think we're always prone to something when the seasons are changing," I said, dishing out the stew onto the plates. "Is that enough for you, Alice?"

"Plenty, dear. Thank you. I do appreciate you asking me up here. It's such a beautiful place."

"Yes, it is. I love Rosehill."

"Me too," Marcus said, smiling at me then sitting down at the table.

I didn't want Alice to feel as though I had only invited her to Rosehill in order to question her about Harold, but part of me suspected she already knew. Her handbag sat on the floor beside her chair, heavily protruding an obviously large item.

"How long have you lived in the village, Alice?" I asked.

"All my life, dear. I was born at Kingsway and my father was a farm labourer. We lived in one of the Dene View cottages."

"That's the place on the other side of the village," Marcus pointed out. "Vera Thompson's son owns it now."

"That's right. He's making a good job of it, too," Alice said.

"And did your husband live in the village?" I asked.

"Oh yes. His family owned Dene View Farm. His father and mine were best friends."

"I take it William didn't want to work on the farm?"

"No, he wasn't interested. He always wanted to be a sailor. His father was disappointed but Harold worked on the farm for a few years, before he opened a shop."

"I believe Harold had a DIY shop on the outskirts of Brannington. Am I right, Alice?" Marcus asked.

"Yes, he did. He loved that place, too. He and Bernard Slater ran it together."

"I don't know that name," Marcus said.

"Their family moved away a long time ago. Bernard was the youngest of six brothers. They're all scattered around the country as far as I know."

"Did the shop do well?"

"For a while. After..." she paused. "After Harold died, Bernard ran it himself for a few years then he sold it. The new owners turned it into a newsagents but it never took off, there was already a paper shop within the post office. It just became a house after that."

"And your husband worked away at sea?"

"Yes, for a long time." She looked down at her empty plate.

"Some more stew, Alice?" I asked.

"Not for me, thank you. That was absolutely delicious."

I got up from the table and reached for the plate of cakes I had left out on the worktop. "How about one of these?" I said. "I made them myself."

"They look lovely. I don't do much baking these days," Alice said. "I haven't got the inclination." She took one of the cupcakes.

"I didn't know you baked," Marcus said, taking a cake too.

"Don't get used to it," I laughed. "It doesn't happen often. I made these this morning."

Alice looked at Marcus then back at me. "Am I right in thinking you two are together?"

We both smiled. "You are. We haven't told anyone yet." I looked proudly at Marcus as he was just cramming his mouth full of cupcake. "I'm waiting for Marcus to make the announcement. I think it'll sound better coming from him."

"Why's that?" she asked.

"Well, I think with him being the vicar and well known in the community. I don't know many people round here yet."

"There's one or two talking about you at church, you know." Alice sat back in her chair, carefully breaking off bits of her cake before popping it into her mouth.

"Who's talking about us?" Marcus asked, his mouth still full of food.

"Oh, you know, ladies at church. We notice things in a small village, vicar."

"Of course you do. I realised that when I first moved here." Marcus finished chewing and took a drink.

"There's no shame in it. Everyone's thrilled for you. A man in your position should have a wife by his side." I looked over at Marcus who was looking surprisingly comfortable after what Alice had just said.

"We're not married, Alice!" I said.

"Oh, I know that, but you should, you make a lovely couple. And you can both cook. That's a lot more than most couples I know. In my day, it was a woman's privilege to cook for her husband, or any man for that matter. Times change, and to be honest, I think in that respect, they've changed for the better." She helped herself to another cake.

"I don't mind cooking for Marcus," I said, "but the first time we had dinner together he cooked a gorgeous lamb stew. I think I should leave him to it." Marcus pulled a face at me, his idea of cooking for me perhaps meant once in a while.

"The last vicar that was here, he got married later on in life. He met his wife when he was on holiday. Next thing we knew she was living in the vicarage with him. They'd had a private wedding down south where she came from. If you two decide to get married one day, you must let us villagers know, it should be a celebration."

I smiled. "We'll be sure to let you know, Alice," I said, watching Marcus help himself to another cake.

"Do you have much to do here now?" Alice asked, looking round the room.

"Just a few rooms left to renovate. But they're not urgent. The house is big enough that I'm rattling round in it as it is."

"Much too big for one, eh?" Alice winked at me, before glancing at Marcus. I loved her sense of humour.

We finished the last of the cakes and drank our tea, Alice seeming quite comfortable in our company. I suggested we moved into the lounge as I wanted her to be completely relaxed when I talked about Harold and the diary.

"Can I get you a sherry, Alice?" Marcus asked, as we walked through the lounge door.

"That would be lovely, vicar. Just a small one though, I have to drive home."

"You can call me Marcus if you like." He smiled before reaching for the decanter. I could feel spirit presence in the room, an energy shifting from side to side, probably as nervous as I was. It was a feminine entity and I suspected it was Jane. But she was reluctant to show herself, as though waiting in the wings to hear what I had to say.

We sat down and Marcus handed out the glasses of sherry. I noticed how he had left a respectable gap between us as he sat down on the sofa beside me, perhaps his professionalism as a vicar hovering on the surface.

"Alice," I began, "do you mind if I talk about Harold?" I couldn't wait any longer; the desire to speak about him was burning.

She looked around the room. "Is he here?"

"I don't think so, not right now." I made a note of where the energy was most prominent. "No, I'm quite sure he isn't." I didn't think it wise at that stage to tell her that Jane could have been with us.

Alice looked at Marcus. He was looking straight at her, waiting for her reaction when I mentioned Harold. I continued.

"You see, the thing is I found something the other day, which belongs to him."

"Harold?"

"Yes," I replied.

She smiled at me. "He lived here for a while, did you know?"

"I've realised that recently." I smiled back at her. I felt she wanted to talk about when he lived at Rosehill, about the memories she would always have of their involvement. But I needed my questions answered.

"Alice?" I looked towards the reluctant shadow now hovering in the corner of the room. "I found Harold's diary. It was in the room where I carry out my readings with clients." She stopped smiling. "I suspected there was something hiding inside the chimney and when I went to feel about in there, I found it. I'm not sure why Harold would have hidden it but I have read some of it."

Alice nodded, taking a large sip of sherry. It was obviously no secret to her why the diary had been hidden, and therefore no surprise to her that the diary existed in the first place.

"What have you read, my dear, you must know an awful lot about me by now."

A wise woman, I thought. "He writes about you, about your affair." I turned to Marcus who was still staring at Alice. "He also writes about the child you had. He says you named the child Jane."

It was at that point the energy crossed the room; I felt a blast of cold air brush past my face. Spirit now stood beside her mother, still unprepared to manifest yet willing to make me aware of her presence.

I continued. "I think the child in the photograph which William showed to me, is Jane. His anger at learning he wasn't the father made him do something terrible, didn't it Alice?"

Her eyes had started to fill up with tears. "What are you saying?" she asked.

"There's no easy way to put this. He got away with murder, didn't he?" I hoped I hadn't pushed her too far.

"It's all right, Alice," Marcus said. "You're amongst friends. We won't say anything to anyone, you have our word."

"Did you know about the murder," I asked, grateful of Marcus's understanding.

She looked from him to me, then back to him again, tears now flowing steadily down her face. "What could I have done?" she said, as she shrugged and shook her head. "The police would never have believed me. In those days we had a local bobby on the pavements, popping into houses for morning coffee. William was my husband. I had to be loyal to him."

"He found out about you two, didn't he?" I asked.

Alice finished her sherry, placing the empty glass onto the coffee table.

"I've lived with it for many years. But I had a young child to bring up, a child who needed a father. Women didn't leave their husbands back then, they stuck by them through thick and thin. Not like today.

A man only needs to say a cross word to his wife these days and she's off to the solicitors." Alice tutted.

"You told me William knew nothing about the child not being his. Was that true?"

She looked down at her trembling hands. "Yes," she said, quietly. "I let him believe Jane was his daughter. She had a family resemblance. He loved her more than anything. Much more than he ever loved me." Marcus took Alice's glass and refilled it before placing it back on the table before her. "She died, not longer after William. It was nearly five years ago. She was only forty one. Vicar, you've seen her photograph, haven't you?" Alice looked at him for clarification. He smiled at her before turning to me.

"Of course I have. She was very beautiful." He turned back to Alice. "She looked like you." Alice just about managed a smile, the tears continuing to fall.

It was then that Alice completely broke down, sobbing with the heaviest sighs as she sat uncontrollably emotional.

"Did she live in Aberdeen?" I asked, almost in a whisper. "Is she the daughter who married a consultant?"

Marcus moved to sit by her and held her against his shoulder. I reached for the tissue box.

"Yes, she was happy there. But she left her husband and moved back in with me. She was devastated after William died." I watched Alice's grief as she sipped her sherry, glad of the comfort from Marcus. "It was like losing my best friend."

"How did she die?" I asked.

Alice blew her nose then scrunched up the tissue, a determined expression on her face. "She died here."

"At Rosehill? In the house?" I asked.

"Yes. After William died I told her about Harold being her father." Alice couldn't look at either Marcus or me. "It was him she should have been grieving for, not William. William didn't deserve her grief."

"So what happened to her?"

"She fell on the stairs." I gasped and Marcus held my hand.

"What was she doing at Rosehill?" he asked.

"I told her it was where Harold had lived. She wanted to come here. I don't know what made her go upstairs but something did. The house was very unstable, as you know."

I turned to Marcus. "Did you know about Jane's death?"

"No, of course not. I would have said something if I had."

"I made sure no one knew. I told people she'd died of a heart attack. She had no reason to be here other than her interest in where Harold lived. And if I went into too much detail about her death, I would have had to explain about Harold, too."

"So who found her?" I asked.

"I did." Alice reached for another tissue. "When she didn't come home that night I had a feeling she might still be here. I walked around the house, came into this room a few times because I kept hearing noises. But then I went towards the stairs because the noises seemed to come from there too, and there she was, face down at the bottom of them."

"Oh, Alice. I'm so sorry."

"She wouldn't have died if I hadn't told her about Harold being her father. But I couldn't let her think that William was. I just couldn't carry on lying to her."

I paused for a moment, realising Alice had obviously been deeply traumatised by the events surrounding Jane's death.

"Alice," I said. "I think William has realised he's not Jane's father since moving on to the spirit world." I waited for her to compose herself and for Marcus to move back to the sofa. "After he showed me the photograph at your reading he moved away, he had an angry expression on his face."

"And you think he was telling me he knew?"

"Yes, I do." I sensed Marcus's discomfort as he crossed his legs, not sure whether to look at Alice or me. But Jane's presence was becoming stronger and I felt Alice needed to know the truth. "I feel Jane is with us now. She hasn't shown herself to me yet, but she is near. I can feel her energy."

Alice once more looked around the room, unable to see the invisible entity. Marcus also seemed to search for a being he couldn't see, a look of alarm covering his face.

"Perhaps Jane didn't visit us during your reading because she knew William was here. Did you expect her to?"

"Of course I did," Alice replied, wiping her tears and sitting up straight. "I also wanted Harold to visit, too, but neither of them bothered did they?" Her anger began to show.

I suddenly thought about the spirit that I had thought had been present at the reading, leaving me unsure as to its identity. "They have visited Rosehill since, many times. Both Jane and Harold directed me to the diary. They obviously wanted me to know the truth." I needed to comfort her now. "But you should know they are together in the spirit world. I feel that Jane is trying to communicate through me in order to contact you."

"Can you speak to her?"

"I can feel her with us. She's saying she wants you to forgive William."

"Forgive William?" Alice raised her voice a little. "He killed her father. Why would she ask me to do that?"

"Jane saw William as her father, Alice. She only knew the truth just before she died. She loved William."

"But why?"

"Like girls love their fathers I suppose. I never knew my real father. But I know that Jane still thinks of William as hers, despite what he did."

"He loved her, alright. They were inseparable for a long time. He was distraught when she moved away to get married."

"There's also another reason she wants you to forgive, Alice." I looked at Marcus who seemed increasingly uncomfortable at the conversation. "If you don't forgive William, he'll never be free. He could go on to haunt Rosehill and even have a hold over Harold for eternity. You loved him, didn't you?"

"Yes. But I loved Harold, too."

"He knows that. That's why he's so angry all the time with Harold. I need to release their spirits, let them continue their journey in peace. Unless you're willing to forgive, that can never be possible." Marcus squeezed my hand, and shifted on the sofa.

"But what about William? Where is he in the spirit world?"

"He lingers, Alice. He committed a terrible crime. There is always justice in the spirit world."

"And where will I end up? With William or Harold?" Marcus rose from the sofa; his mood was evident.

"You will end up where you want to be" I answered. "Should that be with Harold and your daughter then that will be up to you. You shouldn't worry about that now, you have a life to live here."

Marcus moved to the window, staring out. Jane stayed by her mother's side, desperately wanting to make contact with her and waiting for my help. Her energy was now strong. I realised it was her who had been so determined to possess me, testing me to see if I would communicate with her mother. I had been wrong; thinking the energy had been that of a strong male and allowing her to trick me. I vowed then, never to let it happen again.

"I'm seventy eight years old. I do worry about dying. "

"If you want to see the diary, you can. But I think it should be kept here, at Rosehill." I hadn't intended to offer but perhaps she needed closure.

"I might like to have a look one day. Have you read it all?"

"Not yet, I've read up to Jane's birth. There were some missing pages after that, it seemed like they had been torn out. Did Harold visit you after Jane was born?"

Alice eventually calmed down and Marcus returned to the sofa. "Yes," she answered. "He came every day until William got back. But William never went back to sea after he came home and saw Jane; he was totally smitten with her and decided to find work nearby."

"So what happened to Harold?" I asked.

"He still visited us, but William was always at home. Harold became the doting uncle. I was able to come up here, bring Jane with me, because William didn't suspect." It was beginning to make sense.

"I wonder if they were the pages which were missing."

"Did Harold write anything else after that?" Alice asked, shuffling on the sofa, brushing her shoulder as if shooing a fly from its resting place. I suspected Jane had tried to comfort her and she had felt the invisible hand.

"There are more entries, but I haven't read any of them yet. I wanted to talk to you first, try to understand everything."

"Shall I make some coffee?" Marcus asked.

"That's a lovely idea. Would you like a cup, Alice?"

"Not for me, my dears, I need to go. I've been here far too long and it's way past my bed time." It was nine o'clock.

We both stood up, Alice bent down to pick up her bag. She opened it up, carefully reaching in to reveal the item that had made it seem so rounded.

"I thought you might like to see this," she said, passing it to me.

"It's lovely. Who is it?" I looked at the familiar faces in the picture.

Alice pointed at the people in turn. "That's William," she said, "and that's Harold. Can you see the family resemblance?"

"Definitely," I replied. "They were very much alike."

"That's me, of course, and that is Jane." She stroked Jane's face. "She was so beautiful."

Harold was stood beside Alice, his hand on her shoulder, his expression melancholy. William, who held Jane against his body, was almost laughing, portraying the father figure proudly. I looked at the background of the image.

"The place looks familiar," I said.

"It was taken here, at the front of the house. Harold invited us up one Sunday lunch to introduce us to his new lady friend." Alice held the photograph in shaking hands. "She was a nice woman, but her mother didn't approve of their relationship. I remember her telling us. I felt as though we had something in common right from the moment I met her." She seemed unable to move her gaze away from the black and white image, now resting in my hands.

"Did they marry?" I asked.

"Oh no, they weren't together very long. But I liked her." I gave the picture back to Alice and she returned it to her bag, closing the zip as though to protect her lost happiness.

"Did she take the photograph?" I asked.

"Yes. Harold didn't seem keen when I suggested one of him and her together."

Marcus helped her put on her coat. For a woman of such late years she was still able to drive about the countryside, enjoying her independence, perhaps more than being alone.

"Don't forget, you two," she began, "be sure to make the announcement when there's a wedding." She took gloves out of her coat pocket and put them on, then continued, "you can't keep secrets in this village."

"You'll be the first to know," Marcus said, opening the back door.

I hugged her before she left. "You're welcome to come up anytime. If you want to read the diary just ring me. Or if you just want some company, I'm always here."

Her face touched mine as we embraced. "You haven't read the best bit," she whispered into my ear.

I stepped back with astonishment, remembering I had heard the words spoken only a couple of nights previously, but by someone I suspected was from the spirit world. Alice seemed as surprised as I did as we stood a few feet apart. Marcus was hovering at her car, holding the door open, a little impatient as he began to hop from one foot to the other. I doubt she knew what had just happened as I wondered which entity had possessed her.

We watched at the door as she drove away, feeling as though we had just said goodbye to a very dear friend. I couldn't end the night without taking another look at Harold's diary, Marcus would have to understand my haste at needing to find out what "the best bit" was.

Chapter Thirty-Four

*I*t was deathly quiet in the house. Marcus chose to go to bed on his own, a little reluctant. With the diary held tightly in my hands I went back to the four-poster guest room and resumed my position on the bed, sitting upright against the headboard. I stretched out my legs, placing the diary onto my lap. I leaned over to switch on the bedside lamp and the bulb blew, prompting me to switch on the torch I had left there earlier. With the glow from the torch I was just able to see the words on each page. Excitement ran through me when I should have been in a state of fatigue. With a possession having recently taken place at Rosehill I knew I had to get to the bottom of Harold's mysterious life.

I opened the book, removing the bookmark. There wasn't much of interest as I flicked through the pages, it more of less told me of Harold's job and his obvious unhappiness in the situation with Alice. I was feeling quite tired, but I continued to read on nonetheless.

The silence is the room pursued. The atmosphere was beginning to appear a little uncomfortable and I shifted position, unsure of the sudden feeling that I was no longer alone. I looked around the room upon hearing a few footsteps coming from the opposite corner, some tapping sounds beside me, a high pitched cry yearning for my attention, seemingly from near the north facing window. I turned my concentration back to the diary, determined not to let distractions cause me to close the book.

1st April 1965
I met someone today at work, a beautiful young woman, polite and gentle. I want to ask her out for dinner but I didn't take her phone number. She only came in to buy a saw. But I can't get her out of my mind. Going to ask Bernard if he knows who she is.

5th April 1965
I couldn't believe it, the woman came into the shop today; she's called Betty, and she shook my hand. I've asked her out tomorrow night. I feel a bit disloyal to Alice, but why? What's wrong with me? Oh well, suppose I need to move on. If it works out with Betty I'll invite William and Alice to Rosehill for dinner, so that they can meet her. She lives in Woodley, looks about mid twenties. I've never seen such beautiful hair on a woman in my life, brown and shiny, I think they call it brunette. She looks nothing like Alice, though they're both beautiful in their own way. I don't think I'll mention to Alice that I've met Betty. Not sure how she'll take it. I know she wants to stay married to William, but I keep getting the impression that she still fancies me. I'm not going to say anything, though. I'll see whether Betty will go out with me and take it from there.

I smiled, realising that Harold was portraying himself to be somewhat of a philanderer. It was almost midnight. Hearing heavy footsteps in the corridor outside the bedroom, I wondered why Marcus had got out of bed, and went to the door. Perhaps he wanted to sleep with me, snuggling into my bed alone being the colder of the two options. I opened the door and peeped into the hallway, expecting to come face to face with him. But the corridor was empty. It was oppressively dark as I leant against the casing, confused at having nothing to see. The footsteps shifted into the bedroom, heavy shoes of which I suspected belonged to a male entity, now with me as I turned around, closing the door behind me.

I could feel spirit's eyes boring into me, watching me, waiting for my next move. I was uneasy, afraid this spirit had brought negative energy into my home. I got back on the bed, making myself comfortable as I picked up the diary.

"Who are you?" I asked out, noticing the sudden temperature drop. The sensation of being watched continued. I tried not to let spirit see that I was worried; if it was a negative force it would only have wallowed in my fear. I opened the diary again and began to read from where I left off, a part of me wondering if the negative force was trying to stop me reading. But the determined fire within me reached down, turning the pages into sense as I tried hard to banish thoughts of the possible angry spirit.

Tapping started, like the rhythm of a heartbeat. I pointed the glow of the torch onto the page which lay before me. A line had been drawn through some of Harold's words; I suspected he must have changed his mind about what he wanted to write. My attention returned to the north facing window as a sudden gust of wind appeared to blow towards me. The pages of the diary flapped about in my hands, turning over and losing the words I was just about to read.

24th April 1965
Betty stayed last night. She was amazing. I didn't think I could love again after Alice, but I think I'm falling in love with Betty. We made love for the first time. I can't believe our relationship has moved on so fast but I've never felt this excited before. She loves being at Rosehill with me so I think she will be happy living here. Alice and William are coming for lunch tomorrow. I'm really looking forward to introducing them to Betty. Alice has never been in touch. I realise she doesn't want me involved with Jane's upbringing but I keep thinking how nice it would be to see her, not just as an uncle.

The tapping became louder, accompanied by heavy breathing. I was annoyed at spirit's determination not to present before me, yet to distress me with invisible noise.

"Why don't you show yourself?" I asked. "I'm not scared of you. If you want to communicate that's what I'm here for."

I realised it could have been William; his name kept coming into my head. That scared me. Each time William had visited Rosehill, he had brought a negativity which I didn't like. I knew he stood near the window; it was as though his energy was circling like a cyclone ready to explode. But I had to stay strong, make him see that I wasn't afraid of him even though he continued to knock against the opposite wall. His presence only inspired me more, as I wondered what he could be so upset about when his brother had met someone else. Harold no longer wanted to be with Alice. The love of his life now seemed to be a lady called Betty.

26th April 1965
Lunch went well yesterday. I thought Alice looked a little uncomfortable when they first arrived but then again she could have been tired. Jane was asleep in her pram. I kept looking at her, wondering if she will ever realise who her real father is. William took an instant liking to Betty, I could tell with the way he kept touching her arm. I was a bit annoyed when I caught Betty flirting with him in the kitchen. We took a few photographs with William's new camera, very state of the art. Betty took a photograph of the rest of us. William was holding Jane in his arms, I stood next to Alice putting my arm around her and expecting her to brush me away, but she didn't. I hope Betty didn't see how sad I was. She stayed again last night and I left her in bed this morning. I was late for work, the shop didn't open up until 8.15. But it was worth it. Lying next to her soft skin is the best feeling in the world. I could have stayed there all day, making love to her, kissing her beautiful lips. Part of me wishes I'd met her before I fell in love with Alice, perhaps things would have been different. But then again, I wouldn't have Jane.

The pages blew in the make shift breeze once again, taking me to the first week in May.

A warm day, birds singing, buds beginning to flower. Rosehill is glorious at this time of year. I keep thinking about asking Betty to marry me, but I don't know if it's too soon. She seems really keen on me and she's always eager to stay at the house over night. I think some of the locals have been talking about us. I'm not going to stop inviting her to stay just because they think it's wrong. It's nothing to do with them. I suspect old Mrs Smythe is one of them. She was in the shop last week and I noticed she was looking at me funny. They can all keep their noses out.

I sensed the spirit was becoming restless as the bed began to shudder. With the door shut and the lights off, even I felt anxious. Should I have been able to make contact, I would have known whom the spirit was that seemed steadfast in keeping his identity a secret. I still suspected it was William, warning me about reading the diary

10th May 1965
Betty doesn't know about Jane but perhaps I should tell her. I want our relationship to be based on trust, not just love. Bernard keeps laughing at me, says he's never seen me this happy. Sometimes I'd love to tell him about Alice and Jane, but I know there's no point. He'll never understand. I'm not sure I understand myself. I saw Alice in the village yesterday, pushing Jane in the pram. I didn't bother to stop and say hello because I noticed the couple from the Blacksmith's cottage walking towards her.

11th May 1965
I heard the ghostly voice again last night. I couldn't make out what it said but it was like a high pitched scream near the window. I went to have a look but nothing there. There were lots of tapping noises too. Not sure what this means.

I've decided, I'm definitely going to ask Betty to marry me, but I'll choose the right moment. I'll get my hair cut in town and buy a new pair of trousers. Might even stretch to a new tie.

Further entries in the diary confirmed to me that Harold did indeed occupy the guest room as his bedroom. I felt a strong sense of belonging to him, as though reading his diary had been something I was always meant to do, even before finding Rosehill. My eyes were hurting, feeling like stones were caught between the lids. It was time for me to close the book and return to Marcus. The diary would have to wait until morning, providing Marcus didn't have other plans. Of which I thought he might.

The floorboards creaked on my way back to bed, unusually loud. I knew someone walked behind me, the footsteps told me so. Rather unnerved I reached my bedroom, the door slightly ajar. Marcus was sound asleep, facing the old Victorian chest of drawers. I could hear his gentle breathing, his sighs washing away his daily routine as I climbed in next to him, softly snuggling up to his warm body trying not to wake him. He stirred, turning over to lie on his back, his arms lifted above his head. And then he spoke the words to me; the words I had heard twice before.

"You haven't read the best bit." But it wasn't his voice, it was that of another male, a snigger in his tone.

I sat up and looked at him but he didn't wake. The ambience in the room was edgy; my eyes scanned the darkness as it closed in around me, the words echoing through my mind in a bid to have me understand. The spirit which had followed me along the hallway now stood at the foot of my bed, fully manifested, waiting for my reaction. Red eyes bore into mine as a smile rested upon a superior expression. I felt threatened, more than I ever had since discovering my mediumship. Marcus continued to breathe softly, oblivious to his side of the bed being jolted.

"What do you want?" I whispered, my eyes averting to Marcus to confirm I hadn't woken him. "Are you William?"

No words left spirit's mouth, yet his smile broadened as his laugh became prominent; a high pitched sound screeched through my ears causing me to cover them.

"I want you to leave. You have no business here. Leave, and allow Harold to rest in peace." The laugh got louder, the screech almost unbearable. "Get out!" I shouted realising my voice was bound to awaken Marcus.

It did. His sudden movement as he sat up in bed caused spirit to fade, a mist hovering in its place.

"It's okay, I'm fine," I said, as Marcus reached for me, pulling me onto his chest.

"Has something happened?"

"No, just a bad dream." I stroked his silver chest hair, my heart at last slowing down as calm once more overwhelmed me.

"Do you want me to get you some water?"

"Just hold me," I replied. "I just want you to hold me."

"I didn't hear you come to bed," he whispered. "I must have been dead to the world."

"You were." I felt secure again. Once more wrapped in the arms of the man I loved.

Chapter Thirty-Five

We spent the next morning together, walking through the late spring fields, watching the wildlife parade for our entertainment. We managed to catch four deer, grazing in a stock field, seeming to be fearless at our presence. They kept on looking up at us, perhaps desperate to see us walk in the opposite direction. It was a rare sunny day, clouds scattered like bits of cotton wool against a blue collage. "What was your dream about last night?" Marcus enquired, catching me mid thought.

"What do you mean?" I asked, not wanting to talk about the presence that visited me in my bedroom. "I don't remember dreaming anything last night."

"You were shouting in your sleep. You can't have been in bed long."

"I read a little more of the diary. It's an interesting book. Perhaps I was dreaming about that." I smiled, hoping to divert his attention to another subject. I thought about telling him of the words he spoke, unknowingly through the voice of a spirit. But I decided not to.

"I'm sure it is interesting. I'll read it when you've finished."

I slipped my arm through his, resting my head on his shoulder. If only it could always be like this, I thought. Marcus and I could be good together.

"Has Anne been back, do you think?" I asked, a little cautiously.

"I don't know. Why do you ask?"

"I've noticed how you seem to believe me more about spirit contact."

"I don't find it easy."

"I don't expect you to. I imagine it's deeply concerning for you."

"Of course it is. If anyone finds out about what's been happening, that'll be the end of me at the church."

"Oh, I doubt that, Marcus," I said. "The parishioners love you. You're a popular vicar."

"Perhaps. But I still shouldn't be having these conflicting beliefs. It's wrong, Camilla. You know that as well as I do."

"But you're not going to lie to yourself. You've admitted to me that you've seen Anne."

"Only you. I'm struggling to admit it to myself right now."

"What do you mean?" I stopped.

"I hate myself for this. I'm a vicar, a man of God."

"Yes, but you're also a man. You have thoughts and feelings, you're allowed to have a different opinion to the average mind."

"That's just it though. I'm not. I made a vow to God and now I feel as though I've broken it." He raised his voice and turned his back on me. "I knew I shouldn't have told you about Anne."

"But why, Marcus." I moved to stand before him so he had no choice but to face me again. "I can help you. I've accepted your beliefs, and I assume you've accepted mine. Why are you so angry with yourself. It's not your fault that Anne has contacted you. She's done that for a reason."

"She's done it because she's selfish. I talked to her about joining the church before she died. She hated the idea of me being a vicar, of her being the vicar's wife. That's why I didn't do it when she was alive."

"So, do you think she's come to you because she doesn't want you to be a vicar anymore? Or is she angry with you?"

"I'd say it was both reasons." He carried on walking, looking round at the landscape before he stopped again. He sighed. "I don't want to talk about Anne right now," he said, kissing me softly on my lips. "There's no one about."

"We're in the middle of a field," I laughed, glad of the change of subject.

"Yes, in the middle of nowhere." He caressed my neck with his mouth. "I wanted you last night."

"I know, I'm sorry about that." I found myself succumbing to his advances, sinking to the ground as he held out his arm and protected me from hurting myself.

"So, now you can make it up to me."

"You're completely irresistible, do you know that?" I sighed, as he lay on top of me.

"So are you."

He left later that afternoon and even though I was sad to say goodbye to him I felt excited at the prospect of night fall when I planned to resume my position on the guest bed with Harold's diary. I was more determined than ever to reach the best bit. I had no idea what it meant of course but with my heart beating faster than previously, told me it meant something important, something connected to me.

The room was once more quiet, an eerie silence piercing through the shadows as moonlight filtered in. I closed the curtains, large, heavy drapes, the work of a local tapestry-maker. I felt no spirit presence and so I sat down in comfort upon the four-poster, opening the diary and removing the bookmark. With the torch in my right hand I flicked through a few pages with my left, some of which again had been crossed out. I was glad to be alone; Rosehill had a wonderful knack of wrapping itself around me, banishing the coldness that often came with spirit and I loved it for that reason alone. With excitement running through my veins, mysterious thoughts continuously finding their way to the surface, I resumed reading, wondering once again if I would at last find "the best bit".

12th May 1965
William has returned home unexpectedly. He wasn't supposed to be back for two weeks but he came into the shop to tell me he resigned. A part of me thinks he was dismissed but I don't want to ask. He has invited Betty and me round for supper next week. He says he wants to discuss Jane's Christening. I feel a bit cross at the thought of him arranging something that I should be involved with. I have to be the uncle yet I am the father. I don't know how long I can keep up the pretence. Perhaps for the sake of Alice I will have to.

To think that Jane will grow up believing her father to be William is starting to grind me down.

I don't want Betty to notice my despair. I've decided not to tell her about Jane. It will only put her off me, I'm sure. It might even cause a fall out between the four of us when we seem to be getting on so well.

13th May 1965
Betty came round. I decided the time was right to pop the question. She was over the moon when I asked her and even though I don't have a ring to give her, I am ecstatic. I'm taking her into town on Saturday, to look for an engagement ring. I hope she isn't expecting too much.

16th May 1965
We found a beautiful ring for Betty. It didn't cost too much but we need to save up now for the wedding. I want to get married soon but I think she would rather wait until we have enough money to make it a lavish affair. That's okay, I want to please her. She deserves that. We're going out with Alice and William tonight to celebrate our engagement. They're taking us for a meal to The Smokey Corner.

As I reached to turn over the page of the diary, I felt something touch my hand. I recognised it as that of a spirit hand, a gentle touch wanting my attention. I had been, until that point, unaware of spirit presence. The room remained quiet, yet now felt oppressive, my heart racing once more. I dropped the torch and it rolled off the bed, falling onto the floor and I muttered to myself as I leant over to retrieve it. Pulling myself back up, I turned around to see a face, staring at me from the other side of the bed. Naturally startled, I jumped and looked at the manifested spirit which now sat completely still, watching as I tried to calm myself.

"What the .." It sat there, bold and determined, waiting for my obvious reaction. "Mother!"

"Sit down, Camilla," she said, her voice drowning out the sound of my heart thudding against my chest.

"Mum, why are you here?"

"I need to talk to you," she said, as she sat on the bed next to me. "It's time you learnt some things about your life."

I repositioned myself on the bed, feeling a little apprehensive at her unexpected visit. Her voice was as clear as if she had been living. Yet here she sat, in her world of death, communicating to my world of life. She was beautiful. The creases on her face had disappeared and she appeared youthful, much younger than I ever remembered her to be. Her hair sat upon her shoulders, soft curls hugging her face, a little old fashioned in style perhaps but still a glamorous look, one which young women would have yearned to wear during the 1960's. I had photographs of her taken during that decade so I was able to recognise the style in which I saw. She pointed towards the diary.

"I knew you would find it."

"Did you know about this?" I asked.

"Yes, I did. Your grandmother did, too. That's why she brought you here."

"She wanted me to find Harold Baxter's diary?"

"Yes, my darling." She stroked my face. I sat completely still, emotions rushing through me as I could feel my eyes welling up with tears.

"You need to know the truth. You have a right to know."

"To know what?" I asked. "Why do I keep getting messages telling me I haven't read the best bit? I don't understand."

Her eyes glared into mine. I heard a noise from the far corner of the room as a stream of smoke etched its way towards us. The room had suddenly become heavy, the smell of tobacco prominent. My mother stopped stroking my face and pulled away from me. She looked towards the trail of smoke which continued to glide in our direction, her expression had become fearful.

"I have to go," she whispered. "I shouldn't have come." A white mist began to cover her, slowly wrapping itself around her ghostly presence as it appeared to swallow her in a desperate bid to escape from the oncoming smoke trail.

She was gone, as quickly as she had appeared. And I was left with the smell of tobacco burning through my senses. I frantically began flipping through the book, turning each page, wondering what I needed to find. The smoke circled beside me. I had no idea what it meant.

The following day, the phone rang. It was Ross asking if he could come over. He arrived within the hour, somewhat apprehensive as he walked into the kitchen.

"Are you okay," I asked. "You seem a bit nervous."

"I'm fine." He sat down at the table. "I've booked a flight to California."

I tried hard to stop the disappointed expression take hold. "When?"

"Next week."

"I see. I knew you were thinking about it."

"I want to go, Cam. Being over here just isn't for me anymore. I want to get back. I contacted my friend, Tommy the other day, you know, the guy who owns the bars and wants to open another. I told him I was thinking about going back and he wants us to talk about going into business together."

"Are you unhappy over here?" I put the kettle on the Aga to boil.

"I'm lonely. I don't know anyone here anymore, apart from you and the kids. They have their own lives and you, well, you're with Marcus all the time."

"I'm always here for you, Ross."

"I know, but as a friend." He rubbed his mouth with his hands. "I want more."

The kettle reached the boil and I made coffees, passing one to Ross. "What do you mean by that?" I asked.

"While I'm over here I can't stop thinking about you." I sat down opposite him, feeling rather uncomfortable. "I know you and Marcus are an item and I don't want to come between you. But I need to move on with my life; I need to find something else to focus on. Someone else, perhaps."

"What about your ex-girlfriend. Didn't you keep in touch?"

"We phoned each other occasionally, but like I said, she didn't seem to care about us being apart." He sipped his coffee. "And when I came here for that reading last year, I realised I didn't want to be with her anyway."

"It's too late, Ross."

"I know it is. That's why it's time for me to move on. I'm not going to torture myself anymore, thinking there could be a chance for us, knowing underneath that there isn't."

I felt awful. I thought back to the few occasions Ross and I had been alone together; at Rosehill, then at Lucy's house when we were sorting out her things. I hadn't led him on but maybe he thought I wanted more than friendship, too.

"I don't know what to say, Ross. I'm sorry you're going back, I really am. But I'm in love with Marcus. You and I are just friends. I hope we always will be."

"Of course we will. Maybe one day, you and Marcus will come to California and stay with me."

"Maybe," I said. "Have you told the kids that you're going?"

"I rang them yesterday. They're quite excited I think. They're planning on a gap year and asked if they could spend it with me."

"That's a lovely idea. You'll have a great time."

"I'm sure." He drank the rest of his coffee. "I just wish things had been different."

"Don't, Ross. There's no point dwelling on what could have been. We had something once, but that was a long time ago. You moved on before I did."

"Yes, and now I regret leaving you."

"But there's no point having regrets. Life is what you make it. You've had a wonderful time in America these past twenty years. I got on with my life in Edinburgh."

"I upset you when I left, didn't I?" He put his cup on the table.

"Yes, you did. But I was old enough to accept it. I'm not prepared to live by what-ifs. I'm happy, Ross. I'm happier now than I've ever been. Of course I wish Lucy was here, but I've found someone to love me, someone to share my life with."

"I love you."

I stood up and went to the window. Ross stood up, too, his chair scraping across the floor.

"I'm sorry," he said. "I shouldn't have said that. I'd better go."

I turned to face him, his eyes filled with tears. "You didn't have to say that. I love you, too, Ross. But as a friend. That's all." He nodded. "Will I see you before you leave next week?"

"I've got a lot to do. My flight's on Monday. Jacob and Rebecca are taking me to the airport. They're staying with me for the weekend."

"I hope it works out for you, I really do." I moved towards him. "You will be happy, Ross, I know you will."

He smiled. "And what about the girl I'm supposed to marry?" he asked.

"Maybe she's your ex. But I know what I saw."

"I'll keep in touch, Cam." He kissed me on my lips, a caressing sensation, with a reluctance to pull away.

I put my arms around his neck and closed my eyes. Right at that moment I wanted him. All other thoughts had banished from my mind, even ones of Marcus. I had missed being with Ross in this way and ever since he'd come back to the Borders I'd been fighting my emotions towards him. It was proving too much as he continued to kiss me, passionately running his fingers through my hair. I knew we were in danger of it going further but my body seemed locked in his embrace, unable to pull away and make sense of a situation that shouldn't have been. He gently forced me back into the kitchen towards the table, pushing me against it, before placing his arms under mine, gently lifting me. I was drowning in lust, remembering the times we had been together, so many years ago, happy, until he left. It was then that I finally pushed him from me, and moved away from the table.

"What are we doing?" I said, the shock in my voice forcing him to stay back.

"I'm sorry, I thought you wanted it."

"No. No, Ross, I don't want it. Not now, not ever."

"I want you so much, Cam."

I straightened my clothes and ran my fingers through my hair. "We've been through this. It isn't going to happen. I don't want to lose Marcus. I think it would be better if you left now."

He opened the back door and stood for a moment with his back to me.

"We could have been good together." He turned round to face me, his eyes filled with regret. "Don't be angry with me for loving you."

"I'm more angry at myself. I shouldn't have let that happen. And neither should you."

He nodded. "If you ever need me, get in touch. I'm only a phone call away."

I stood still, unable to speak for a moment. "I won't ring you, Ross. I won't let you get in the way of my relationship with Marcus."

"But I am in the way, aren't I."

"No!" I raised my voice. "You and I can never be lovers again. And I'm not sure we can continue being friends either."

"I'm sorry. I really am. Bye, Camilla." He got into his car and closed the door. I was reluctant to go outside, waving to him was no longer an option.

I hated myself for almost letting passion overwhelm me, knowing the feelings I had towards Marcus were increasing by the day. I closed the back door and went back into the kitchen. His empty cup still rested on the table and I picked it up. I ran my fingers around the area in which his lips would have touched, before tears flowed gently down my cheeks.

Chapter Thirty-Six

*I*t was like a part of my life had ended. Like all those years ago, I thought about the times I spent with the man I had loved so much; the one who had devastated me when he moved away. I was twenty-five when he first moved to America and my mother was gravely ill. The idea of me moving with him was out of the question, but he went anyway, fulfilling his dream and starting afresh. When he left, I doubted he ever really loved me at all. I spent a long time pining for him, trying to rebuild my life and forget we ever had a relationship. But he was always there, at the back of my mind, niggling at me whenever I came close to forming a new relationship.

I needed to be in the guest room; my quest to find the best bit was prodding me, forcing me to look further for the end. It was still morning, daylight shining vibrantly into the atmospheric room where I immediately sensed spirit presence. But I couldn't find the diary. Having left it on the bedside table a few nights previously it seemed to have vanished. No one had been in that room apart from me. Perhaps spirit had moved the book, for its own amusement maybe or just to confuse me, but it was no longer in the place I had left it. I opened drawers, wardrobes, looked under the bed. Spirit stood over me, jeering as I searched. A poltergeist had once more been through my home and moved books, but this time with new reason, haunting me as I struggled to concentrate.

"Where is it?" I asked, whilst on hands and knees, desperately looking under the bed for a second time. "How dare you move it." Anger was rising inside, the morning had been bad for me, and spirit was making it worse. "Who are you anyway? What are you doing here, in my home?"

The energy moved to the window, tricking me into believing the diary had been put there, perhaps in the box beneath the sill in which I kept bed sheets. I opened it aggressively, lifting each blanket and pillow case from their neatly folded shapes, realising as I neared the bottom that the diary wasn't in the box.

"Put it back and get out of my home." The sound of laughter emitted through my head, a man's voice, cruel and insensitive.

I could feel my face flushed with anger. I was so tired and felt drained after everything that had happened. Why couldn't I find the diary and somehow place the last piece of jigsaw in my life's puzzle? And why did Ross have to leave? Questions whizzing around my head, my heart thumping as I stood in the middle of the room, sobbing like a child who felt her whole world was caving in around her. The past year at Rosehill had been so wonderful; having found my dream home, discovered a history, found my mother again. It hadn't been all good, losing Lucy had upset me deeply, and now I felt I had lost Ross too. Perhaps it was my own fault. Maybe his. The love we had for each other had been in the past, yet I knew that my feelings for him went beyond a simple friendship. He had been gone from my house for only half an hour yet I missed him. The thought of never being close in his arms again terrified me; a life without him at the end made me feel lost somehow, empty inside.

I threw the bed sheets back into the box, slamming it shut. As I walked towards the bedside cabinet, thinking it could have been in there, I realised the spirit which tormented me was sat on the bed, perhaps waiting for me to join it. But I had no intention of staying in the room. Rosehill was my house; I didn't accept malevolent spirits in my home and I was in no way going to encourage this one to stay. My heartache at Ross leaving overwhelmed me once again. I no longer wanted to read the diary; it was as though the presence was forcing me away from it, encouraging me to leave it be. Never in my life had I allowed a spirit presence to get the better of me, but this was different. I was scared. As I looked around the room I could feel spirit taunting me, laughing at my weaknesses. It was if spirit enjoyed seeing me in this state of helplessness.

I left the guest room, closing the door gently behind me. I wiped the tears from my eyes as I walked back to the kitchen. I hadn't arranged to see Marcus that day but I needed him to hold me. I knew it was for the wrong reason but I still needed him. More than I'd ever needed him since we'd been together.

I rang him and asked him to come to the house. I must have sounded upset because within fifteen minutes, he drew up in the driveway.

"Hey, are you okay?" he asked as he came into the house.

"I am now," I replied and wrapped my arms around him. He held me tightly against him, rubbing his hands up and down my back."

"What is it?"

"I'm not having a good day." I pulled away from him. "I'll make us a drink."

"What's happened?"

I put the kettle on to boil. "I thought I'd read a bit more of the diary, but I can't find it." I hoped he didn't pick up on my sadness, too.

"Well, where did you put it last?"

"I left it in the guest room in the west wing. I've been reading it in there and I put it on the bedside table. It's gone."

"How can it have gone?" he asked, sitting down at the table.

"Well to me it's obvious."

"Do you think it's been moved?"

"Yes, I do. And I think I know who moved it." I made the coffee.

"Who? Are you saying someone's been in the house?"

I nodded. "Not someone, some*thing*. I think it could be William Baxter, Alice's late husband. He's visited me a few times and always comes with a negative energy."

Marcus sighed before sipping his coffee. "Are you sure? I find that hard to believe."

"I thought you might," I said, wondering if the day could get any worse. "But there you have it."

"Take me to the guest room." He stood up. "I'm interested to see where you could have left it. Maybe we can look together."

"Fine," I said, "follow me." I led him to the room and opened the door. As we entered the room he looked immediately at the table where I had left the diary.

"What's this?" he said, picking up the book.

I stared at it. "It's the diary," I said, totally baffled as to how it had got there. "I swear to you it wasn't there earlier when I came up here. I wanted to read it."

"Are you tired?" Marcus put it in my hands and I looked down at it.

"Yes, I am. But I know it'd been moved. I'm not stupid. The energy in here was making fun of me earlier."

"Perhaps you need to get some rest. Come on, I'll finish my coffee then leave you to go back to bed for an hour."

"But, Marcus, it wasn't there. I'm not too tired that I didn't even see it. And look," I pointed to the bed linen box. "I emptied that because I sensed someone was standing near it, telling me the diary was in there." I went over to the box and opened it. "See." The sheets were in the same state I had thrown them back in, which I have to admit, was a relief.

"Okay, I believe you. But don't worry about it now, you've found it again. Take it downstairs and put it somewhere else."

We left the room and went to the kitchen where Marcus sat down again and carried on drinking his coffee. I put the diary in a drawer, hoping it would still be there when next I had chance to read it. I was finding it difficult to smile as I joined him at the table, still thinking about Ross.

"There's something else, isn't there?" he asked.

I looked at him. "No, I'm fine."

"No, you're not. I've known you long enough, Camilla. I know when something's troubling you. What is it?"

I stood up and went to the sink, gazing out of the window at the beauty of my fields. Marcus knew me too well and I was determined not to keep things from him. I turned to face him.

"Ross is leaving. He's going back to America in a few days time."

Marcus shrugged. "And why are you upset about that?"

"Because he's all I have left of Lucy."

"What about Jacob and Rebecca?"

"They have their own lives now, I doubt they'll ever come back here."

"But aren't you their godmother? Surely they won't lose touch with you." He had a point, but I could sense he didn't believe I was telling him everything.

"I'll stay in touch with them, of course I will, but it won't be the same without Ross around. I've known him such a long time; he was my connection to Lucy."

"Are you sure there's nothing else to it?"

Perhaps my face said it all but I knew I couldn't fool him. "He kissed me, Marcus."

"Kissed you? When?"

"This morning. He came over to tell me of his decision to go back. Before he left he held me, then kissed me. I didn't intend it to happen." I sat down again and buried my face in my hands, unable to look at him. "And I didn't lead him on, if that's what you're thinking." I slowly lifted my head when he didn't answer.

"I don't know what to think if I'm honest." He looked at me, crestfallen, arms hanging. I'd hurt him, I knew I had. And I didn't blame him for being upset and troubled at my confession. But he didn't speak, only continued to stare.

"Please say something. Anything," I begged. My heart raced. "Have I destroyed what we have?"

"You two have a history," he said eventually. "I knew there was something between you. I could tell when we all had dinner together; the flirting, him making remarks to you, referring to your past."

"There's nothing going on between us, Marcus. I can assure you."

"Of course there isn't, now," he said his voice raised. "He's obviously left you again, hasn't he. And you're devastated.

I opened my mouth to defend myself, but he cut me short.

"No, don't say anything. Nothing that you say would make it better." His knuckles were white.

"Oh, come on, don't be like this, please. I love you, Marcus. I feel nothing towards Ross."

"Then why did you kiss him?" Pain soaked his words.

"He kissed me. I'm just telling you because I don't want to keep secrets from you." But I was still lying. I had enjoyed the kiss and if I hadn't pushed him away I was sure it would have led to much more.

He got up and walked towards the door. I trembled, tears stinging my eyes, I could only see him through a blur. How could I have been so stupid to let this happen? Why did I feel so confused about these two men?

"How do you expect me to trust you now?" He grabbed his keys from the sideboard. "You need to think about who you want, Camilla. I'm not sure you really know." I had never seen him this hurt, this angry, and this lost. And I was the cause.

"Marcus!" I called after him in a last attempt, but he was already out the door. All I could do was watch as he got into his car. He started the engine, unable to look at me. "Marcus! I'm sorry. I love you, not Ross." But he drove away. I no longer wondered if the day could get any worse. I had never felt so low since the death of my mother. I still stood in the doorway, unable to feel the cold, just hot tears streaming down my face as heavy sobs shook my body. When I finally closed the door, I sat at the table and let my emotions take over.

I was torn between wanting to phone Ross and needing to phone Marcus. I knew I should've called Marcus but I couldn't bring myself to do it. He was angry with me, the first time he had ever shown real aggression in his voice. And I didn't blame him. I deserved it. But I loved him deeply and I needed to make him believe that. We had enjoyed such a wonderful time together, I couldn't have contemplated not being with him. Even Alice had seen how good we were together, the mention of marriage having passed her lips when she spoke about our relationship. The locals hadn't said anything to me but I got the feeling it was no longer a talking point in the village.

Chapter Thirty-Seven

*N*ight fell and I stood at the front door for some fresh air, moonlight struggling to break through the clouds. An owl hooted in the distance, its declaration of night being broadcast to the countryside. Bats frantically glided around me, searching for a resting place to hang, seeking a tiny break in the stonework of the house. I could hear the whir of their flight, resonating above me. I walked around the front of the house, gravel driveway scrunching beneath my slipper clad feet. My car sat, silent and rested; the hammock seat stood perfectly still, no breeze able to lift it from tired hinges.

Suddenly able to tune into an unstable atmosphere, my heart raced and my eyes dashed from left to right. I realised I had been joined by an astral presence, one which seemed to wait for an invitation into the house. The spirit of Harold held out his hand to me, asking to be led into a warm home, his spirit manifested as clear as seeing his human form before me.

No words were needed; I knew why Harold wanted me to take him inside. It was like he had come home, wanting me to invite him into the house that he acknowledged now belonged to me. I led him to the guest room, gently opening the door and allowing him to walk ahead of me into his bedroom. He fumbled about first, picking ornaments up, putting them down again, opening a few drawers and searching through contents. He was looking for the diary. His frustration at it being moved was plain to see; I felt sorry for him. His brother still tormented him in the next life, when all Harold sought was peace.

He turned to me, his eyes drowning in sadness. "Where is it?" he said. "I need you to read it. I found it for you earlier when you were searching and left it here." He pointed to the bedside table.

"I'll go and get it," I said, rushing out of the room. I found it in the drawer in which I placed it earlier, grabbing it then running back to the guest room. "Why me?" I asked, softly when I returned.

It was at that moment that Harold turned towards the bed. Anger overwhelmed the sadness in his eyes as he stared. William had joined us, clearly manifested and lying against the headboard, arms folded, and legs crossed, smiling with smug arrogance.

I stood in the doorway, shocked at seeing William. His faced terrified me when I noticed his red eyes and an evil-looking smile.

"You bastard!" Harold roared, leaning towards his brother. "Why can't you leave us alone? Betty never loved you. You didn't make love to her, you just used her and cast her aside the way you did Alice."

I was unable to move. This wasn't what I expected to find.

"Betty and I loved each other," Harold continued, "but you had to spoil it didn't you. You were never there for Alice. How could you have expected her to live like a married woman when she lived the single life?"

William smirked at his brother. "She was my wife, Harold. You deserved everything you got."

"I deserved some happiness," he paused, "with Betty." Harold was beginning to cave, the anger started to subside as his sadness once more glazed his eyes.

"And what about Jane? My daughter, until I find out she isn't." William said, leaning forward.

"You let Alice believe that you knew nothing of what happened between me and her. You humiliated her. She could have been happy. But you had to keep her trapped all those years." Harold spat his words of disgust.

"I loved Alice. I still do. Despite the fact she slept with you and bore your child. " William looked as if he was about to jump up.

"Stop!" I couldn't watch this any longer. "You're brothers and a lot of years have passed. Isn't it time to forgive now?"

Both men looked at me.

"You don't even know half the truth," William said, a frolicking expression on his face.

"Stop diverting the subject," Harold said in a brisk manner, turning his attention to his brother. "Answer me two questions. Why did you kill me?"

I was desperate to get to the bottom of the family feud yet unsure I was happy to continue listening to two astrals tear each other apart, even after death. The coldness in the room had seeped into my bones as I wrapped my arms around my body, rubbing my hands against me. Curtains began to flap in the enraged energy which banded insults and accusations in a guest room at my beloved Rosehill.

"You stole Alice's heart. You fathered Jane. And then you got Betty, too. I had nothing. Like always. Nothing." William looked down towards trembling hands. "You had mother's undivided attention when we were boys, and you were always father's golden boy. I was just William, no one special, a trouble causer in most eyes."

"You killed me out of jealousy?" Genuine surprise showed on Harold's expression. Thoughts raced around my head as I continued to try desperately to make sense of a brother's heartache.

"Of course I was jealous of you. When you and Betty got engaged I couldn't take it anymore. I had to get rid of you."

"But why try to take Betty from me?" I urged Harold to ask the question.

"She loved me. Can't you see that? The only reason she agreed to marry you was because she was carrying your child. She didn't love you, you stupid man. It was me she wanted to be with. But I didn't sleep with her. I wasn't unfaithful to Alice."

Clearly stunned, Harold stared at William, unable to answer the last proclamation. He turned to face me, his eyes almost bursting from his head with tears. Thoughts impressed on me, a secret having been found out before his death was becoming clear.

"I'm sorry, Camilla," Harold said. "That's why I wanted you to read the diary."

"What do you mean?" I asked.

William laughed. "You're going to have to tell her now, aren't you?"

Harold turned to his brother. "Shut up!" He hollered, making me jump. Then he turned back to me and continued. "I wanted you to know a long time ago, but I wanted you to see Rosehill, to be able to find out about me. That's why I asked your grandmother to bring you here."

"My grandmother?"

"Yes. She was reluctant at first, she didn't want the truth to come out, or so I thought. I think she was scared of the effect it might have on you. She didn't approve of me, you see."

"Didn't approve? Do you mean when you were still alive? How did you know my grandmother?"

William continued to smirk whilst sat on the bed. He seemed to enjoy watching his brother reveal what I had waited so long to know.

"She's Betty's mother." Harold almost whispered to me as he looked down at the floor.

"Betty who? Do you mean the lady you were engaged to?"

"Yes."

I thought about it for a moment before realising what Harold was telling me. I lifted my hand to my mouth, gasping in disbelief at what was being revealed.

"Betty, Betty....isn't that short for Elizabeth? But my mother's name was Elizabeth....what are you saying?"

My legs gave way as I fell to the ground and Harold raced over to assist me. I knew there was no need to continue looking at the diary having now learned the truth about why my grandmother brought me to Rosehill. I sat on the floor, unable to stand, my limbs weak.

"Who put the diary inside the chimney?" I asked, as Harold sat on the floor beside me, his energy almost surpassing mine.

"Your mother did. I asked her to. I wanted you to find it one day." Harold smiled at me as he sat alongside, his hand on top of mine. "I told her to hide the diary, after I'd died."

I glared at Harold. He told me something that I couldn't quite comprehend. William continued to sit upon the bed, no longer seeming smug or cruel. Yet appearing a little sympathetic, kind even, his eyes no longer red but the brown in which they would once have been. He and Harold looked very much alike.

"Are you saying my mother was .."

"A medium, yes," Harold nodded. "But she didn't broadcast the fact. She preferred to keep it a secret from the world. Your grandmother tried to help her, encouraging her to be open, but in those days it was something looked upon rather unfavourably. She would have lost many friends had people known. I guess she preferred to be without her ability to communicate, but it never left her. When I passed on, I was able to contact her, tell her things about me, about Alice." He paused for breath, still presenting in human resemblance. "I've watched you grow up, Camilla. I encouraged your grandmother to bring you back here, hoping you would fall in love with Rosehill the way I did."

My father had looked after me throughout my life after all. He had been there for me, maybe not in body, but in spirit. And to me, that was all that mattered.

"Why did you never make contact with me before?" I asked, still holding his hand.

"I couldn't. Even though your grandmother wanted you to know the truth, she never liked me. She knew about Alice and me."

"And she didn't say anything to my mother? Why?"

"I guess she could see that your mother was happy with me. At first, anyway. Until William swept her off her feet."

"I didn't sweep her off her feet," William said, through gritted teeth.

"Of course you did," Harold snarled, turning to face his brother. "She fell in love with you while she was carrying our child. And I was helpless." He turned back to me. "I wanted you to find my diary, read the entries, and learn a little about me first. The last few dates tell of Betty's pregnancy, of how I loved her, of the future I craved with her."

"And Alice? Didn't you love her anymore after you met my mother?" I wasn't sure I needed to hear the answer, but Harold had been kind enough to reveal the truth to me, allowing me a glimpse into his life.

"Yes, I did love Alice, but I couldn't have her. She was already married to William. And even though they had Jane who was mine, I knew I would never truly have Alice. Her loyalty belonged to her husband."

I frowned. "So my mother was second best for you?"

"For a while, I guess she was. But then I fell in love with her, the way I had done with Alice. Even though I still loved Alice, your mother was the one I wanted to be with. Knowing she was having my baby and knowing we were getting married was all I needed in my life. She gave me everything I ever wanted." He turned to face William who was now perched on the end of the bed, his head in his hands.

"Alice knew I would go to prison should I have been found out for killing you. That's why she never told. She couldn't bear for me to have been sent away again after Jane was born."

"You're wrong. She would have been better off without you." Harold yelled, anger overwhelming his expression. "I had a life ahead of me and you took it away. You had no right."

"It's in the past," William said.

"You destroyed my past. You enjoyed a life with Alice. What did I get? Forty years of knowing I had two daughters who I could never have a life with. Not to mention the love of a woman."

"Which one?" William asked, laughing and jeering as he got off the bed.

"I could have had either of them once."

"Alice would never leave me no matter how much you wanted her, and as for Betty, all she wanted was Rosehill. If you haven't worked that one out yet, there's no hope for you." William was now standing in front of Harold. "You're an idiot. You would never have been happy with either woman."

Harold became furious as he stood facing his brother, his fists clenched as though getting ready to hit William. "I'm no idiot," he said, backing away slightly. "What about Alice? She's lived with this secret all these years and kept it to herself. I'm not surprised she told Jane about me. How could any mother allow her child to think an evil murderer like you is her father? It must have been heartbreaking for her."

"You're deluded, Harold. It was me she wanted, just like it was me that Betty wanted. Face facts." William once more laughed.

Harold raised his arm, his fist still clenched, then he punched his brother, full on against his chin. William fell to the ground, still laughing. "What are you trying to do, Harold? Kill me?"

"I should have killed you before you killed me. You're an evil bastard and you're no brother of mine." William got up and faced Harold again. I was scared about the drama unfolding before me.

"Stop it! Both of you, this isn't the answer." I yelled, hoping my voice would carry above William's laugh.

But Harold hit him again, once more knocking him to the floor. This time William stayed down, propping himself up with his elbow.

I was starting to feel Harold's energy slip away. William looked at me, showing no remorse. Harold's life had been snatched from him at the hands of his brother. He had forty six years of catching up to do, with me. I wanted to turn back time and bring him back, grow up with the father I always yearned for, the real father, instead of the man which my mother allowed me believe was he. I had once felt resentment towards her for not allowing me the right to know who my real father was, but now, I realised why she seldom visited me from her astral plane. She knew I was destined to find out his identity, once my grandmother had led me to Rosehill, it was imminent.

"And Jane?" I asked.

"She's your half-sister. She's been trying to communicate with Alice since she died. Alice blamed herself for Jane's death after she told her about me. But together, we've been trying to encourage Alice to understand that it wasn't her fault, none of this was her fault."

So Jane had wanted me to know that she was my half sister whom I never had the chance to meet. Having only passed away five years previously, it could have been possible for us to know each other, for us to have had a relationship and form a bond.

"Does Alice know who I am? Does she know I'm Harold's daughter?" I hoped my question would tempt Harold to use my energy to come back to the guest room and help me understand the last four decades of my life. "Harold, are you still here? You've faded, I can't feel your energy, please come back. I need you."

"Alice doesn't know who you are." William answered, himself beginning to fade. "Betty moved away after Harold died and we heard no more from her."

I froze, disgusted at the spirit which had told so many lies, hurt people, even killed a man in order to keep what he felt belonged to him. I couldn't look at him anymore. He had taken my father from me, taunted me in my own home, tried to prevent me from knowing the truth. But a part of me felt sorry for him. He no longer had Alice in his life; he no longer had a life. And for the rest of his astral journey, I was quite sure that Harold would stay out of his way. William Baxter would have died a lonely man.

Thoughts were racing round my head though I was unable to decipher them. My mother's cries would have been an indication of the heartbreak she felt when she discovered Harold was dead. I was sure she loved him. William was wrong. She didn't talk about him much after Eric, the man I thought was my father had left, but she did tell me once that we could have been happy together, as a family unit. Of course I knew nothing of my past. But with my grandmother's help and her determination to introduce me to Rosehill, it was inevitable that I would one day understand who I was.

I felt as though I grieved for a man I didn't know. I sat on the floor, staring into the empty atmosphere that now prevailed in the guest room. A part of me wanted to communicate with Harold again, have him answer the questions that were burning inside me. I was also seething with anger at the thought of my father being brutally murdered by his jealous brother. Only to spend the next forty six years trying to make contact with me. And then there was my mother. I wondered if any of them would ever be allowed to rest in peace.

Chapter Thirty-Eight

*M*onday morning arrived, the day Ross was leaving for America. I sat and stared at the clock, thinking about him at Edinburgh airport. I didn't want him to leave my life, not like this. But I knew that if my relationship with Marcus stood any chance of surviving, Ross would need to be out of my life completely. I couldn't live with jealously, knowing that Marcus was hurting deep inside and worrying about me wanting to be with someone else. It wouldn't have worked, we both knew that.Ross's flight to Heathrow was at eleven o'clock. I imagined him boarding the plane, taking notice of the stewardesses as they guided him to his seat. I thought about the sadness he might have felt as he stared out of the cabin window, watching another plane take off into the sky. I looked at the phone, telling myself to pick it up and dial Marcus. But I held back. I wanted Marcus to trust me; I thought if he saw my grief at Ross leaving, it would make the jealousy resurface again.

I managed to eat a sandwich at lunch time, still chasing the hands on the clock. I switched the television on, anything to distract me from the sadness I felt. Since my discovery about Harold, I had tried hard to summon communication between us, but he'd stayed away. Perhaps he thought I needed space to come to terms with what I knew. I thought I'd sensed my grandmother in the hallway earlier, but could have been mistaken when I realised it was raining outside, tiny patters brushing against the windows.

I sat in the lounge for a while, the television on, background noise emitting around the room yet failing to reach my thoughts. Then the phone rang, its usual shrill which made me jump and ask the question, "who could this be?"

"Hello?" I answered.

"It's me."

"Marcus." It was so good to hear his voice. "How are you?"

"I'm fine. How are you?"

"I'm okay." It went quiet for a few moments.

"I miss you. Can I come up?"

Tears filled my eyes as the relief at hearing his voice shook me back to reality. "Of course you can. I'm in all day."

"I won't be long." He hung up. I thought I sensed hostility in his voice, but I could have been wrong. Paranoia had perhaps set in. After all, he said he'd missed me.

I ran upstairs and made myself look presentable. I only hoped he wasn't coming to Rosehill to break up with me. His car drew up ten minutes later and I opened the front door. He didn't say anything when he got out of his car but just walked towards me. He wasn't smiling.

"Is everything okay?" I asked, as he walked past me and into the house.

"Not really." My heart sank. I looked at him, discomfort enveloping my emotions.

"Would you like a drink?"

"No thanks. I've been doing some thinking these past few days."

"Do you want to come in here and sit down?" I beckoned to the lounge door. He followed me in and sat in the armchair.

"I want to talk to you about Ross." I thought as much.

"What about Ross?"

"He went back today, didn't he?"

"Yes, he did." I tried to hide my disappointment.

"And do you miss him?"

"Why should I miss him?"

"Because of what you two had together. I know it was more than a friendship, Camilla."

I smiled at him and shook my head. "Twenty years ago it was more than a friendship. I won't deny that. But we're nothing more than friends now. In fact, I don't think I'll ever see him again."

"How can you be so sure?" Marcus's eyes fixed themselves onto mine.

"Well, I'm not sure I guess, but I'm not going to depress myself about it."

"You see I have a problem." He sat back against the chair and crossed his legs. "I want to believe you, but I don't."

"Why? What's making you doubt what I'm telling you?"

"I had another visit the other night."

"Anne?"

"Yes, Anne. I thought I was dreaming at first, she seemed to be standing next to the bed and she was looking at me."

"And you don't think you were dreaming?"

"No, I'm quite sure I wasn't."

"What did she say?"

He looked away. "She told me you were pining for Ross."

"Why would she say something like that?" I asked, amazed at him believing a spirit, when he was angry at himself for believing in them in the first place.

"She said it and I don't know why. But I want you to tell me that's she's wrong." He turned to me and sat perfectly still. "Are you pining for him?"

"No! Absolutely not. How dare she say I am." I became angry as I confronted him. "So I'm taking it you believe she's here then?"

He sighed and put his head in his hands.

"Marcus, are you okay?" I asked.

"I don't know anymore. And yes, I do believe she's here. I've always believed she's here but I didn't want to admit it. The church won't allow me to have these beliefs."

I moved and sat on the floor by his legs. "I'm not pining for Ross. It's you I'm pining for. I've missed you."

He lifted his head to face me, his cheeks were tear stained as he looked into my eyes.

"Please don't lie to me."

"I'm not. I can't believe you think this." I stood up and went back to the sofa. "Ross is gone. I doubt he'll come back here."

"I want to believe you, I really do."

"Then believe me, Marcus. What can I do to make you understand that I'm telling you the truth? Lucy was my best friend and I guess I'll always have connections with the family, especially through Jacob and Rebecca, but not necessarily with Ross."

He stood up and went to the fireplace, standing with his back to me.

"Ross isn't the only reason I came here to talk to you."

"Oh?"

He turned round and faced me. "I'm not sure I can carry on working for the church."

"I see."

"It just feels so wrong now. The feelings of jealously towards Ross that I've been having, believing that Anne's here, and sitting with you and Alice the other night. It doesn't make sense to the vows I took."

"What are you going to do?" I asked.

"I'm not sure yet. But I know one thing; Anne's visits have caused me to doubt my faith. It's as though she's here, constantly trying to make me do what she wants. I need her to leave me alone, to leave you alone."

"Would you like me to help set her free?"

"How?"

"We'll need to do a séance, try and make contact. She'll only come forward if she wants to. But if she knows you're here then it might encourage her." I shifted position. "Are you absolutely sure about this?"

"Yes. I can't go on like this. I'm living a lie." That was true.

"Then we'll try our best," I said, as he joined me on the sofa, resting my head against his shoulder.

<hr />

"May the light shine on us and protect us from negative forces who may wish to make contact." Marcus and I sat at the table in the reading room. The candle was lit in the centre, the only light that illuminated an otherwise dark room. My eyes were closed so I was unable to see whether Marcus's were too, but I trusted he believed in what we were doing. It was as though he had become so desperate in his mission to move on, that releasing Anne was the only way forward.

I opened my eyes and looked at him. He was holding both my hands as he faced the table. "You can open your eyes now," I said. He did, lifting his head and looking around the room.

"Can you feel anything?" he asked.

"Not at the moment, but you need to concentrate. I want you to channel all your energy into thinking about Anne, about how much you loved her, about the good times you had together. We need to encourage her to come forward with love and friendship."

He nodded. "I'm remembering our wedding day. She looked so beautiful, dressed in white, flowers in her hair and a bouquet of roses in her hands."

"That's good, keep thinking about her like that."

"I was so proud when I saw her walking up the aisle towards me. We were young and in love." Noises from the fireplace distracted my attention. "It was a beautiful sunny day."

"What was the date?"

"Saturday, 14th June, 1975."

I concentrated hard, the noises from the fireplace were becoming more distinct as I realised it wasn't just twigs which were breaking the silence. A white mist appeared, hovering in front of the hearth. As I stared at it I noticed in the corner of my eye, that Marcus was looking towards it too, seemingly transfixed on what was about to manifest.

"What is it?" he asked.

"I think it's Anne," I whispered. "Just stay still and keep remembering your wedding day. Think about the honeymoon and the memories you have of being happy with her."

"We went to Devon for our honeymoon," he said. "It was a quaint bed and breakfast, all we could afford. But it was perfect."

Anne was becoming clearer as her manifested spirit started to show itself. She looked at Marcus, smiling. She was dressed in white.

"Can you see her?" I asked.

"Yes. I can see she's wearing the wedding dress." His voice was trembling and tears had formed in his eyes. "She looks stunning, just like she did on our wedding day."

"She's presenting to you as your bride."

He let go of my hand and shifted in his chair as though about to stand up. I grabbed his hand and looked at him. "Please, stay at the table. Let her come to you."

"But she needs me," he said, unable to take his eyes off the ghost which now stood before him.

"She doesn't need you, Marcus. She needs the light. She has to go onto her next journey."

"Anne!" he whimpered, as tears fell down his cheeks. "Why did you do it?" I stayed silent and looked towards Anne.

"I couldn't take it anymore," she said. "You didn't understand how I felt. No one did. My life was over as far as I was concerned."

"Of course it wasn't over. I was there for you. We could have got through it together."

"I wanted that, Marcus. But you accepted it too quickly. You didn't hurt like I did."

"I did hurt, Anne. I hurt because I could see how upset you were. Can't you understand that?" Marcus's voice rose. I squeezed his hand in comfort.

"Why did you want to be a vicar?" she asked.

"Why are so you against me being a vicar?"

She moved towards us. "Look at you, sat here with this woman. You see the world in a different light. You're not cut out to be a vicar, Marcus, don't you see?"

"Anne," I said, "you can't dictate to Marcus what he does with his life. He enjoys his job." I turned to him. "Tell her."

He looked at me and I noticed the doubt in his expression. Then he turned his head back to Anne. "You're right. I'm not cut out to be a vicar." He put his head down and looked towards the table. "Sitting here, talking to you, Anne, it's proof that I'm not a true vicar. I never can be. I see that now."

"Because of me?" she asked, before looking at me. "Or her?"

Marcus lifted his head towards me. "Both of you," he said. I smiled at him, realising how difficult that must have been for him to say.

"Anne, you need to let go now. It's time." I stared at her, seeing the tears fall as she continued to be transfixed on Marcus. "Let us release you. I want to help you find peace and move on from the torment you've been feeling these past twenty years."

"I don't want to leave," she cried. "Marcus, come with me. We can be together again."

"No, Anne," I said. "Marcus can't be with you now. He's still got a life to enjoy on the earth plane."

Marcus looked at me and smiled. "Yes," he said, "I have a life to enjoy here." He turned back to Anne. "I want you to move on, leave us in peace."

I was so proud of him. It would have taken a great deal of courage for him to have sat in that room with me, talking to the spirit of his dead wife, telling her about his desire to continue life with another woman. Anne's face was full of sorrow, tears continued to fall as she leant towards her beloved husband. The candle flickered as she neared the table. Her face now inches away, her lips touched his as she reached in for a kiss. He would have felt the coldness of her skin against his face and he puckered his lips, obviously accepting her parting gesture. I turned away, letting the ghost of Anne say one last goodbye to her husband whom she had loved so deeply. I could feel her pain in my heart as my own eyes filled with tears, thoughts of her frantic depression overwhelming my mind. I pictured her sat in the disused building, a box of matches in her hand, face tear stained and unable to focus on anything other than ending her life.

She moved from Marcus, leaving him bewildered at the touch of her lips. We both watched as she backed away towards the fireplace, once more standing in front of the hearth. The mist that had first indicated her appearance began to form again, moving upwards and covering her astral body like a circle of smoke. Marcus reached out towards where the mist now enveloped her, showing only her face as she smiled at him weakly.

"Anne!" he said. "I did love you, my darling. I'll never forget you." Anne continued to smile at him, before she glanced at me.

"Go towards the light now, Anne. Begin your next journey with our love." I continued to hold Marcus's other hand as he still reached out to the fading image of his heart-broken wife. I realised it had been difficult for her to see him happy with another woman but what we were doing was the right thing. Her astral journey awaited as our earth journey was about to begin.

The room fell silent. The mist dispersed like smoke rising in the sky. Marcus and I were once more in the reading room alone. I stood up and switched on the light before blowing out the candle. He sat still for a moment, probably reflecting on the last few moments of his time with Anne. He'd made the right decision to set her free. Anne was right, he couldn't go on being a vicar knowing he believed in the spirit world the way I did. And I was relieved that he had realised that himself. I rejoined him at the table, once more holding his hand.

"Are you okay?" I asked.

He faced me and wiped his tears away. "I think so." His voice was still wobbly but he seemed more composed. "We've done the right thing, haven't we?"

"Yes, we have. It needed to be done. She couldn't go on haunting you the way she was."

"She didn't want me to be a vicar, did she?"

"No."

"And now she feels as though she's won."

I stared into his eyes. "Anne hasn't won, Marcus." I wiped his face. "She's lost her life, and probably more importantly to her, she's lost you."

"I'll always love her, Camilla."

"I know you will. But by her leaving, it's giving you a chance to move on with your own life. She's given that to you."

He nodded. "I think I'd like some fresh air, shall we go for a walk?"

I stood up again. "That's a good idea, come on."

Chapter Thirty-Nine

We put our coats on and gathered the dogs together before leaving the house. It was a beautiful sunny day, perfect for a walk in the fields. Bird song lifted our moods while an eagle hovered high above us. A slight breeze blew, rustling the leaves on the hedges. A tractor sounded in the distance, gathering early silage, whilst a micro-glider buzzed in the skies, its pilot probably looking down on the patchwork quilt of the countryside.

We walked hand in hand, the warm sun on our backs as the breeze warranted me to fasten my cardigan.

"Are you warm enough?" he asked.

"I'm fine. If that breeze would go down I'd be lovely and warm." He put his arm around me, pulling me into him. I noticed his mood had mellowed, his words softly spoken as he seemed totally relaxed.

"I love it up here," he said.

"I know, you've said often." I laughed.

"No, I mean I *really* love it. I could be immensely happy here."

I looked up at him as we continued to walk. He breathed in the fresh air.

"On a day like this you get panoramic scenes when the sun shines. It's an incredibly beautiful view."

"I've the most beautiful view right next to me." He stopped walking, pulled me even closer into him and kissed me passionately. I responded by putting my arms around his neck. My heart was beating in excitement at his tender touch. He pulled away from me and cupped my face with his hands. His soft eyes sank into mine.

"I love you," he said.

"I love you, too."

He looked around our vicinity and took my hand, before leading me the few steps to a tree stump which seemed to appear just for us. I sat down on it and looked towards the horizon. The hills in the distance seemed closer than usual as I imagined being able to reach out and touch them. Everywhere was so calm, just how I liked it to be. Rosehill once more wrapped its soul around mine as Marcus turned to face me. He stroked my cheek before pulling something out of his trouser pocket. It was a small, navy blue box. I looked at it, my body feeling as though it were floating above the scene which played in that sun drenched field.

Marcus lifted the lid. The beauty of a diamond took my breath away as I remained motionless and overwhelmed. A gold band hugged the single diamond as it almost begged me to touch it. I looked at him.

"Marry me," he said.

I was unable to speak. My mouth was open yet no words escaped. He kissed me again.

"I love you," he said. "I want to spend the rest of my life with you."

I smiled, my mouth increasingly sweeping upwards into a dazzling grin.

"Yes," I answered eventually. "Yes, I'll marry you." This time, I kissed him, flinging my arms around his neck once more and hugging him with every ounce of strength I had within me.

He took the ring out of the box, his shaky hands struggling to position it on my finger. It fit like a glove. I stared down at it, repositioning my hand to get the best angle. It was like all my dreams had come true at once. There we were, at my beloved Rosehill, having just made a decision about the rest of our lives. It was perfect.

"We'll have to tell the locals," he said, and laughed when he saw the look of horror on my face.

"I think I might leave that to you."

"I haven't been this happy for such a long time, Camilla."

"I'm happy, too. I've never been this happy, ever." I snuggled into him. "When will you tell Julia?"

"I'll go and see her in the morning," he said with a sigh. "She'll be okay about it, I'm sure."

I chuckled. "I'm not. She made it quite clear that she doesn't like me. This might tip her over the edge."

"She's not that bad, you know. She was just sick of the rat race in London, that's why she moved to the countryside."

"She doesn't like me, it's a fact!"

He laughed. "Well, whatever. It's not up to her. I'll tell her tomorrow."

I looked over at the house which stood proudly on its hill as it guarded the surrounding fields. "I think we should get married at Rosehill," I said. "It'll be the perfect place." I turned back to him. "I can see it now; a ceilidh at night and the locals having a wonderful time."

"And us."

"And us," I said, reaching towards his face for another kiss.

"There is one thing," he said.

"Which is?"

"How would you feel about me moving into Rosehill?" He was also looking towards the house.

"I think that would be perfect." I said.

"It would be nice to live here with you."

"Then that's what we'll do. The church won't mind if you don't occupy the vicarage, will they?"

He turned away from me. "No. No, I'm sure they won't mind." I sensed a little deflation in his tone. "How would you feel if I told you I'm going to resign?"

I stared at him. He pulled away then looked towards the fields again.

"Resign? Why?"

"I can't really see anyone accepting our marriage round here, can you?"

"But that's silly. It's not up to people round here. It's up to us."

"I know that, but people will talk. They know what you do and I'm well known in the district. It wouldn't bode well if I were to carry on preaching whilst coming home to a house full of spirits."

I laughed. "People like me round here, as far as I know. I've got to know a few of the locals. But when you put it like that, I guess it wouldn't bode well. You shouldn't let gossip dictate your life though."

"I have no intention of letting gossip do that. But I don't want anyone bad-mouthing you."

"I don't know what to say. It's your decision, of course, but it seems a bit drastic." I snuggled into him again.

"I want to start a new life, here with you. Make a fresh start without having the guilt of being a vicar and believing in..., well..., you know..."

"The paranormal?"

"Yes, if you like. What's happened with Anne has proved to me that the priesthood isn't the right job for me."

"And what are you going to do instead?"

"I'm not sure yet. I thought about going back into teaching."

I kissed him. "You seem to have it all worked out. But maybe you should speak to the church first. They might not accept your decision."

"They will. I have a strong enough case to leave."

"Are you going to tell them about me?"

"Of course I am. I want to tell everyone about you. You're my new life." He kissed me, his lips pressing hard against mine. He moved his arms up and down my back. The grass once more invited us to lie on it as he gently pushed me down, gathering me in his strong arms.

The sun shone on us and the breeze had calmed. I no longer felt cold but could feel the warmth running through my veins as the flames in my heart burned, smothered by Marcus's love. I wasn't sure it would have been the right moment to announce to Marcus that we weren't alone; that we had been joined by a small gathering of smiling faces watching proudly as a loved one's dreams had finally come true.

Thank you for purchasing a copy of
Discovery at Rosehill by Kathryn Brown
www.crystaljigsaw.blogspot.com